WHAT PEOPLE ARE SAYI

"As an avid reader of mostly bestselling authors, I was curious about this new book *Come Find Me*. I found the intrigue a pleasant surprise. Ruth Waring cleverly wove mystery from the beginning to the end of her novel. You were never sure what was behind the sadness or where new found happiness was leading Evelyn. In the end, the reader was left with many possible endings. I like that. Although not a comedy, certain events made you smile or laugh at the simple things in day to day life, be it the antics of the family pet or the joy of a newborn child. Laughter is good. The reader is left with a feeling of warmth and satisfaction at the end of the story that things can and will change for the better. I would recommend this book to one and all. A believable story without the coarseness so often found in today's writings."

SUSAN DUKE, Insurance Broker
Mississauga, Ontario

"Deeply moving, inspiring, compassionate and real are phrases I would use to describe *Come Find Me*. Those who read it can't help but grow in understanding, trust and zeal in seeking the heart of Him who calls, 'Come, find me.'"

KATHY LE GRESLEY, Elementary School Teacher
Lindsay, Ontario

"Loved it! Stayed up till 2:00 a.m. to finish it. I was lying in bed wiping my eyes. I loved the ending. That certainly was a surprise. I didn't see it coming. Super book!"

LINDA HOLLYWOOD, pastor's wife
London, Ontario

"*Come Find Me* captured my heart! I really enjoyed the imagery throughout—especially the scene with the birds fighting and how that related to Evelyn's personal turmoil. I enjoyed the Jewish history as well as the surprise ending. Awesome!"

DARLENE TURNER, Business Process Consultant
London, Ontario

"Wow! I find it hard to find the words to tell you how much I enjoyed *Come Find Me*. It was gripping. The characters each had a life of their own and I laughed and cried along with them. The author should be very proud of her accomplishment. If *Come Find Me* is any indication, I'm sure her next project will be awesome!"

DONNA GALLAGHER, Special Ed Teacher
Cameron, Ontario

"I was enthralled by *Come Find Me*. The writing was so elegant, the characters so real and authentic, and the setting so life-like. It reminded me of something I might have read once by Margaret Laurence or Carol Shields. *Come Find Me* chronicles the journey of a Jewish woman struggling with her faith in God. The story spans her entire life, making the book very much a portrait of a woman. Obviously, to pull this off, the central character would have to be exceptionally handled, and it is. The character of Evelyn is vibrant and alive. Her struggles feel significant and easy to relate to. The complexity of characterization Ruth displays in her writing is, in my experience, a very rare skill."

EVAN BRAUN, Editor
Winnipeg, Manitoba

Ruth Waring

COME FIND ME

ISBN-13: 978-1-926676-59-3

Printed in Canada.

Printed by Word Alive Press
131 Cordite Road, Winnipeg, MB R3W 1S1
www.wordalivepress.ca

Dedicated to

LORNA MAY MACDONALD

my dear friend and mentor

ACKNOWLEDGEMENTS

One morning in February 2004, after an evening of challenge and motivation with my writer's group, I awoke at 5:00 a.m. and went directly to my computer. Several hours later, the life of Evelyn Sherwood (a.k.a. Evlyna Cohen) faced me on a legal-size sheet of paper, drawn, charted, and text-boxed! I believe God knew I had something to say, and I will be forever thankful that He, by His grace and wisdom, allowed me to say it through the characters I developed and lived with over the following few years.

Beyond this, I want to express deep appreciation to the four ladies in my writer's group: Darlene Turner, Heather Joyce, Lisa Wilson, and Stephanie Nichols. Their encouragement, critiques, challenges, and humour pushed me to completion. Giving birth to WWC (*Women Writing for Christ*) surprised me and then inspired me by filling an unknown void in my life. Through its birth, WWC gave me the gift of friendship from four unique women. *Thank you!*

My husband Doug smiled when I told him I intended to write a novel. He encouraged and supported me from the beginning; patiently listened to my frustrations, applauded my successful moments, and never laughed once, even when he found me crying at the death of one of my characters. (He even suggested I rewrite the chapter so the character wouldn't die. I told him it was too late!) He is the best, and no wife could ask for more, especially a novice writer! *Thank you!*

A special thanks to Harvey Katz and Sharon Berman who, without their help, discernment, and newfound friendships, I would never have been able to capture an authentic Jewish element in *Come Find Me.* Harvey, I listened with intent, grateful for all that you taught me, and I will be forever indebted to you for introducing me to Sharon. And to you, Sharon, I can only thank God for bringing you into my life, not just for your willingness to be the first to read my novel and offer your insight, but for your loving spirit and the new friendship that has resulted. You are my sister in Christ and a rose, indeed! *Thank you!* And to Dr. Marvin Rosenthol, with whom I spent only an hour and a half, *thank you* for your candidness, your suggestions, and your corrections. You spurred me on with your belief in my work.

My *new* friend, Kathy LeGresley and my *old* friend, Laura van Zanden, painstakingly edited, advised, and encouraged me as they read through my work. Their willingness to deal with faulty grammar, spelling errors, word errors, and incorrect verb tenses was daunting, and yet they marked, circled, underlined, and listed errors! What can I say, Kathy? Your friendship is an unexpected and delightful gift. And Laura, well, you've always been there for me when I needed your expertise, and your friendship is irreplaceable. Words don't seem to be enough, but... *thank you,* both!

Life is full of gifts, but nothing compares to family, especially my children—Stewart, Jennifer, and Bradley, and my daughter in-law Christine and my son-in-law Greg. *Thank you* for being part of my life and, in your own way, supporting me on this adventure.

A special *thank you* to all those unnamed people whose lives are built into my characters and to the many others who asked how my book was coming along, who encouraged, supported, and challenged me.

Why did I write *Come Find Me*? Initially it began as an assignment with my writer's group. It grew from there and I began to pray that the story of Evelyn Sherwood's spiritual journey would relate to someone on a similar journey, that maybe a life would be changed from having met her.

As the story and characters evolved, I began to realize that *Come Find Me* was not just about entertaining you—as one who enjoys reading—although I hope you will find yourself smiling, maybe even laughing at times! It was about making a difference. I wanted to challenge your thinking, your faith, your own spiritual journey, as mine was challenged each time I sat at my computer. I wanted you to stop and ask yourself, as I did, *Would I have done it differently? Would I have been stronger? Would I have believed?*

As I wrote *Come Find Me,* I gave much thought to the often-asked question, *What is life all about?* Motivated by this time-worn question, I sought to provide hope not only for my protagonist, but for my readers as the love and faithfulness of our all-forgiving, true, living God is experienced.

Ruth Waring

And ye shall seek me, and find me,
when ye shall search for me
with all your heart.
JEREMIAH 29:13

PROLOGUE

Toronto, Ontario
1939

Pack my things! Why?" Evlyna's voice pierced the silence as her eyes darted from corner to corner. The cover on the piano keyboard lay closed. Linens, piled neatly on a chair, waited their turn to be placed in a nearly-full barrel. Drawn drapes almost blocked the late afternoon sun and the premature darkness added to Evlyna's growing fear. The steady ticking of the mantel clock had ceased. It lay on its side on the dining room table beside assorted dishes, piano books, and the few pictures that had hung on the wall for most of her life. She watched as her mother and grandmother carefully packed their china into two crates that stood three-quarters full by the sideboard in the small dining room. She could hear whispered monotones as they wrapped the family heirlooms, but their eyes remained locked on their task, shoulders bent as though they carried a great burden.

Evlyna became conscious of something else: the absence of freshly baked bread from the bakery downstairs. For all of her thirteen years, or certainly as far back as her memories would take her, the aroma of bread and pastries had permeated their home. Cinnamon or cloves or the different spices of the various holiday seasons perfumed the draperies, her clothes, the bedding, her father's beard, and all too often her own hair. The fragrance seemed to cling in her nostrils even when she sat in her classroom at school, five blocks from home.

Now there was nothing.

Evlyna counted the days. *Three in a row,* she thought. Her father had not opened the family bakery for three days in a row.

"Mother, what's happening?" Evlyna whispered. "Where are we going?" Casting guarded glances at the eerie shadows dancing on the naked walls, she imagined impatient ghosts waiting to haunt the remains of their earthly possessions.

"Evlyna, please don't ask questions. Just do what your father asks."

But Evlyna Cohen needed answers. She ignored her mother's imploring voice and turned to her grandmother. *Were those tears?* A second look at her mother only intensified her growing fears. A terrible realization of what was happening overwhelmed her and Evlyna spun around to face her father.

"No! We can't just *leave.* There's got to be another way. So what if people don't talk to us. We can make new friends. You can find new customers." She spun again. "Mother, please talk to Father."

Her pleading proved futile.

"Father, I beg you!"

Jóózsef Cohen drew himself up and stood directly in front of her. "The bakery is sold and the apartment has been rented to another family. We have new names. Our life here is over."

Evlyna shied from her father's uncommonly loud voice, but more from what he said.

"Now go and pack. We leave in the morning on the eight o'clock train." Although ending on a quieter note, her father's words hung heavily in Evlyna's ears.

She looked into her father's eyes. *What's he afraid of?* The thought caused her to pause, but only for a moment. Her young years and her own fears overruled and words spilled out, slowly, but with a determination that could not be missed on her audience.

"I'll never forgive you for this. Never! This is your God's fault. I hate Him!"

"Evlyna, please..."

But Evlyna fled to her room, away from her father, away from his God.

Pressing her door closed with her back, Evlyna slid to the floor and gave into the tears she'd fought so hard to hide.

New names? The thought terrified her. "How can they just walk away? How can they just turn their backs on *who* they are and pretend this life never existed?" Her whispered words fell heavily in the silent room. She flicked her shoes off and threw her sweater to the bottom of the bed. It missed and landed in a heap on the floor. It was only then that she noticed the two open suitcases and satchel at the foot of her bed.

"This can't be happening," she said, glancing at her desk. "I've got a school project to finish. It will affect my marks." Then reality struck in a surreal way. It was not the packing in the living room. Not the bare walls, or the full crates, or her father's announcement. It was her desk! She suddenly realized she would never see her friends again. She would never be pestered by Ronnie in English when Mr. Nichols faced the blackboard. She would not be handing in any project; she would not be finishing the Mother's Day gift at Mrs. Harding's sewing class. She would never again walk to school on the snow mounds at the edge of the road, pushing and shoving with her lifelong friends. Never again would she race up the back stairs after school to sample the new baking her father had created. No more projects, no more friends, no more *anything* that made her life normal and Evlyna pulled her knees to her chest, lowered her head, and wept.

Time passed. The room became dark long before Evlyna raised her head, and it was only the quiet tapping that aroused her.

"Go away!"

"Evlyna, it's Bubi. Please, child, open the door."

Her grandmother's voice was gentle, and Evlyna could imagine her standing close to the door, pressing her hand on it as though touching hers. She rolled to her side and stretched her cramped legs before opening the door.

Rachel Feldman stood head level with Evlyna, "small in stature, but mighty in person," as her son-in-law had often described her. But the once strong and determined grandmother now stood before Evlyna frail and tired. *She didn't look like this when I left for school this morning.* Evlyna clenched her fists. In defence of her beloved grandmother, her concern fuelled her anger toward her father. *She looks...*

"May I come in?"

Evlyna nodded and stepped aside, her thoughts left unfinished.

"May I?" pointing to the bedside light.

Evlyna nodded again.

"Come, sit here beside me." Her grandmother had carefully placed the suitcases on the floor and patted the bed.

"Bubi, I just don't understand. Why is he doing this? Why do we have to leave?" Evlyna flopped beside her grandmother, noticing that her grandmother's feet never reached the floor.

"I can't answer that, at least not in a way you would accept. All I can say is that your father and mother are doing what they believe to be the best possible thing given their circumstances."

"Do you agree with them?"

"It doesn't matter, child. I must comply and so must you."

"But I won't! I can't. I don't agree with what they've done. They've just turned their backs on their faith and are choosing to believe in something that's completely opposite to all they've ever believed, all they've ever taught me. How can I comply?"

Rachel Feldman remained silent as she removed her pearl necklace, lifted Evlyna's long dark hair, and anchored the strand around her neck. "These pearls belonged to my mother; she gave them to me on my wedding day. I'd like you to look after them for me, and maybe someday you will give them to *your* daughter."

Evlyna looked in her dressing table mirror and, for the first time in several hours, smiled. "They're beautiful. I've never really noticed them before, only that you always wear them. Maybe that's why I've never paid too much attention to them."

"Sometimes we fail to see the things that are always in front of us." Her grandmother patted Evlyna's hand and smiled an understanding smile before continuing. "Your life here is like these precious pearls: invaluable. These pearls may break, may even be lost, but the memory of them will always live in your heart. Just like your life here. You will never forget it. It's sealed in your memory forever. But you have to choose, my dear Evlyna. You have to choose how you move ahead: with sadness, for sure, but determination, or with bitterness and resentment. Perhaps these pearls will help you choose." Without another word, she gently touched Evlyna's cheek and slipped quietly from the room.

Morning came too soon for Evlyna. She'd been up for hours. Her desk was clear, her project in the wastebasket. Her dresser drawers were empty. Her closet was bare. She had complied, but... *I'm sorry, Bubi, I'll never forgive him.* Although her grandmother had gently pointed out her options, Evlyna would never forgive. There would be no more tears. Resignation had won, but there would be a price.

"Evlyna, we are ready to leave." Her mother's unsteady voice broke the silence.

Evlyna opened her door, turned for one last look, then closed it as Evlyna Chava Cohen and opened another, as it were, as Evelyn Crawford, her new name for her new life. She wore her grandmother's pearls; but out of sight, hidden from her father's eyes was her own necklace, her own identity, her own *Star of David.*

PART ONE

1

Be not hasty in thy spirit to be angry:
for anger resteth in the bosom of fools.
ECCLESIASTES 7:9

June 1964

Evelyn Sherwood avoided gatherings that required socializing and yet a sea of faces stretched before her. She could feel her heart racing and the familiar desire to run mounting within. She had surrendered to her daughter's urging to come to the speaking competition at Thystle Creek High School, but with each passing moment, Evelyn regretted her decision. A protective wall stood between her world in Thystle Creek and the dark secrets she had harboured since her thirteenth year, and now this world she regularly avoided extended across the width of the high school gymnasium.

A widow with a teenage daughter, Evelyn had resigned herself to a self-inflicted isolation rather than torment herself with what she believed to be an unattainable peace. To survive ordeals such as this—although she seldom exposed herself to such torment—she wore a mask: a smile, skilfully applied each time she walked out her front door. It appeared as though an artist had taken pity on her inner sadness, and with a simple but artful stroke removed all appearance of inner pain.

Tonight she wore her mask.

Students she recognized from the library where she worked, and others she had never seen before blended into one large mosaic. She slipped into the third last row. With her umbrella tucked under her seat, Evelyn straightened her skirt, closed her eyes, and forced herself to breathe deeply.

A sudden crack of thunder startled her and added to her growing agitation. Raindrops had pelted the dry ground as she'd approached the school. In fact, it had begun pouring with such a vengeance that small tributaries to the major runoff rushed down Lasington Street, creating puddles in the irregular dips in the road.

Evelyn shifted in her seat. *It's just a speaking contest. What could possibly be so important to bring me out on such a night?* She recalled overhearing conversations earlier in the week among the students at the library about the annual public speaking competition. But she had shut her ears to anything further, even at the expense of learning how the reputation of the school involved her daughter. Her interest centred on the library, not the gossip that filtered down from the students. And despite the excitement generated throughout the town each year, she had never understood the hype about a high school public speaking contest.

The library was the only element of the outside world of which Evelyn allowed herself to be a part. When Lewis had brought her as his bride to the small town of Thystle Creek in Central Alberta, she had worked as an assistant, stocking the library shelves, signing out books for students and children, and learning the Dewey Decimal System. Over the years she had taken on increased responsibilities until she finally attained the title of head librarian. Unwittingly, the new responsibility had contributed to her escape from the real world. She'd welcomed the opportunity and buried herself deeper into her world of books.

A growing uneasiness haunted Evelyn as she scanned the crowd for her daughter. She noticed that the inclement weather had not dampened the spirits of those hustling into the auditorium; the laughter and excitement could not be missed. Greetings filled the gym to a buzzing magnitude as dripping coats hung on a portable coat rack at the back of the gym. Galoshes and rubber boots sat under their owners' coats or jackets in their own puddles, and umbrellas perched open on the floor. As each moment passed, Evelyn felt the panic rising. Where was Lucy?

She watched Wil Douglas exchange an awkward handshake with Jim Broughton.

"When's the cast coming off, Jim?" she heard him ask.

"Oh, don't let him fool you, Wil," Jack Ramsey chimed in, helping Jim settle himself onto a chair. "He's milking this almost as much as Dave's milking his cows."

Leave it to Wil, Evelyn thought as she watched the young school teacher interact with those well beyond the age of his peer group. She recalled hearing via the library grapevine that Jim Broughton had been crushed between his bull and the walls of its stall. The word had been that he was lucky it had only been his shoulder that had taken the weight of the beast.

Watching the scene unfold, she studied Wil. Regularly in and out of the Sherwood home, he acted as the older brother Lucy never had. From childhood, he'd been her trusted friend and Lewis had loved him like a son. But even after all these years, Evelyn kept her distance, unable to express gratitude for the positive influence and friendship the sixth grade teacher had with her daughter.

"Hi, Mollie. You cooking up a storm these days? Nasty one out there right now." Evelyn heard voices behind her and saw Charlie Wheaton exchange greetings with Mollie Henderson as she shook her wet jacket before hanging it on a hook. Original proprietor of the local diner, Mollie replied with a nod and her famous grin before heading to a seat on the far side of the gym, pausing briefly to interact with Wil. Evelyn felt a pang of envy. *If only I could be more…*

"Sue! Oh, Sue!" Evelyn turned slightly to see Ruth Norton, sole owner and operator of the local pick-your-own strawberry farm on the north side of town, waving frantically to Sue Victors from across the gym. She watched as the two middle-aged women linked arms like teenagers and chatted all the way to their seats, stopping briefly to check on the progress of Jim Broughton.

"Hello, Evelyn, nice to see you. Nasty out there tonight."

Evelyn spun around and faced the front. "Oh, h–hello, Cliff," she responded quietly and then watched Cliff Moses move on to sit nearer to the front of the gymnasium. With his boots sitting off-centre of his dripping jacket at the back of the gym, he walked gingerly across the floor in his socked feet, refusing help from anyone. The most senior of the senior citizens of Thystle Creek, Cliff had been christened *Uncle Mo* long before Evelyn married Lewis, and at eighty-two, he was the patriarch of the town, respected, admired and loved, despite his stubbornness.

The noise level increased with the arrival of numerous families. Children ran and slid in their socks on the slippery floor, ignoring parental protests. Men back-clapped one another, women hugged and shared greetings as though years had passed since their last encounter. And babies cried their objections at every coo or ogle as they were passed from woman to woman.

The social interaction proved too much and panic won the storm raging within. *I can't do this.* Evelyn rose to leave, but noticed Wil watching her. His relaxed posture changed when their eyes met. The foot that had casually rested against the back wall of the gym slid to the floor, leaving him standing almost at attention as though intent on sending her a message. She followed his gaze to the front of the gymnasium and found the reason she'd come sitting in the second row. *Lucy?* It took only a moment for Evelyn to realize why Lucy had not eaten her supper. Why she had kept to her room when she'd come home from school. *This is why she left early, why she had me promise I'd come. She's speaking tonight!* Evelyn stared at the back of her daughter's head, willing her to turn around.

Lucy Sherwood sat between two boys and two girls, with another girl and boy to her left, and risked rudeness by ignoring them. Her feet were planted firmly in the squares on the gymnasium floor and her hands twisted in the folds of her skirt, the only external evidence of her inner turmoil. She closed her eyes and sighed, pushing back a lock of her light brown hair that had fallen loose over her face. Three weeks had passed since she'd accepted the challenge to represent her school in the Regional Public Speaking Contest, or the RPSC as the students had tagged it, and as she sat waiting, reviewing the topic she had chosen, she wondered if she'd made a mistake.

Lucy sighed again and shook her head as disturbing thoughts provoked her. *What in the world was I thinking? I should have told Mom. Is she even here?* Pointless rambling came to a halt when Lucy glanced at her watch. *Five to seven... a little late now.*

She tried to centre her thoughts on what she had prepared to say, but failed, and reluctantly focused on what it was that really made her nervous. Lucy knew it wasn't the contest distracting her; she had been in too many debates. Just a month earlier she had stood before her peers confidently defending her belief that sex before marriage was wrong. She'd led her team to victory, hands down. Lucy knew what it meant to face the opposition and stand firm. No, this gnawing fear was not centred on winning or losing. The mounting apprehension within had another source, and she turned and found that source watching her from the back of the gym. About to wave, Lucy stopped short, recognizing the all too familiar expression on her mother's face. She lowered her arm. Her smile faded. *Your mask can't fool me, Mom.*

"Lucille Sherwood will open our competition," Lucy heard her principal announce, and she found herself on her feet heading toward the podium. She no longer needed to wonder how her mother would react to her speech. Her fear was about to be realized.

This is a mistake, Lucy thought. She placed her cue cards before her, acknowledged the judges, and then turned to her audience. Mercifully, her thoughts began to focus on the reason why she stood before this crowd. "I am a tree whose green head reached high into the sky yesterday. Today my head is still high in the sky, but it is no longer green…" and Lucy's speech became automatic as her mind flooded with memories of her father.

The late Lewis Sherwood had been part-time mayor of Thystle Creek and owner of Sherwood's Hardware Emporium. A little eccentric by some standards, Lewis had chosen *Emporium* over *Store* because, "It's more than just a *store,* we have everything you need!" He'd been slightly overweight with thinning, sandy-coloured hair, and those who'd loved him called him Louie.

Lewis had loved his hometown where he'd lived his entire forty years, apart from the time he'd spent overseas during World War II. The grin he extended to strangers passing through town generally drew an involuntary nod or smile. He'd loved nature, the animals, the forests, and the freedom of walking on blankets of creeping wild thyme in the spring or crunching fallen leaves underfoot in the autumn. To Lewis, nothing compared to a crisp winter day as the snow fell and the temperature dropped, freezing the town's namesake into silence. Known for his enthusiasm and love for his hometown, he would often be quoted when a stranger commented on the beauty of the surroundings, "You can only find it in the North." He'd been zealous about protecting his woods from intruders, especially city folk seeking an adventure to brighten their mundane lives, and yet often stood by helplessly when nature all too often threatened to ignite the parched forest in the middle of the summer. His focus on the protection of the forest and its wildlife had won Lewis the distinguished position of mayor when he was a young man, newly married and fresh home from the war.

Lewis had lived his adult life by the Good Book. He would often quote from the Bible to his regular customers if they came into the Emporium anxious about some "very important" or "life-changing" decision they needed to make. Predictably, "Rest in the Lord, and wait patiently for him" would resonate throughout the store just before Lewis offered to pray for their particular need, and often they left feeling a whole lot better than when they came in.

The little white church on Grant Street had come to be *home* every Sunday for Lewis and his daughter. They had their favourite pew, right alongside Josh Graham, who had been instrumental in introducing Lewis to the source of peace he eventually adopted into his everyday life. Each time he worshipped, Lewis would lift his hands in celebration and his voice could be heard by everyone who sat within three rows behind and in front of him. It was obvious to all that he was tone deaf—and nobody knew that better than Lewis—but he was always ready to quote Psalm 98:4, "Make a joyful noise unto the Lord, all the earth: make a loud noise, and rejoice, and sing praise," quickly adding with a boyish grin, "It didn't say the joyful noise had to be in tune!"

Memories of her father vied for her attention and Lucy struggled inwardly. Yet the well-rehearsed words flowed from her mouth. "Yesterday my arms offered a playground for squirrels and chipmunks, a home for birds that enjoyed the safety of the forest. Yesterday I held the nest of a mother robin. Snuggled beneath her belly, her five babies' chirping demands could be heard over the treetops each morning. Today, only the charred remains of a faithful mother and her family can be found in what is left of my outstretched limbs." Lucy's voice filled the auditorium. "Yesterday I looked out over a bed of soft green moss. Today, as far as I can see from my great height is to the horizon where everything is black, desolate, and dead. Soon I, too, will be dead."

2

Greater love hath no man than this,
that a man lay down his life for his friends.
John 15:13

Lucy's speech painted vivid pictures and Josh Graham quivered involuntarily.

"Was that you, Mr. Camper, who never took time to appreciate the beauty that surrounded you? Living in your asphalt cities with treeless streets, were you not able to understand? Could you not conceive the need to protect the comfort and shade we offered you? Did you not realize we held life in our limbs, that we provided a home for the smallest of insects and a temporary landing for eagles as they awaited their dinner far below? Was that you, Mr. Camper, who never understood the importance of being fire-wise?"

Josh didn't wish Lucy silent. On the contrary, he understood the need for her to speak out. He hoped this would bring her some healing, perhaps closure, for it was all true... there had been a forest fire. Her father had died saving him. His best friend had given him the ultimate gift: his life.

"Was that you, Mr. Camper, who assumed the smouldering fire that had cooked your breakfast earlier that morning would go out on its own? Did you shake your head in disbelief hours later as flames rose over the very spot where you had taken refuge in our forest the night before? Did you not understand the role you had played in the destruction that followed?"

Josh stared straight ahead. As Lucy's voice filled the room, sounds filled his head. The shouting, the screaming, the sobbing.

"Did you not understand how lives—animals and humans alike—would be changed forever when you allowed your beautiful weekend home to become a fiery furnace?"

Josh rubbed his right thigh. It had been four years and healing had been quick, but he continued to experience stiffness on damp days. Tonight his leg ached, and in listening to Lucy, he could smell the fire, feel the suffocating heat, hear the sound of Lewis's voice.

"Josh! Josh! Where are you? Oh God, please help me find him. Josh! Josh!"

"Louie? Is that you? I–I can't see. The smoke's too thick. I'm over near the embankment pinned under a tree. I think my leg's broken."

"Hang on, son, I'm coming. I'm almost through the... I can see you, Josh, I can see you now!"

Josh remembered Lewis talking to him, dragging him out from under the fallen tree, pouring water from his canteen onto a handkerchief to wipe the gash on his forehead. He recalled the sound, the sharp, breaking sound that often precedes the thunderous noise as a tree succumbs to its enemy and falls with a final thud to the fiery forest floor.

"Louie! Louie! Watch out... the tree!"

Josh remembered Lewis looking up at the threatening sound. He remembered Lewis pushing him down the hill seconds before the treetop broke from the main trunk. He remembered rolling, and with each tumble feeling the excruciating pain as his broken leg hit the ground beneath him. He remembered hearing a scream and then realized it was his own voice screaming in horror, knowing he had left behind his best friend buried beneath the tree. He remembered waking up in the hospital miles from home wishing he could stop remembering.

His memories often evoked nightmares that robbed him of sleep, resulting in the ongoing battle between flashbacks and reality, and the should-have, could-have syndrome. Sometimes he won the battle. When he didn't, he was left exhausted and overcome with grief. On the good days, he vowed he would never forget the sacrifice his friend had made.

"Louie Sherwood personified John 15:13," Pastor Cribbs had said the day of Lewis's funeral. "Greater love hath no man than this, that a man lay down his life for his friends." Josh had hung his head, aware of the magnitude of Lewis's sacrifice and the role he'd played, yet he had wanted nothing more than to see Lewis walk down the church aisle with his usual grin and firm handshake.

Josh glanced around the gymnasium and noticed Evelyn. He watched as she struggled with each breath. He couldn't help noticing others watching her as well, and although he marvelled at the fact that she'd come, he ached for her, knowing how much pain Lucy's speech would cause.

"Do you feel the shame? Can you sense the loss?" Lucy's voice broke through his thoughts. "Animals fled the fiery inferno desperate to survive, and people braved the flames frantic to save what the fire had yet to destroy. Lives were injured. Lives were lost."

And Josh remembered his friend.

Since childhood he'd known Lewis as Mr. Sherwood. He'd grown up hearing stories of Lewis and, having lost his own father as a ten-year-old, Josh had latched on to Lewis as a father figure, trying to emulate him in his young life. He became a regular at the Emporium, offering to unload boxes from delivery trucks or stock shelves. When he was a teenager, his charisma and willingness to listen and learn had landed the much coveted after-school job at Sherwood's Hardware Emporium.

Within the first month, Josh knew every size and type of screw, nut and bolt found within the walls of the Emporium. Yard goods, canning supplies, electrical needs, nothing missed his attentive eye. His vivid imagination led to a new slogan endorsed by Lewis and everyone in town: *Why look elsewhere when SHE's got it.* Much to the delight of his new employer, he'd renamed Sherwood's Hardware Emporium to match her initials.

Josh worked hard. His eagerness to please and his punctuality resulted in a raise of ten cents an hour by the end of his third month and the encouraging words of his mentor: "You deserve it, son. You're a good worker and if you keep it up, you'll go places."

Josh smiled now, remembering Lewis's words, and despite the sorrow Lucy's speech was creating, he silently thanked her for reminding him of the unique friendship he'd had with her father. He knew he'd done more for Lewis than keeping his customers happy and sorting stock. He'd not been in Lewis's employ long before he'd shared his beliefs and brought religion into Lewis's life, not the soft, comfortable kind, but the kind that seeps into one's soul. He had introduced Lewis to the concept of being able to talk to God as though He were his best friend. Josh was thrilled when Lewis decided that his life needed the kind of communion with God that Josh had so often and so easily shared.

"You mean it's that simple?" Lewis had exclaimed in disbelief.

"That's all I have to do? That's it?"

"You couldn't be more exact, Mr. Sherwood. Jesus meant for little children to understand why He came and died, so you adults shouldn't have a problem," Josh had quipped. "Jesus loves you, Mr. Sherwood, and accepting His gift of love and understanding that He died for your sins makes you a Christian, by the Bible's standards."

Josh could still see Lewis scratch his head, could still hear his quiet response: "Out of the mouths of babes…"

During his first year, Josh had been known as the "Gofer at SHE," a nickname that stuck until he left for university at nineteen. When he returned home in the spring of '58, he was welcomed with a strong handshake and a bear hug from Lewis. "How ya doing, Gofer? Welcome home!"

"Thanks, Mr. Sherwood. It's sure good to be back. You know…" Josh hesitated. "…the big city can't measure up to *this*." His outstretched arms enveloped the surroundings and he smiled, knowing he affirmed his older friend's deep-felt belief.

"Look me up when you get settled, Josh. I've got an idea I wanna run by you. And call me Louie, will ya!" Lewis had added as he waved and headed toward the Emporium.

"Sure thing, Mr. Sherwo… Louie; I'll be over this afternoon."

That afternoon Lewis had offered Josh a full partnership in the business. Two years later, Lewis was dead.

Josh remained silent at the conclusion of Lucy's speech. He knew a tribute had been paid to the memory of Lewis and who better than his own daughter to have done it? Quiet sniffles led to hushed struggles as purses clicked open for the ever-faithful tissue. Several men seemed to find something on the ceiling that demanded their immediate attention and others felt the need to study the pattern on the tile floor under their feet. Children sat quietly. Babies stopped fussing.

Josh was glad Wil broke the deafening silence, sending applause rippling forward from the back of the gymnasium until everyone stood, relieved that they could express some emotion other than what was buried deep within. Everyone stood but Evelyn.

She had been present in body, but Evelyn's thoughts had been elsewhere. Her daughter's words opened a wound so deep she was forced to stifle her gasps when her chest refused to expand with air. Her rapid pulse pounded in her ears and her eyes filled but refused to empty. She sat motionless and stared straight ahead, willing her mind to focus on anything but what she had just heard. All day she had been reliving a memory of the day her life changed forever and there had been no reprieve tonight. Memories flooded her mind and she shuddered as they took over her conscious thought. The ever-present inner voice taunted her: *How could she? What right does she have? She's obviously thinking more of this contest than of you! Don't sit around and watch people applaud her. Get out of here!* Somewhere deep within Evelyn could hear the sirens as Lewis's lifeless body was rushed to a hospital, but as Wil's applause penetrated the stillness of the room, the shrill of the sirens became distant only to be replaced with a festering rage.

Amidst the growing applause, Evelyn stood up and walked out.

3

My soul is weary of my life;
I will leave my complaint upon myself;
I will speak in the bitterness of my soul.
JOB 10:1

Aspen Avenue, like many streets in Thystle Creek, flaunted its beauty year round. At the height of the summer months, branches of aging Manitoba Maples would arc the road, providing a canopy from the misty summer rain. The autumn months would turn the canopy into a majestic blanket of orange, red and yellow before the leaves scattered to the ground below and retired the canopy for another year. Then, with winter months looming ahead, the neighbourhood would launch long-established traditions. Families would drag fallen leaves to the edge of the road where young children would enjoy endless tumbles in three-foot high piles of summer's bounty. Those who laboured over the rakes would feign objection as they hid their own laughter behind their busyness, remembering days gone by. At the first sign of snow, shovels and trucks with ploughs would replace rakes and lawnmowers, readying the street once again for a long, cold winter.

Eleven-fifty-one Aspen Avenue had been home for Lewis Sherwood, and in the four years following his death, Evelyn had lost herself as much in adding to the beauty of their street as she had in her books at the library. Each spring, her gentle hand encouraged tulips and crocuses to flourish under her front kitchen window, only to give way to the Alberta wild rose, calla lilies, and a large display of poppies during the summer months. Under the large white pine on the front lawn, clusters of lemon mint multiplied under her watchful eye and a grove of white birch stood to the right of the centre walkway, shading the living room window. The north side provided home for the less tamed flowers that grew as nature intended. Large upturned blooms on the white bell flowers shared space with purple prairie crocuses and soft carpet moss, and late in the fall, on the verge of frost, fringed gentian flowers thrived in the dampness that insured their survival.

However, the surrounding beauty disappeared in the shadow of the raging storms, one created by the Almighty, the other by His created being.

Evelyn struggled, head down against nature's assault and her ability to reason. Losing the battle, her anguished cries echoed the earlier voice and dissolved in the wailing wind. "How could she? How could she?" Fuelled by anger and disbelief, she hurried along Aspen Avenue, allowing the storm to have its way with her. The wind blew against her back, pushing her down the tree-lined street and her umbrella strained in its effort to keep her dry. Water snaked around her feet, forming small puddles in her path. Treetops danced furiously as the wind swirled pellets of rain in every direction.

She could envision her daughter standing before the large group of people talking about the fire. Talking about how Lewis had died. *Everything is black, desolate and dead. Soon I, too, will be dead...* reverberated in Evelyn's head, and she unwillingly relived the fire that had killed her husband.

I don't need to be reminded. Evelyn's thoughts raged at her absent daughter. "Your father was killed!" she shouted in the storm. "Remember?"

Evelyn stumbled up her path as the wind blew the branches of the pine tree, rocketing cones to the ground on the front lawn. Her tears ran freely as she struggled with the key to the front door. When the latch finally released its hold, Evelyn pushed herself free from the wind, closed the door against the storm and collapsed on the front hall carpet.

As was her habit in defence of her bitterness and rage, she turned to an unseen God and cursed Him. Tears ran until the cavern within emptied and the ensuing stillness became a threat. It was a reminder of how alone she was, and that was too much to bear. Evelyn rose from her cramped position, placed her umbrella in the hall stand, and walked into the darkened living room. It was not that she wanted music in her home; it was more that she couldn't stand the silence, the aloneness, so Evelyn pressed the button on the hi-fi.

I'll be faithful, I'll be true, loving you… The whispered voice crooned soft words, and as Evelyn stood facing the night blackness and the volatile storm, waiting for her daughter, memories soothed her soul, if only temporarily. She locked her arms over her chest. *Winter, summer, springtime too, loving you…* She closed her eyes and relived a memory, a happy memory that kept her husband alive, a memory of his embrace as they glided around the kitchen floor.

4

A time to weep, and a time to laugh;
a time to mourn, and a time to dance.
ECCLESIASTES 3:4

In a home where an unspoken disquiet was often apparent but seldom addressed, the dancing had been a fresh respite. It had been sporadic, Evelyn would admit that, and it was not true dancing, as most would define it. Rather, it was an endearing moment when her family forgot their pain and indulged themselves in an infectious laughter that brought with it the warmth of much-needed contentment. It was a laughter built on a love that denied everyone's perception that the Sherwoods were not a happy couple.

The dancing always happened in the kitchen on a Thursday night when music from a prescheduled radio program echoed throughout Evelyn's home. The kitchen sat to the left of the main entrance, off the front hall, and extended the depth of the house. The bay window created a small alcove that housed a kitchen table and chairs, and afforded a full view of the temporary dance floor. Anyone passing by could see Evelyn with her husband, embracing, laughing, swirling.

They couldn't begin to understand the temporary release, couldn't begin to grasp the freedom felt in forgetting, even for a brief moment. They could just witness it.

Lost in Lewis's embrace, Evelyn would relax in the gentleness of the moment. *I will spend my whole life through, loving you, just loving you* quietly played; time paused and Evelyn's pain would cease to exist.

Unlike a bashfulness that enveloped Evelyn while her husband embraced her, Lewis's behaviour proved he didn't understand the meaning of shy. Suddenly, *Blue Suede Shoes* filled the kitchen and overflowed into the rest of the house, and much to the delight of their daughter, her husband would join the voice of the latest teenage idol and sing louder than necessary in an effort to prove to the world that he, indeed, had a voice to be reckoned with.

Twirling Evelyn safely to the kitchen chair, Lewis would reach for Lucy as she stood parroting him in the doorway and spin her into his arms in one sweeping motion. Lucy's laughter would reach borderline hysteria until she was released to join Evelyn while Lewis continued to entertain his family with his personal imitation of the latest trend in music, strumming on an invisible guitar.

For a brief moment, Evelyn's world was coloured with the sounds of laughter, excitement and pleasure, but only for a brief moment. Blind to the human eye, the one who was always present, always ready to deceive, always ready to accuse, whispered in her ear. *Who are you kidding? This won't last. You're living in a dream world*. Each time her countenance would change, although the transformation was lost on the two doing their own imitation of a hound dog, and she would quietly slip by the father and daughter duo and assume an act of busyness at the kitchen sink. Choking back sobs, she would lower her head in submission to the voice of the accuser, reminded once again of her secrets known by no one, not even her husband.

Evelyn's image reflected in the living room window as lightning cut jagged slices of white and yellow across the tumultuous sky. The ensuing thunder and her own reflection invaded her memories and pulled her back to the present. At thirty-nine, her outward appearance often caused heads to turn her way. Current fashion never demanded her attention, yet her choice of clothing remained fashionable. Her walnut-brown, shoulder length hair required little attention except to brush it in place or out of the way as she laboured in her garden or worked over a stack of books at the library. The summer sun lightened it and gave it a shine that lasted into the winter months, and to everyone but Evelyn, she would be considered beautiful.

Evelyn could still hear Lewis's voice…"Our daughter sure got your good looks." His touch had been gentle and his whisper more so as he cupped her face and kissed her. Seeing her hesitate, he never failed to add, "I love you, Evie girl."

Evelyn's shyness from his endearment still haunted her. She'd loved Lewis, but she'd never felt worthy of his praise, and the ever-present voice was always ready to remind her: *If he'd known about your past would he have still loved you?* "Had you known, would you have given up on me, Louie?" Evelyn whispered in the darkness. The night sky lit up again and the roll of thunder accompanied her inner battle. Anger. Guilt. Defeat. She shook her head in a feeble attempt to erase the memories.

Through fresh tears she lowered her head, remembering her husband's gentle spirit. Haunted by her refusal to listen to him and acknowledge the One who could lift her burden and release her from her self-inflicted prison, she recalled a conversation that had taken place just two days before Lewis had died.

She hugged herself to squelch a shudder. She willed her thoughts to cease, but failed, and with her eyes closed, submitted to the memory.

"Evie, your sadness pains me," Lewis spoke softly. "The other day I read in a book by C.S. Lewis that true Christianity 'means that every single act and feeling, every experience whether pleasant or unpleasant must be referred to God. It means looking at everything as something that comes from Him.' Evie, your unpleasant experience … "

"Don't minimize my pain with the simplest of words. Unpleasant!" she hissed as she unleashed her anger. "How can you define God's act of cruelty and disregard for life with one word? Please don't talk to me about pleasant or unpleasant experiences, Lewis. Your God can't help me. No one can."

Evelyn recalled using her husband's formal name intentionally in an attempt to end their conversation, but Lewis had continued, ignoring her plea to be left alone.

"You haven't given Him a chance, Evie. Knowing God has brought me a freedom I'd lost in my youth, a peace that's released me from the pain of my war memories. When I accepted Christ, I knew I was loved, accepted and forgiven, and freed to love Him in return. He can do the same for you, but you've gotta want it, girl. You've gotta understand that you're hardening your heart to the One who can set you free."

Evelyn continued, as though deaf to her husband's pleadings. "Any thoughts I have ever had about God were born to me by my parents, but He was their choice, not mine; their God, not mine; their God who was supposed to love and protect. How could a God … " She stumbled over the strange words and began again. "You claim He is a healer and a provider, One who is—what is it you say?—all-sufficient and a lover of my soul. What does He know about love?" Evelyn's anger and pain attacked further as tears emptied on her face. "How could the God that you claim loves and protects be the same God who stood by and watched Bobby...watched innocent people die?" Her composure gone, she ceased struggling with couching her words. "I've asked your unseen God that question again and again and the response is always the same: Silence! He's either not there or doesn't care!"

Evelyn trembled, remembering the scene. That was the last time her husband had spoken to her about God, and now he was gone. It was too late to retract her words, too late to assure Lewis that her anger was not at him but at his God.

As she wrestled with the memory, her thoughts returned to the events of the evening and her anger toward her daughter rekindled.

5

Let him kiss me with the kisses of his mouth:
for thy love is better than wine.
SONG OF SOLOMON 1:2

Lucy burst through the front doorway, partly from the wind blowing behind her, but mostly from excitement. She turned within the protection of the front hall and waved to Wil and his parents, shouting over the thunder, "Thank you for the ride home." She hesitated before turning on the lights. Where could her mother be? To her relief, the hall light revealed her standing in the living room, looking out the window.

"Mom, I won!" Lucy exclaimed, overlooking the darkness of the living room in her excitement. "I brought home the trophy. For the first time, TCH has won and I did it! You should have seen them. They laughed, they cried, they clapped. I even got a hug from Mr. McTavish. That was a shock! Everyone laughed. He was so excited." But Lucy's enthusiasm waned. "Mom, are you okay? Why did you leave so early? I was worried you were..."

"Why did I leave?" Evelyn interrupted Lucy. "Why did I leave?"

Her voice escalated as she slowly turned around. "Lucy, how could you do that? It was hard enough to live through another anniversary of your father's death, but to spend it listening to you talking about *forest fires.* You talked as though you were a bystander, unaffected by it!"

"You know that's not true," Lucy came to her own defence. "Daddy is ... Daddy was everything to me." Her voice dropped to a whisper. "I miss him, too, you know." Tears filled her eyes, but her words fell on deaf ears.

"'I am a tree ...'" Evelyn imitated her daughter with a sarcasm that wounded Lucy more than if her mother had raised her hand to her. "Really, Lucy, to belittle your father's death like that! He's gone and no amount of pretence or make-believe or talking about it can change that. And no competition or award ..." She left her words hanging with a cursory look at the trophy in Lucy's hand.

Her mother's attack continued, taking another direction, one for which Lucy had no response.

"Your father told me once—just days before he died—that *everything* that happens comes from the God he believed in, the One you worship. Well, look what your God did to your father! He died a cruel, horrible and needless death. That can only prove one thing: your God isn't concerned about you. He never was. Your worship—as was your father's—is wasted on an unseen, uncaring God." Evelyn continued, thoughtlessly disparaging her daughter's belief. "It's one thing to have a childish fantasy in some supreme being, but it's time for you to accept reality and grow up, Lucy. Your father's dead and you can see where the worship of his God got him: nowhere, just dead!"

Lucy stood in stunned silence as her mother continued to deride the faith Lucy once shared with her father. She stood in silence because she knew in her heart she felt the anger toward God her mother was accusing her of and it frightened her.

"Why would He kill a man who worshipped Him, who faithfully spoke words from a book he held in reverence? Why? Judging from your avoidance of church and your lack of answers now, it's obvious you know that what I'm saying is true." Her words softened. "We're on our own, Lucy, we're on our own." And Evelyn ended her pronouncement of disbelief in God with a quiet sob and sank wordlessly into the chair by the window where she had been standing for so long.

FLEE!

Lucy laid the trophy on the coffee table in the darkened room and retreated to her own. She felt the loss of her father, too, but in a way that no one could understand. She buried her face in her pillow and sobbed. He had been more than her father; he had been her confidant, her friend, the one who understood her. He had loved her through the lonely years of growing up in a home where two parents lived, but only one had provided the nurturing a growing child needed. His death had left a void that had been filled with an anger directed to the One who could have prevented his death.

Conscious of the rain pelting on her window, she imagined for a brief moment that God was attempting to cleanse her bitter spirit. She had felt Him moments earlier urging her to escape her mother's tirade, but she refused to acknowledge Him, a refusal she had enacted many times over the past four years. Her worship of God had been shared with her father and he was gone. It was over. It was that simple. *Maybe in time,* Lucy considered briefly, trying to console herself; but it proved in vain. She had never been able to curse God, but she had consciously made a choice and she turned her back on God's quiet prompting once again.

A sudden gush of water falling from the eaves into the water barrel in the back corner of the house distracted her. With new determination, she quickly resolved that no amount of *verbal* storm she had just endured could wash away her victory, and she relived the evening that had just taken place.

I won! She smiled in the darkened room. She had seen her mother leave and her heart sank. Then she saw Wil applauding. Lucy folded her hands under her chin and squeezed herself, remembering the shivers of excitement that had raced through her as the applause built into a wave and everyone stood, even the children.

Despite her mother's rejection, despite the spiritual vacuum she now felt, Lucy allowed herself the freedom to enjoy the moment of victory. Of course, the true victory hadn't come until the end of the evening, after the judges had deliberated and found her the winner. Then the realization had hit: Thystle Creek High School had won the RPSC for the first time and she'd brought it about.

Adults and students had crowded around her and she could still feel the bear hug from her principal. *That was weird.* Lucy shuddered, remembering. Handshakes, pats on the back, words of congratulations continued to come into focus, along with the kiss.

Wil had hugged her and planted a kiss on her cheek. "Way to go, Luce. I'm so proud of you," he'd said, hesitating slightly before releasing her. In the dark, Lucy touched the spot where he'd kissed her. *Did he linger or did I just imagine it?* Lucy squeezed her pillow as she relived the moment. *He's kissed me before, like a brother,* she chided herself, but she couldn't deny that this time something was different. *Funny, I've never noticed his dimples before. Wonder why I'm noticing them now?* Conscious of sobs coming from the living room, she muffled a giggle and turned on her side in search of some elusive answers to some surprising and perplexing questions.

As sleep slowly engulfed her, Lucy's thoughts pivoted between the awakening feelings she was experiencing and the kiss that meant something more than congratulations, and she was determined to find out what!

Evelyn recoiled as her daughter's parting look haunted her, but absorbed in self-pity she could only go as far as declaring herself a terrible mother. She couldn't go beyond the barrier that she had put up between herself and her daughter. She couldn't bring herself to seek forgiveness and receive comfort. *Why bother?* the ever-present voice whispered in her ear, and Evelyn listened. Past ghosts surfaced. Images of two men vied for her attention, and in the shadows of her life she saw two innocent babies, one son who never had the opportunity to grow beneath her heart and another who never had a chance to take his first breath. There was yet another image, but she refused to acknowledge it. Rather, she cursed God.

Hours passed before Evelyn rose, extinguished the only light shining in the Sherwood home, and left the house in darkness, not unlike her own soul.

6

Rejoice, O young man, in thy youth;
and let thy heart cheer thee in the days of thy youth,
and walk in the ways of thine heart...
ECCLESIASTES 11:9

All day Friday Wil had been anxious to talk to Lucy about her mother and the way she had responded to Lucy's speech, but between his teaching schedule and basketball game with his sixth grade boys at night, he'd missed her. Now it was Saturday. He knew exactly where to find her.

Wil had encouraged Lucy to return to work at the Emporium not long after her father had been killed. Although she had been a young teenager then, she had been part of the atmosphere of the Emporium since she was old enough to tag along with Lewis and entertain customers. Even so, it had been hard for Wil to convince her.

"I don't know, Wil. Mom isn't doing great and besides, I think it'll be too painful to..."

"Luce, your mom sold Josh the other half of SHE, right? I figure it was something she had to do to try and move on. Either that or it was just too painful to hang on to. Now that Josh has full ownership, he might be glad to have a part of Lewis around. You've got his smile, you know," he added with a smirk.

Lucy's choice to go back created no noticeable change in her mother, but it had led to a discovery that Lucy had shared with Wil not long after her return.

"You were right. There are lots of memories, and Josh is really glad I came back."

A car horn took Wil from his memory as he turned his truck onto Lasington Street and saw Jim Broughton flagging him down. They each waved a greeting and Jim strolled over with the update that his shoulder was coming along fine. Both enjoyed some small talk, but inevitably their conversation led to Lucy winning the competition and the disappointment it must have been for her to see her mother walk out at the end of her speech.

Moments later, with his truck parked in front of the Emporium, Wil sat and watched Lucy through the storefront window as he ruminated on her decision to return. *Good choice, Luce, good choice.* He smiled, nodding, as though she were there reading his mind. *Just like your speech. Despite your mom, Thursday night was another good choice. If anyone had the gumption to take on that challenge, you did.* He wasn't quite ready to let go of that evening.

He remembered scanning the crowd from the back of the gymnasium and finding Lucy sitting near the front, very still, like a statue. He saw her check her watch and involuntarily had done the same. Thinking now, he wondered if she'd been nervous, but Wil could not recall a time when her boldness and courage hadn't won over fear. He remembered her as a four-year-old bundle of energy when her father had brought her to church for the first time. As a young lad of nine, Wil hid a grin behind his hymn book when Lucy stood on the pew, firmly grasped her father's shoulder, and then proceeded to wave to everyone in the congregation who was looking her way. His grin had turned into giggles that resulted in a firm hand on his own shoulder by his mother and a stern, "William, face the front."

Nothing has ever daunted you, Luce. You're quite the young woman. About to climb out of his truck, the thought struck him. *Young woman! What happened to my 'kid sister'?* He closed the truck door, hugged the steering wheel, and stared in Lucy's direction again, arrested by confusion, then disbelief. Lucy had been the closest thing to a sister Wil had known growing up. He was the youngest in a large family of two older sisters and an older brother, and early in his life he'd learned what a *change of life baby* was—he was one of them. His brother and sisters had married and moved away. With all the appearances of being an only child, Wil had welcomed the chance of being a big brother to Lucy. As he grew into his teens, he had often felt the need to watch over her, perhaps even when it wasn't necessary. The night of the competition was no exception. He'd watched Lucy turn from her mother's look. He'd noticed her shoulders droop with obvious discouragement, and he'd felt powerless to help her. But he had felt something else, too. When Lucy had taken her place at the podium, he'd no longer seen a teenage girl that needed the protection of a big brother, but a young woman who held her head high.

And then, there was the kiss. *Where did that come from?* Wil relaxed his grip on the steering wheel. He closed his eyes, threw his head back against the seat, then bolted upright and started to laugh. "Of course!"

The revelation was simple, yet startling. It had been screaming in his ear on Thursday night and he'd ignored it. Now he smiled with realization and acceptance. "I'm in love with Lucy!" Embarrassed somewhat, he looked around to be sure he hadn't been heard, then shook his head in wonder and amazement. *This girl's been my friend most of my life, and now—*

A tap on his truck's door startled him.

"You okay, Wil?"

"Yeah, just fine, Doc. Just great! How's about you?"

"*I'm* okay, but *you* should be more careful who sees you talking to yourself. Might be cause for some good old-fashioned town gossip," he added with a wink and a tip of his hat before continuing on his way.

Wil watched him go and wondered if the doctor had actually heard his declaration of love for Lucy. But he shrugged the thought away, climbed out of his truck, and headed for the Emporium.

He paused inside the front door when he couldn't see Lucy. Still alone with his thoughts, he continued to marvel at this unexpected revelation. He knew now he'd loved Lucy when she was baptized at twelve, sinking into the creek and coming up with an overzealous splash that reached everyone unlucky enough to be close to the shore. He smiled, remembering, willing himself not to laugh aloud. He'd loved her at thirteen as she screamed in denial of her father's death. He'd loved her even as her rage had been directed at the One who had created his love for her.

I love Lucille Jacqueline Sherwood, Wil almost shouted, and then suppressed a laugh thinking of the scene that such an announcement would create. He'd loved her as she'd searched the crowd at the competition, looking for the only face that mattered. And he'd loved her even more when she'd momentarily bowed her head at her mother's apparent rejection. Now he was faced with the possibility of their relationship becoming more than just platonic and discovering if what he was feeling could possibly be reciprocated.

Intent on surprising her, Wil found Lucy stacking a new shipment of light bulbs on the shelf at the back of the store, and fearing a potential accident, he approached her openly. "Hi, Luce." His greeting masked his emotions.

"Hi." Lucy groaned as she stood from her crouched position.

"I've been trying to catch up with you since Thursday night. What'd your mom say when you took the trophy home?"

Lucy responded to his question with a shrug and a weak smile, a signal to Wil that things hadn't gone well. He'd offered to go in with Lucy when his parents had dropped her off during the storm, but she'd assured him that things would be fine, so he hadn't pressed her.

"It was pretty bad. I haven't seen her so angry in a long time. I thought maybe things were getting better, but after the other night, I'm not so sure." Lucy headed toward the counter and rang up a sale for Mr. Cleaton, nodding politely as he expressed how much he enjoyed her friendly smile. Turning to Wil, she continued on a lighter note. "Are you doing anything tonight?"

With what once would have been a natural suggestion, Lucy had unwittingly stirred the new emotions that Wil had been focusing on just before he saw her. He found himself staring, dazed by her suggestion.

"Wil?" She repeated her question under the watchful eye of Mr. Cleaton as she packaged up his bag of screws, electrical tape, and six new sets of electrical boxes.

"Oh, sorry Luce, a lot on my mind I guess. Yeah, I'm free. I've just got some papers to grade and then finish my reports by next Wednesday. I can't believe school's finished next week," he added absentmindedly. "But tonight's not a problem. What do you have in mind?"

"Nothing special. I thought maybe we could bike to Miller's Mountain. It's been a while since I've seen one of our famous sunsets. You interested?" Lucy asked, with a hopeful smile.

"Sounds like a plan to me. Wear your bathing suit just in case we decide to cool off after the ride. Never mind with the face! You'll be glad you wore it if the water's not too cold. I'll meet you at the curve in front of Ruth Norton's road. About six?"

"Six is fine, but I'd rather not wait on the road. I'll meet you at the top. Now, I'd better get back to work before I'm fired."

Wil left and Lucy turned to help Irene Morgan find a box of mason jars she needed in anticipation of her new batch of Saskatoon berry jam. All of a sudden, Lucy didn't mind coming to work today. She held the door for Irene and reached up and flicked the bell that announced the arrival or departure of a customer.

"Isn't it a beautiful day, Mrs. M.?" Lucy asked, unaware of her flushed cheeks and Irene Morgan's knowing smile. She turned back to the crate of packaged light bulbs that had been momentarily neglected; however, her thoughts were far from aligning the light bulbs in any particular order. As though a form of electrical osmosis had struck her, a light had come on and she smiled as she realized she had been humming *Love Me Tender.*

"Mom, Wil and I are biking to Miller's Mountain. We might stay for a swim if it's not too cold, but I won't be late."

Evelyn sat at the kitchen table, nursing a cup of coffee. She'd spent the day in the garden trying to stay ahead of the weeds, but also trying to forget the scene that had taken place a couple of nights earlier. Up until now, neither she nor Lucy had mentioned the argument; in fact, they had missed seeing each other entirely. When Evelyn had come downstairs Friday morning, Lucy had already left for school and the trophy was no longer on the coffee table. Evelyn had found it on a shelf in her daughter's bedroom beside a picture of her father.

"That's fine, Lucy," Evelyn responded, aware that Lucy had gathered her things and was heading for the front door. As an afterthought, she called after her, "Lucy, I'm sorry about..." and then checked herself. She changed the subject and the near-apology was lost on Lucy. Her next comment surprised even herself. "Lucy, are you getting serious about Wil?"

So totally out of character, she regretted asking it when she saw the look on her daughter's face, but committed to it, she continued. "You've been friends for so long... I was wondering if there was something more. You two remind me of your father and... when we used to visit the mountain." Evelyn's voice trailed off when there was no immediate response.

Lucy backtracked to the kitchen doorway and impulsively hugged her mother. "Nope, we're just good friends. See ya later." And the moment ended.

Lucy turned her bike toward the road just west of town, leaving Aspen Avenue behind. The rare comment her mother had made about her parents' visits to the mountain had opened an old memory, a quiet moment when her father had talked about the condition of the world when he met her mother. They were on the mountain, a month before he'd died.

"We met during a time when the world was being torn apart by war. It was as though the tentacles of a monster had reached across an ocean into cities and towns, as well as farming communities that seldom feel the effects of a local city, much less a war on the other side of the ocean." His voice had been pensive, his words melancholic. "It was a war that snatched, separated, and swallowed up lives. No one was spared," he'd said. "Babies who had been conceived during a desperate attempt to shut out the inevitable separation that loomed ahead entered a world where a madman ruled and fathers and brothers fought in battles that would scar the world forever. In battles where the fear of death permeated every moment of every day and the passion to survive spawned every breath taken. In battles where one witnessed a lifelong friend die a cruel death, and where one was left to wonder *if* or *when*."

Lucy had sat quietly, afraid to move for fear the spell would be broken. She had never heard her father speak with such eloquence, with such passion, with such pain, and she wondered if these words would be found in his diary.

In the years following her father's death, Lucy had read much on the war that had invaded, and yet had joined, two lives. She'd read that it had brought a different kind of life for those who would never see a battlefield, but a life where even the separation of an ocean could not protect them. A life controlled by fear, temporarily abated when the long-awaited letter finally arrived and was devoured daily to keep alive the author. For others, it was a life when prayers and petitions to the Creator were constant, and for those who didn't or wouldn't look beyond themselves for answers, it was a life filled with anger and dread, intent on cursing the One who was suffering alongside those who cursed Him. For some, it was a life that took on new meaning when the telegram arrived or the official car pulled up in front of their home. Petitions reached the heavens beseeching the Almighty to prevent the occupants of the car from coming to their doorstep. Instead, a life of hopelessness for the new widow and the fatherless resulted as the reality of war swept into their lives. The ocean could not offer protection from the madman who orchestrated his own desires and fulfilled his own passions to improve the human race.

Lucy raised her head to the wind as her bike wheels crunched over the gravel road that led toward the lookout at Miller's Mountain. *Dad was quite a man.* She wondered if the townspeople realized how lucky they were for having known her father.

7

Am I a God at hand,
saith the Lord, and not a God afar off?
Can any hide himself in secret places
that I shall not see him? saith the Lord.
JEREMIAH 23:23-24

Evelyn had stood in the doorway of their home as Lucy pulled her bike from the carport. Not being in the habit of watching her daughter leave, it never occurred to Evelyn to wave, yet Lucy had, just before heading west on Aspen Avenue. Evelyn returned the gesture, feeling slightly embarrassed, and then shut the door and returned to the kitchen for a fresh cup of coffee.

Memories of Miller's Mountain filled her thoughts. When they were younger, before Lucy was born, she and Lewis would drive to the base of the mountain, park by the well-worn trail, climb to the ledge, and slide out on the smooth rock, facing west. Nature had provided a natural seat, enjoyed by many before them and no doubt many more to come. This place had become sacred. Promises were made, first kisses were given and received, proposals were offered, and tears of both joy and sorrow had spilled onto the moss-free rock.

Coming from a province that boasted of its mighty waterfall, Evelyn would always remember her first visit to Miller's Mountain and its testimony to the majesty of Northern Canada. Until that day, she only had Lewis's word on the beauty of the north. Her first visit to Miller's Mountain changed everything. It was love at first sight. Lewis had led her blindfolded to the flat rock that overlooked Thystle Creek. Securing her hand in his, he'd guided her over unseen roots and stones until he had carefully positioned her on the flat rock facing the sunset.

"Welcome to your new home, Evie girl." He removed her eye covering and sat back to allow the mountain to vaunt itself before its new convert.

A pallet of red, orange, and yellow had stretched for miles, dotted with faithful evergreens that stood as guardian angels over the valley. Rich forests extended down the sides into the fertile valley below, and blotches of meadows had created a patchwork of multiple shades of green and yellow across the land. Cows mooed in the distance and their echoes bounced across the valley. A screech owl unwittingly alerted potential victims to scurry to safety and added to the battle of the survival of the fittest. Evelyn remembered the hawk. It had soared high above them in a current of air, then flapped its wings in a smooth and steady rhythm, circling, waiting, before it pierced the sky earthward like an arrow fresh from a bow and retrieved its dinner. She remembered thinking, *Something didn't survive.*

Reflecting on the beauty that had stretched before her on that first autumn night, Evelyn found herself holding her breath, willing the moment to return. Instead, she remembered another night and she grasped her coffee mug as though drawing strength from its warmth.

Her gaze drifted to the back garden and the tall spruce trees where Lewis had stood and openly expressed his love for the Creator of all that had lain before her on that first night on Miller's Mountain. "But I could never fall in love with your God, Louie," she whispered, her voice echoing in the stillness of the kitchen. Saddened by this thought, she struggled as her first memories of a supreme being surfaced. *Don't go there!* the ever-present voice warned. But she did.

Her knowledge of God had been ingrained in her as a child. But her thoughts and opinion of God and any form of religion had changed when her parents became believers in Jesus Christ the year she turned thirteen. Even now she shook her head, bewildered. *How could they just turn their backs on* who *they were and forget their heritage?*

Her rebellion ensued over the following years. Confusion, rejection, and eventually a deeply seeded anger lead to a rejection of the God of her parents. Yet, thinking back on her first visit to Miller's Mountain, Evelyn realized she had come very close to paying tribute to someone or something for the awesomeness that had stretched before her but was unable to submit to a quiet, inner voice that had simply said, *COME*. The protective wall had been in place for too long.

Evelyn sighed. With her second cup of coffee finished, she stood reluctantly to begin the task of cleaning the kitchen. Her thoughts were elsewhere, however, having been sparked by her memories of Miller's Mountain, and with the leftovers in the fridge and the dishes air-drying in the sink, Evelyn headed for the living room. As though anticipating an exacting ordeal, she paused before sitting down in front of Lewis's desk that shared the space with a chair in the front window. Evelyn removed a few sheets of writing paper from the bottom right-hand drawer and began a letter.

Saturday, June 20, 1964

Dear Father and Mother,

It's been a while since I last wrote. I hope this letter finds you both well.

How's Bubi? She'll be having a birthday soon, won't she? How are you managing as you care for her, Mother? I'm sure an aging parent can produce unique demands. I don't relish the day when it falls upon Lucy.

There was a public speaking contest at the high school Lucy attends and she was chosen to represent her school. Her school has never won the competition, but this year Lucy changed all that. She won the trophy. I'm afraid I was unkind to her since the topic was too painful for me to appreciate, but I don't need to trouble you with all that. Just know that you would be honoured by the kind of granddaughter you have.

I'm still working at the local library. It fills my day during the long winters here in the north, and in the summer when school is out, the library is only open three days a week. This gives me lots of time in the garden. The flowers here are different than back home, stronger, hardier. They need to be to survive the long winters. But fortunately strawberries still grow in late August, and since we have a local strawberry farm just out of town, I have taken advantage of their abundance, although I have grown to appreciate the local Saskatoon berry.

Do you remember the young man I have mentioned before, William Douglas? Folks here call him Wil. He teaches a Grade Six class at our public school and has known Lucy all her life. He was five when Lucy was born and has been like a brother for Lucy ever since. You would like him. I think there's more than a friendship kindling, but it seems neither Lucy nor Wil are aware of it.

Miller's Mountain still brings its own wonder and beauty each season. Louie and I used to go there and watch the sun set behind the mountain on the other side of the valley. He took Lucy there often. I never went with them. Now Lucy is going with Wil. I'm quite certain I've shared the beauty of this mountain with you before, but now that Lucy is sharing it with Wil in a special way, their visits have prompted pleasant memories for me.

Lewis would be proud of Lucy. I like to think that he's watching, but I know that's not practical. My heart has never healed and I have doubts that it ever will. I know that I'm often unkind to Lucy, but an inner voice continually shouts in my ear at how painfully unfair life is and I find myself listening. I wish I could pray, but then again, to whom would I pray? I don't believe as you do.

I will close for now. I miss your voices and your smiles. Please hug Bubi. Tell her she would be proud of her great granddaughter.

I will write again, I promise.

Your daughter,

Evlyna

Folding her pages in half, Evelyn removed an envelope from the bottom desk drawer. Her hand paused for a moment before writing and when she did, she whispered the words, *Mr. and Mrs. Jóózsef Cohen.* With what seemed like great effort, she rose from her desk chair, left the living room, and returned moments later with a small wooden box. Unlocking it, Evelyn lifted the lid and set aside a small, cloth jewellery bag that lay on top of two piles of envelopes. She ceremoniously untied the satin ribbon that bound the larger group of envelopes and laid the newly written letter on the top. Retying the ribbon, she placed the pile of letters, now increased by one, back into the box.

She turned to the smaller pile, all addressed to Evelyn Crawford in Halifax, all unopened. As so often in the past, the temptation to read even one surfaced and then quickly evaporated. A tear fell on *Crawford* and her hands shook. *What's the point?* the voice taunted. *They had their chance.* Placing the jewellery bag in the box, Evelyn closed the lid, fastened the lock, and bowed her head. As the tears flowed, Evelyn struggled with the same thought she had each time she added a letter to the pile: *Why?*

8

Come, and let us go up to the mountain of the Lord,
and to the house of the God of Jacob; and he will teach us
of his ways, and we will walk in his paths.
MICAH 4:2

Lucy was looking forward to the time with Wil even though she still had not reckoned with her interpretation of his kiss on Thursday night. *Strange,* she thought, *I've never felt this way before when we've made plans to go anywhere.* Despite the breeze, Lucy felt her cheeks flush and she smiled in anticipation of the moments that lay ahead.

She arrived early and set her bike in the grove of trees at the end of the road as a signal for Wil. Winded from biking uphill, she took in the view behind her and complimented herself at her agility to make such a gruelling ride. *Driving would be faster, but not as much fun.* She turned toward the mountain, but not before looking over her shoulder with a grin. *Downhill all the way.* She giggled at the idea, and then strolled along the path to the familiar rock and inched herself out on nature's hard seat.

"Beautiful," Lucy whispered, and then challenged herself that the word didn't seem to be enough to describe the view. For a moment she considered "awesome," but then remembered her father telling her that "awesome" should be reserved to describe God. Multiple shades of early summer green lay before her as fresh paint on a canvas. *Each season seems to bring its own paintbrush,* she thought, smiling at her creative analogy. Absorbing the scene as a dry sponge consumes its first drink, Lucy sighed and cupped her knees to her chin.

Thystle Creek spread between two mountain ranges in a small, protected valley. Dropping from the top of the mountain high above town, the creek itself slowed and widened at a flattened spot of the mountainside, providing a swimming hole just to the right of where Lucy sat. It meandered for a few hundred yards then dropped abruptly, cutting a sharp path down the edge of the mountain to the valley below. Many had braved the spring waters and chanced a quick dip, hoping to receive some warmth as they stretched themselves out on the sun-heated flat rock. Others less heroic waited until the summer sun had warmed the elevated pond. Laughter often filtered down to the valley as young and old alike enjoyed God's handiwork.

In an effort to hold on to the contentment, Lucy surprised herself by trying to pray, but the thoughts and words seemed foreign. She tried again, this time to sing, but no song came. *It's gone,* she thought, giving in to the battle that the enemy seemed to confront her with daily. *Why do I always feel this defeat whenever I'm alone?* She took some comfort in knowing Wil was concerned about her spiritual vacuum, yet relieved he never nagged her about it.

On the day her father had been killed, Wil had held her in his arms as she poured out her rage. "I will never love Him again! Never! Never!" she had vowed, pounding Wil's chest. "Never!" And she'd collapsed in Wil's arms in anguish, determined she would never again view God in the way she had when her father was alive. "We've loved Him and worshipped Him together, Wil. Why would He do this? What have I done? What did my father do that was so bad? Why couldn't He stop the tree from falling?" Her questions had escaped like a rushing dam that had broken with no hope of repair.

In his quiet, steady way, smiling through his own tears, Wil had lifted strands of her hair from her face and brushed away her tears. "I don't know. I can't explain why God allows things to happen, why He takes one life and leaves another." Lucy stared at him, unable or unwilling to absorb his words. "But you didn't do anything wrong, Luce. Neither did your father. All I know is that no matter how hard it is for you to believe it, God knows best. He sees the big picture and despite how you feel right now, He loves you, He understands your pain and hurt. He even understands your anger and will always be here, waiting, just like a father waits with open arms to hold his lost child." With the reference to a father, Lucy had broken completely. "I believe you'll find your way back to God, Luce. I believe it with my whole heart. I know you, but better still, God knows you. You'll be back," he said as he rocked her and tried to comfort her as best he could.

They never talked about it after that, but Lucy knew Wil, and she knew he was praying. Because of this, her anger remained hidden, not to be shared, not to be helped, and seemingly never to be healed. Scenes of her mother's anger flashed before her, and Lucy shuddered. *Please, don't let me become like that.*

She shut her eyes and let the sun warm her face. The glare had softened, and the shadows crept across the valley as the sun moved closer to settling itself behind the mountains for another day. The fading ball of light reflecting far below on the river created doubts that they would have a swim. Lucy opened her eyes. The disturbing scene had faded, but the view had not. It continued to kindle a deep memory and despite her attempts to shut God out of her life, she was reminded of the *God Is* game she and her father had played as part of their visit to Miller's Mountain. It was a game that at one time had proven to be the cement that strengthened father and daughter's faith in God and their love for each other. *It wasn't really a game of competition,* Lucy thought now, remembering the challenge she had just faced. It was more an awareness and confession of the greatness of God, and despite her effort to deny it an audience, Lucy replayed the memory of the last word game she'd had with her father.

The summer Lucy had been thirteen had been unusually dry and hot and she'd welcomed the invitation from her dad to cool off in the evening breeze on Miller's Mountain. She remembered even now the sad look that brushed across his face when her mother had declined his coaxing to join them.

"Come on, Evie. We're just going to sit a while. It's hot here and a lot cooler up there. And," he teased hopefully, "it'll be like old times, watching the sun set."

"Not tonight, Louie," was her mother's reply, and father and daughter relied on their usual team spirit to help them climb their personal mountain before heading for the one that God had created.

Settled together on the flat rock, they had sat quietly for a moment until Lucy's father broke the silence with "God is … " But before he could complete his thought, Lucy had jumped in.

"I'll go first, Daddy," Lucy challenged. Curling her legs under herself against the weathered rock, she turned to face her father and the game began. "God is great."

"God is tender." Lewis countered, using a word that began with the last letter of the last word before Lucy finished counting to five.

"God is Redeemer."

"God is righteous."

"God is Saviour."

"God is Rabbi."

"Good one, Dad! God is invincible." Lucy turned and shouted this to the mountains and then laughed as her echo bounced back.

"God is eternal. One, two three four..."

"God is always!" Lucy laughed as she deliberately chose a word that disqualified her and ended the game.

She'd told him that she could have said "God is love," but that it was too easy and had willingly ended the game as the underdog. His comment haunted her, even now.

"But God *is* love, Lucy. Never forget that."

It was then that her father had shared his war experiences, and when he'd finished he'd taken the opportunity to remind her that no matter what happened in life, God was always there. In the war across the ocean. In their life in Thystle Creek. He was always in control. He would always love her. He would always be there for her.

Her father died three weeks later.

Where are you now, God? Lucy shrugged the thought away and turned to watch the shadows of the mountains creep across the valley floor and remembered that as a child she had been struck with wonder and amazement with these same shadows. "Daddy, do the shadows ever change?" she once asked as a little girl. Responding now to her childlike question, Lucy whispered aloud the memory of her father's answer that evening, years earlier: "No, Lucy, they never change. They're always in the same pattern as they have been for centuries." The memory of her father's words continued. "Trees have grown and died, but the shadows of the mountains remain the same. Never become indifferent to the handiwork of God, Lucy. Never cease to marvel at His creation." He'd squeezed her close and she'd sighed somewhat in awe of her father's wisdom.

Lucy tried hard to remember a verse her father often quoted when he was inspired by the beauty that stretched before her. The words came slowly: "Come, and let us go up to the mountain of the Lord . . . and he will teach us of his ways, and we will walk in his paths."

That must have been how you saw God, Daddy, Lucy thought. So much had happened in his life and there had been so much to cope with that Lucy was not surprised her father must have seen God as *permanent* through it all, always there, always strong, forever the same, just like the mountains before her.

"I wish I could be strong like you, Daddy," Lucy whispered to the evening breeze. "I wish I could see you again, to talk with you, to play *God Is* again, to share secrets."

Lucy's heart was heavy with the reminder of the God she'd rejected and the emptiness her father's death had brought. They had shared so much, listening to each other, keeping secrets that Lucy wondered if she would ever feel safe in sharing with anyone ever again. *Especially that one secret we had.* She groaned as her arms encircled her bent knees.

Lucy had unearthed a secret that, had it been pursued further, would have given her a better understanding of why things were the way they were in her home, why her mother never talked about her life growing up, and why her father had been left to provide her with as normal a family environment as possible.

But it was not to be. Her mother's life, much like the subject of the war, was never shared or discussed in the Sherwood home. *Your life may have been locked and buried in a vault, Mom, but I found a key,* Lucy thought now. In fact, it had been quite by accident that she'd opened a door, as it were, that allowed her a glimpse of a secret that its owner had surrendered to the past.

Coming here may not have been such a good idea, she sighed, stretching her knees and rising to leave. She saw Wil at the bottom of the path. He waved to her and she watched him make his way up the slope to join her. *I could tell Wil.* She considered the possibility as he approached her, shading his eyes from the evening sun, and then she knew the desire to share her secret with him went deeper. She *had* to tell him.

Wil plunked himself next to Lucy and took in the view.

"Been here long?"

"Maybe twenty minutes. Long enough to see the sun do its magic with the shadows. Look over there. Those very shadows are the same ones my dad and I used to watch grow across the valley when I was just a kid. Seems like yesterday. We shared so much about God on this mountain. I couldn't help remembering a verse he would say and our game of *God Is.* Did I ever tell you about that game?"

Lucy had been staring across the span of the valley while she spoke to Wil, and as she questioned him about the game, Wil caught the glimmer of a tear. He'd heard of the game many times—and in fact had witnessed it—but it seemed inappropriate at the moment to acknowledge that. But he silently thanked God for revealing Himself to Lucy once again, even though she may not have realized what had happened.

"You okay?" He drew his legs up and faced his friend.

"Just remembering, that's all," Lucy replied. Wil could not miss her attempt at a smile. "Once in a while, the memories take over and as much as I love recalling times with my dad, sometimes they can be too painful. I guess tonight's one of those times. I'll be okay." Lucy turned back to the setting sun.

Wil followed her gaze and didn't pursue it further

"Not much daylight left. Guess we should have left earlier. Are you ready to go?"

"Not just yet. There's something I wanna tell you." But before Lucy could speak, Wil broke her concentration.

"Actually, there's something I want to talk to you about, too, but ladies first," he teased.

The stillness that followed seemed to stretch across the valley. Unaware of the battle going on inside Lucy's head, Wil remained silent, but with each passing moment, he became more concerned about whatever it was Lucy was trying to put into words. Finally, Lucy's voice broke the evening solitude and Wil sat mesmerized as her story unfolded. He watched her face, her eyes, her expressions.

"It was early summer, when I was twelve, my baptism. Remember?"

Wil nodded, slightly entranced. His love for Lucy heightened and he silently thanked God once again, only this time for bringing such a wonderful friend into his life.

9

Cast thy burden upon the Lord, and he shall sustain thee:
he shall never suffer the righteous to be moved.
PSALM 55:22

Summer 1959

"Mother, are you sure?" Lucy questioned her mother with a dreaded fear that she would change her mind. She had just suggested Lucy wear her great-grandmother's pearl necklace the Sunday she was to be baptized. Knowing nothing of her mother's family history, Lucy hesitated.

"I want you to be happy," her mother responded, touching her daughter's cheek in a moment of affection Lucy seldom shared with her mother.

"Then won't you change your mind and come with Daddy and me to the service, just this one time?"

"Lucy, please!" Her mother's tone of impatience made it clear to Lucy that she had no interest in attending church.

Not being discouraged, Lucy pressed further. "But Mom, most of the town will be showing up. Billy's mom and dad will be there, the whole Lambert family and all their kids will be watching Susie get dunked, and even Rachel Perkins's grandparents have come from out of town. Wil and Jason and... everyone! Mom, please!" Lucy pleaded, but her mother had already turned toward the bedroom door without a reply.

Lucy couldn't help wondering if allowing her to wear the pearls was her mother's way of avoiding further confrontation. She would not attend church, no matter how hard Lucy pressed, and Lucy was left standing alone in the centre of her bedroom.

"Not even my own baptism would break down her wall, Wil," Lucy commented quietly, breaking from the past as she remembered her mother's retreat down the hallway. She turned and looked into Wil's face. "You know, that was the first and only time my mother has ever mentioned her family to me. To think that somewhere out there I have a grandmother, maybe even a great-grandmother. I just don't understand, I... but let me finish."

The pearls were on a short strand and Lucy found them lying in her mother's jewellery box on the dresser in her parents' bedroom. Full of the typical excitement of a twelve-year-old, Lucy's hands trembled as she carefully lifted the pearls from the box. She anchored the strand at the back of her neck, thinking of what lay ahead and smiled. *This day will be perfect!* She knew the importance of becoming part of a Christian community and a member of the local church. Wearing her great-grandmother's pearls could never compete with that, but it was a highlight. Lucy had wanted to hug her mother, but her mother's hasty retreat from Lucy's bedroom had made that impossible.

Lucy stood in front of her mother's mirror, wondering in amazement how a simple small strand of pearls could make such a difference. But it did, and Lucy was thrilled, so thrilled that she twirled in circles in front of her mother's dresser, laughing and singing a nameless tune. Suddenly, in a moment of dizziness, she lost her balance and knocked her mother's jewellery box to the floor. Its contents scattered across the carpet, the box landing face down with the lining detaching itself from its frame. Lucy quickly bent to replace the lining and the contents in the box, but something caught her attention, and fortunately so, for it could have been easily mistaken for a scrap of paper and discarded.

"What's all the singing about Lu..." Her father appeared at the bedroom door and found Lucy cross-legged on the floor holding a small piece of paper.

Frightened by an inexplicable instinct that she was holding something she should not be holding, she dropped it into her lap and locked her arms across her chest. "I'm sorry, Daddy. It was an accident. I was just spinning and fell." Tears filled Lucy's eyes. She held up the torn paper and questioned her father as he crossed the floor to console her. "Do you know what this is?"

"Yes," Lewis sighed. "Yes, I do." Lewis bent down to help Lucy pick up the pieces of jewellery. As he did, Lucy thought he whispered more. She wasn't sure what, but she realized she had unearthed something that brought a visible sadness to her father.

"What is it?"

Holding the piece of paper reverently in his hands, her father stretched his legs out on the floor and leaned against the edge of the bed. Lucy watched his face and waited, her own emotions in a whirlwind.

"It only took a few moments, Wil, for Dad to tell the story, but I've never forgotten it."

"Are you sure you want to continue?"

Lucy nodded. "I *need* to tell you, Wil."

"His name was Bobby Jenkins," her father said. "We were in the same regiment and spent long, lonely nights comparing our past and our dreams for the future while we waited to be sent on the mission we were being trained for. He was nice; someone I liked right away. We shared jokes and stories of small town living and our dreams of becoming 'healers of the world.' We both hated the war and took comfort in knowing we were not alone in our hatred. He shared his belief that there was a God who had all things in control, and no matter how the war ended, it was His plan. I found that hard to believe, back then; thought he was a little over the edge." Lewis smiled at Lucy. "Despite our differences on religious views, by the time we were called up on our mission, I began to think of Bobby as my brother, the one I never had.

"He grew up with your mother in a small community in Eastern Ontario, just north of Lake Ontario. Pontypool, I think."

Lucy smiled at the name.

"Coming from a small town in the foothills of two mountain ranges, I found it hard to imagine never seeing snow-capped mountains or forests that stretched for hundreds and hundreds of acres. Most of the land where Bobby lived was claimed for farming, but not everyone lived on a farm. Your mother lived two houses down from the general store; Bobby lived two streets over, behind the grain elevators..."

As she listened to her father, Lucy couldn't help wondering if it was a story he hadn't remembered for many years. His face sobered and she saw a sadness that came from living with someone he loved, someone she began to understand suffered a deep but private hurt.

"At fifteen, your mother was in love with Bobby—she was not much older than you, Luce." Lewis stretched out his arms. With the jewellery back in its box, Lucy settled herself beside her father on the floor as he told the story of her mother's first love.

"Some called it puppy love, but after listening to Bobby tell the story, I believe, had things turned out differently, it would have lasted a lifetime. They'd been neighbours, as was everyone in such a small community, and there were no secrets." He squeezed Lucy and an understanding passed between them. The town could have been Thystle Creek; everybody knew everybody else's business. "But at fifteen, your mother had kept her thoughts for Bobby to herself, at least that's what she thought. But Bobby and her parents were aware of her feelings long before she dared tell anyone. During the long nights in England when there was an ordered blackout, Bobby would share stories about how your mother's parents smiled with the kind of wisdom that comes in knowing why their daughter would become shy and silent anytime Bobby dropped in or his name was mentioned."

Lucy marvelled at how understanding her father was, how he never showed any sign of resentment or jealousy toward the boy who had meant so much to her mother.

"Bobby had never known love until he watched a young girl of fifteen frantically try to save a stray chicken in a crate that had fallen from a farmer's truck on the way to the local market. According to Bobby, your mother never looked more beautiful as she argued the rights of the chicken in the face of its owner. She had failed in her attempt, but vowed never to eat chicken again, much to the amusement of the farmer. And Bobby's heart was smitten. Your mother told me this same story a few years later with a slight twist. She insisted that she convinced the farmer to keep that chicken when the rest were delivered to the slaughterhouse. I think that brought some comfort to your mother, but in her heart I think she knew it wasn't true."

Lucy's father continued his stories, one after another, until Lucy learned how a small piece of paper had come to be such an important piece of a puzzle in her mother's life.

"In January 1942, the war touched your mother and Bobby's small town when Bobby enlisted. He was twenty, your mother seventeen. Conscription was a new word for many, with a terrifying meaning," Lewis spoke softly, "and Bobby wasn't about to wait around wondering if he would be called to fight. When he enlisted voluntarily, he and your mother begged your grandparents to allow them to marry. It had been evident to everyone in town, and certainly to your grandparents, that they were in love, but your mother was underage by a few months. Your grandparents said no, encouraging them to wait until the war was over.

"With her marriage on hold, your mother joined the ranks of many young women as their boyfriends or husbands said good bye and left them standing on the edge of the train station watching the train disappear down the tracks. Years later, your mother told me how she had grasped a small piece of paper in her coat pocket as she watched the train disappear. It had no value or meaning to anyone else, but to your mother and Bobby it was their lifeline that spanned the ocean. They had ripped a two dollar bill in half, each keeping a piece. It symbolized their separation, their being torn apart. It was their way of being united, despite the ocean. They promised to keep the pieces and, when the war was over, they would tape them back together on the day of their wedding. This is the small scrap of paper she clung to, the one you're holding now."

"What happened?" Lucy asked, dreading the answer she already knew in her heart.

Lewis finished the story and fell silent, leaving Lucy holding the half bill with a new sense of awe.

Lucy turned to Wil. "Bobby Jenkins never returned. He was buried in France somewhere. Daddy never asked my mother where. He was never sure if she even knew. All that my mother has left of Bobby is that piece of torn money and her memories. And a bitter heart," Lucy added as she sat staring at the horizon.

Wil put his arm around Lucy's shoulder and hugged her closer to him.

"There's more. I'll always remember my father's story. War became a reality for me through my dad's eyes."

10

Exalt her, and she shall promote thee:
she shall bring thee to honour,
when thou dost embrace her.
PROVERBS 4:8

Lucy and her father sat quietly for a few moments, Lucy still holding the torn two dollar bill as though it had become sacred over the past ten minutes. Finally, she broke their silence with a whispered question, fearing that if she spoke louder a spell would be broken, never to be recaptured. "How did you meet mommy?"

"When Bobby and I met, we were in training in England for the invasion of Dieppe in France," Lewis began again as simply as taking his next breath. "Although we were in the same regiment, we were in different companies and became separated. Each of our commanders had been given orders to fill in the gaps—or the holes—in the cliffs just west of Dieppe, near Pourville. We both made it through the attack, but many died in the withdrawal, including Bobby." Lewis's voice faltered. "Over nine hundred Canadians were killed that day."

The ticking of the bedside clock magnified the silence as Lucy's father paused in his memories.

"We were the same age and although we'd only met a few months earlier, I felt a sense of loss that I couldn't explain then, or now. We hardly knew one another, but in our short time together I felt I'd known him all my life. I knew about a girl back home because he received letters from her regularly while we prepared for the invasion. Bobby was forever saying, 'When this war's over, I'm gonna marry her!'"

Silence occupied every corner of the room until Lucy's father broke it with his story of the faceless name of the girl back home, a friend of a friend who had been his link to sanity and hope for the future. A purpose to breathe, to fight, to stay alive.

"When Bobby died, I sent two letters, one to Mr. and Mrs. Jenkins and one to your mother in care of the Jenkins to express my sorrow at Bobby's death. Two months later, I got a thank you note, postmarked Halifax. Your mother had moved there two months after Bobby had left home to work in a factory that helped build weapons. She told me once that it was her way of "getting even and killing the monster madman." When she learned that Bobby had been killed, she stayed on the east coast.

"After that, we began to write regularly. Her letters were always full of stories about Bobby. I suppose it was therapy for her to talk about him so freely, and it was then that I learned about the two dollar bill.

"When the war ended, I visited your mother as a friend, but I knew that I had already fallen in love with her long before the war had ended. We courted for six months and then, in September of '46, we married and moved here. Nine months later, you were born," Lewis added with a wink in his eye.

"Why did she keep this torn bill?" Lucy asked, overwhelmed with the confidences her father was sharing with her.

"Memories, just memories," was all her father said as he stared straight ahead. Lucy wondered if he was seeing things that were not visible to the naked eye.

Almost depleted, Lucy drew Wil back to the beginning and shared the moments just before she and her father had left for her baptism.

"It'd been a special day, Wil. Except for the conversation with my dad, it had been almost perfect. Not perfect, but almost," Lucy added, emphasizing her determination to lift her spirits despite the heaviness of her heart. "We left my mother standing with her back to us as she always did on Sundays. 'I need to attend to the dishes,' was her unfailing excuse, and that morning was no exception. Mom never turned to see her grandmother's pearls around my neck. She never saw my red eyes. She just never turned around," Lucy whispered, losing her resolve to be positive.

"That explains a lot, doesn't it, Luce? Why your mother is so quiet, so withdrawn. Why she never smiles. I'm so sorry."

"Thanks." Her smile was weak. "I've had to accept my mother's indifference, but at least I know the truth. I just can't tell her I know."

Wil turned Lucy to face him. She welcomed his gentle touch on her cheek and the even gentler kiss on her forehead that finally lifted the heaviness that had settled over them. She smiled into Wil's eyes; no words were necessary, but his expression of affection had accomplished a greater good. The dark cloud that had crept in dispersed, and feeling much relieved, Lucy shifted her story to a part of that day shared not only with her father, but with Wil. They escalated into hearty laughter as they shared memories.

"The sun was at its peak, Luce. Remember? No clouds. And the water…the creek had still been cold from the spring runoff, but not so cold that it stopped you guys from being dunked. You were the youngest, so you had to go first," Wil teased. "You were dipped, trembling with excitement, and came up shivering from the cold water hooting and hollering, splashing everyone who wasn't standing far enough back. Remember Mrs. Bates? She got soaked and had to go home to change. Mr. Bates did all he could to conceal his laughter, but got hollered at all the way to their car. And the Bradley twins? They had been innocently playing on the shore and never saw it coming."

By this time, Wil was rocking with laughter and Lucy listened in amazement that he had remembered so much detail.

"I remember my dad was waiting on the edge of the water, towel in hand," Lucy said, continuing where Wil left off. "His own shoes and pant legs were wet from getting too close to the water. He had tripped on the edge of the towel he was holding for me and almost went head first into the creek, and that only added to the craziness of the moment."

Lucy paused.

"You know what else I remember? If there had been any sadness or disappointment in Mom not being there, Dad never showed it. He was so proud of me and everyone could see that," Lucy concluded quietly.

She recalled that the neighbours and friends had enjoyed the moment and watched the scene unfold as she had embraced her father. If Lucy's mother had been missed, Lucy never heard a word of condemnation from this crowd of friends.

As she relived the day, Lucy watched Wil share his memories. He had been the first to congratulate her. Once she'd cocooned herself in the dry towel her father had given her, she turned and found him standing just back from the two of them, arms folded and grinning from the pure pleasure of watching her with her father. He had stretched both arms out, surrounding her, and then swung her around drawing squeals of laughter from the not-quite-yet young woman. Begging to be released, Lucy had let her lifetime friend spin her round and round.

The reminiscing had done wonders. She and Wil hugged themselves trying to relax the laughter cramps that had invaded their lungs. Then their eyes met. Their laughter ceased when emotional electricity filled the air. The lifelong friends found themselves in an embrace that would set them on a new course neither had travelled before, but one that would change their lives forever.

Dusk had settled over Thystle Creek. Alone with her memories, Evelyn sat with an unopened book in her lap. All evening she had replayed her conversation with her daughter before Lucy had left for Miller's Mountain. *Am I correct? Is there a relationship developing between Lucy and Wil? Have I just imagined it*? The next thought left her breathless with fear. *What will I do when she's gone?*

PART TWO

11

For my thoughts are not your thoughts,
neither are your ways my ways, saith the Lord.
ISAIAH 55:8

April 1968

Evelyn busied herself with boxes of Kindergarten keepsakes, conscious of Lucy's one-way conversation about what to do with her Grade Two spelling book. Evelyn smiled at her daughter's frustration and offered encouraging words. "It's no easy task sorting through years of memories, Lucy." *And trying to decide what should be kept and what needs to be disposed of, if ever so gently, is no easy task either,* she mused as she found herself going down her own memory lane.

With no surprise to Evelyn, her daughter's engagement to Wil had followed the Christmas after Lucy's graduation from high school. They had decided to wait a year before marrying while Lucy moved to Vancouver to help on a "mission of mercy," as Wil had so aptly put it to Evelyn over a cup of coffee in the Sherwood kitchen.

"I met Garry and Jessie Patrick when Jess and I were at Teacher's

College. It seems they've just opened a new eatery on the coast and need some help. Jessie's landed a job teaching Grade Two for a teacher on maternity leave and that limits her to one night a week and weekends to help Garry. As much as I'll miss her, I've encouraged Lucy to go. Hope that's all right with you, Mrs. S."

What could she say? Of course it had been all right. For some unknown reason, Evelyn knew that Lucy *had* to go. Deep inside, she knew the time had come to let go. Their decision to wait a year before marrying had provided her an opportunity to get used to the idea of living alone.

Yes, it had been a good decision, Wil, Evelyn thought now, two years after the fact. And here she sat in the basement with Lucy sorting through her childhood memorabilia, months before her wedding. She pulled a box from the rafters and glanced over at her daughter. She was proud of her. Winner of the Regional Public Speaking Competition two years in a row. Valedictorian for her class of '66. She had matured into a beautiful young woman, culminating in her engagement to Wil Douglas. *Surprise! Surprise!* Evelyn thought as she remembered the night Wil proposed and Lucy received her ring.

"What do you mean in a Cracker Jack box? What was Wil thinking?"

"Honest, Mom, he put it in the popcorn and explained that he couldn't afford a real one and would I accept this imitation until he could? He just said, 'Will you marry me?' It was dark in the car and I couldn't tell any different. I just slipped the ring on my finger and threw my arms around his neck and screamed, 'Yes!' I told him I didn't care what was on my finger. Then, he reached under the driver's seat, pulled out a jar, and handed it to me. It read, *Fine Jewellery and Diamond Cleaner.* It took a few seconds for it to register and then I looked at my ring again. I almost killed him for fooling me."

Evelyn smiled at the memory, but more at her daughter's honesty and enthusiasm for life, and marvelled at how well she had survived a tumultuous childhood. While Lucy had helped the Patricks, Evelyn had spent many long nights dealing with the emotional pain she'd inflicted on Lewis and Lucy. She couldn't land on the *why now* of her introspection, yet she had faced the reality that most of her life had been filled with self-pity, anger, and little regard for husband, daughter or parents.

I certainly had to face a lot, she mused as her hands automatically busied themselves with Lucy's grade school treasures. During the months of her daughter's absence, an unfamiliar longing began to surface, a pain so full of regret and guilt that Evelyn wasn't sure at times if she would survive. Time of day didn't seem to matter, early in the morning before her day began or deep in the night when sleep escaped her. The depth of the longing often left her physically aching and mentally exhausted. Many of her actions and choices had never been resolved, some never would be, but one in particular haunted her on a regular basis: the night Lucy won the speaking competition for the first time, the night she had berated her daughter.

Lucy's speech four years earlier had ignited an anger to a depth that haunted Evelyn into the dark hours of the night, and it was an anger for which she felt great shame. In her attempt to cope with her past, she was too often impeded by the menacing voice, presenting itself unexpectedly and unmercifully. Although it had diminished noticeably over the past months, without warning it would silently whisper words of discouragement, plant thoughts of defeat or rejection or guilt, and often at a time when pleasurable thoughts dared to win over despair. Upon Lucy's return from the coast, it had been evident to Evelyn that she'd been forgiven. Evelyn suspected that Lucy's reconciliation with her God had made that possible. Lucy had been attending church regularly with Wil since coming home. *But forgiving yourself is another matter,* Evelyn thought as she wiped dust from the crate lid that had stood in the corner of the basement since Lucy had graduated from Grade Eight.

Unexpectedly, she thought of her husband and sighed. Lucy glanced up from the stack of grade school textbooks. They exchanged smiles and Evelyn continued to lift down boxes from their storage.

Memories of Lewis always surfaced, but never in a tormenting way; they were just constant. Her life with her husband invaded her dreams repeatedly, and regret often ensued. During Lucy's absence, Evelyn had paced her floors in the darkness beseeching Lewis's forgiveness. Many nights she'd wrestled with words she had spoken, harsh words that cut and wounded deeply. However, there were nights she would remember his embrace, his passion as he held her, touched her, caressed her. She would remember his unfailing love, a love Lewis had expressed despite the many occasions he had endured her explosive anger. Even now, as she dug through trunks and boxes, she remembered his love, and it continued to baffle her. *Was it your God, Louie? Did He give you that love?*

COME.

Evelyn turned sharply and looked at her daughter, expecting her to have spoken. She had not. Lucy's head was buried in a pile of Kindergarten crafts. Evelyn shook off an unsettling feeling, but not before remembering the same feeling months earlier and wondered, for a moment, if this feeling was part of the crossroad she had found herself facing. For reasons that still escaped her, she had come to a turning point in her life. Despite the lack of answers as to *why* or *how,* she knew she had to press on if she were to survive. She knew she needed to snuff out the menacing voice and that could only be done, she concluded, by living in the present instead of the past. What was it she had read somewhere? *Life is not made of wishing this or that, but of looking ahead and not back.* She needed to stop looking back.

Despite the resulting agony the thoughts provoked, Evelyn had welcomed the newness of this invasion in her thought life. Despite the lack of answers, her decision to focus on the present released her from some guilt. Despite the history of neglecting her daughter, the change in her relationship with Lucy had been her reward. A bond had crystallized and Evelyn saw heads turn in surprise as she and Lucy passed on the street, chattering back and forth like best friends.

Opening dusty and well-sealed boxes, Lucy and her mother had found themselves in a time warp. Finally, agreeing with her mother that they would start with the toys and decide what could be used at the children's centre in the library, Lucy had committed the week to finishing the onerous task. Fortunately, the weather had cooperated, with a spring rain over the entire valley keeping most of its residents housebound.

"Look at this, Mom!" Lucy exclaimed as she unearthed a treasure box full of essays, art posters, and crafts. "All the valuable possessions every child believes should be kept forever," Lucy said with a smile. "I can't believe how fast time has gone. I was just a kid when I wrote this essay about the game *God Is* that Daddy and I used to play."

Silence filled the room. Realizing her error, Lucy quickly folded the paper and placed it in the 'keeping' pile of collectibles that had grown throughout the morning. She turned her attention to a doll, a much safer topic that would not weaken the bridge that had been built between her and her mother. She had been quietly watching her mother for the last few minutes and had become fearful of a threatening despondency. She knew all the signs from years of living with a mother who withdrew easily and quickly for no apparent reason. She didn't want that to happen, not today, not any day, not ever again.

"Remember this, Mom? Uncle Mo gave it to me."

Holding up a dusty, crumpled doll, Lucy struggled with what to do. "I shouldn't part with this, should I?" She implored her mother for help as she held her childhood collectable at arm's length. "Mom, should I?"

"Of course not, Lucy," Evelyn replied in disbelief, taking the doll from her daughter and smoothing its tattered hair like a little girl stroking her favourite toy. "It's almost heresy just thinking of giving away Cliff's gift," Evelyn added with a smirk, resting the doll in her lap. Without warning, her humour sobered somewhat. "Did you know that Cliff Moses was rejected at twenty-one by his only sweetheart?"

Lucy nodded, having heard the story from her father as they'd sat in the glow of the setting sun on Miller's Mountain. "He's a lonely man with a broken heart," her father would conclude at the end of each episode, and the warmth in his words and his obvious respect for the older man was one of the reasons why Lucy loved Cliff Moses. Although she was quite young when she'd first heard his story, Lucy had always seen him as a strong, brave man despite his age and reclusive nature. As a child, she'd felt sorry for him, but as she matured, her genuine admiration deepened for the town patriarch.

Evelyn continued with a sadness that seemed to settle like a threatening storm cloud over the two women. "Your father told me Cliff's fiancé left town for a last fling in the big city before marrying, but she never returned. He remained unmarried, and over the years his isolation caused many to think of him as a woeful recluse with a broken heart." Evelyn bowed her head before continuing. "He probably *did* have his heart broken."

Lucy could see her mother slipping and Bobby Jenkins and the torn money came to mind.

"According to your father, all he ever wanted was a brood of kids. And he certainly can't complain about that. He's got more *children* in the neighbourhood kids than Jimmy Brown's rabbits have bunnies."

"And rabbits have bunnies every month!" Lucy jumped in enthusiastically, taking advantage of her mother's mood swing. "When I was a little girl, Wil told me that Uncle Mo was like every child's grandfather. He said that every little boy gets his first ball and mitt on his sixth birthday from Uncle Mo, and no parent would dare intrude on that tradition. The way he told it, I wouldn't want to have been his parents if they'd bought *his* sooner. Lucky for me, I'm a girl," Lucy smirked, lifting the doll from her mother's lap and patting the top of its head. Speaking directly to her childhood treasure, she added, "Little girls don't have to wait as long for their coveted Uncle Mo gift, do they! You came into my life the morning I turned four."

Lost in her own memories for a moment, Lucy continued. "Small kids are admitted where adults fear to tread," she pointed out with a grin. "They uncover a teddy bear nature that few ever see." She gently placed her childhood gift in its own special 'keeping' pile. "Uncle Mo's one of a kind, Mom."

The front doorbell chimed and interrupted the moment.

"I'll get it. Might be Wil." Lucy jumped up from her crouched position and headed for the basement stairs. Taking two steps at a time, she welcomed the opportunity to take a break from the confines of the basement. Sorting through childhood treasures had proved taxing, and she embraced the chance to procrastinate just a little longer. She knew she'd have to finish sorting through the boxes and barrels of clothes, school books, and toys of long ago, but she'd been reluctant about throwing things away, making the task longer and more difficult than she'd imagined.

Racing up the basement stairs, Lucy's mind was still on Cliff Moses. She opened the front door and was startled to find two men squeezed under a black umbrella in an attempt to avoid the steady drizzle. "Uncle Mo!" Lucy exclaimed, genuinely pleased. "For goodness sake, come in. You both look like drowned rats." Lucy cast a wary eye at the stranger. "Mom, Uncle Mo's here, with a visitor," Lucy hollered over her shoulder in the direction of the basement door as she ushered their company into the kitchen. She knew the town's patriarch would never be entertained in the living room.

"Gee, it's good to see you, Uncle Mo. Mom and I were just talking about you. We've been doing spring cleaning with all my stuff in the basement and I found my doll," Lucy said with a twinkle in her eye. She hugged her favourite 'uncle.' The dampness from his jacket gave her a start and she stood back with a scowl. "But what on earth brings you out on a day like this? You should know better. What's it gonna take to get through your thick head that you need to take it easy?" Lucy could hear her own voice and felt slightly embarrassed, especially in front of a stranger, but she didn't let up.

As Evelyn entered the room, Lucy spun around and began again. "Mom, can you believe this?" she said, hands on hips. "It's all but pouring out and this stubborn old coot makes his way over here. Sure hope it's important."

"Lucy!" Evelyn frowned at her daughter. "Sorry, Cliff, sometimes she has a mind of her own. I never know what she'll come out with next. Let me make you some coffee, though, to warm you up, but first, shouldn't you... I mean..." She nodded in the direction of the tall stranger who seemed to be enjoying the current banter.

"Oh, I'm sorry, Evelyn. This is Levi Morsman, MD, my nephew," Cliff announced, squaring his shoulders and acting unusually formal, but obviously very proud. Lucy and her mother exchanged amused looks and mocked a serious face as he continued. "He just arrived in town a week or so ago. Seems my sister thought I needed looking after and *encouraged* Levi to come for a *visit.* I guess my stroke has upset more people than young Lucy here," he commented, throwing a grin in Lucy's direction, accompanied by a shake of his index finger in an attempt to scold his young admirer. "Levi took a leave from the clinic where he works in North Vancouver to spend the next month or so with me. I've already introduced him to Doc Bailey. Levi may be able to help out when he's through *nursing* me," Cliff concluded with a forced scowl. But despite the expected behaviour of a crusty old geezer, it was obvious to Lucy that he was pleased his nephew had come.

Towering over his uncle, Levi Morsman brushed a strand of thick black hair, peppered somewhat with white, from his forehead just before reaching for her mother's hand. His face was already flushed and Lucy wondered if he was genuinely embarrassed at his uncle's accolades. His navy turtleneck sweater hugged his chest just enough to reveal a healthy physique. *He's about Mom's age,* Lucy observed just as he spoke. "Levi is my full name, but my friends call me Lee. Nice to meet you, Mrs. Sherwood. You and your daughter have been spoken of frequently and with high esteem by my uncle. A miracle in itself," he added, bending slightly in an attempt to whisper his last remark.

"That's very nice to hear, and the name's Evelyn. My friends call me Evie... Evelyn." Tactfully, she corrected herself. "And, of course you've already met Lucy."

"Ah, yes, the bride-to-be. How fortunate for the young man to have found such a beauty."

"That's kind of you, Dr. Morsman, but Wil didn't have to *find* me; we grew up together, and for years he's been like my older brother. Then one day things changed and, well, here we are three months away from our wedding."

Lucy's excitement proved captivating, and she was about to prattle on about the wedding when the oldest member of the foursome interrupted her.

"The wedding! That reminds me why I'm here." Cliff lowered his head and paused a moment, leaving his audience in anticipation of what was coming next. It had been obvious that it was important enough to bring him out on such a miserable day. No one spoke, just waited.

"Lucy, I knew your dad ever since he was a little tyke. Watched him grow up into a fine young man, go off to fight for our country and bring home his bride." Cliff smiled and nodded his head respectfully toward Evelyn. "Lucy, I'd be most proud to escort you down the aisle on one of the most important days of your life... out of respect to the memory of your father," he added in earnest.

"Oh, Uncle Mo, that's the nicest thing I've heard since Wil asked me to marry him." Tears filled her eyes. Her mother smiled her approval and Lucy embraced the older man. *How wrong people are,* she thought as he returned her hug.

"Now don't go getting all mushy on me. It's the least I can do." Cliff's attempt to project an air of indifference failed and the excitement that his request had generated led to hot coffee and fresh biscuits and jam around the kitchen table.

Within an hour, the rain had let up and the two men, who had interrupted a day of reminiscing, had created new memories and new friends, and strengthened old ones.

At the front door, Levi turned to his two hosts, and in dramatic form clicked his heels and bowed. "Thank you for a very delightful hour. I've learned much about Thystle Creek and look forward to learning more. By the way, Lucy, I left *Dr. Morsman* in Vancouver. Please, call me Lee." Turning to Evelyn, "It was a pleasure meeting you, Evie, if I may call you that. I'm sure there's more you can share about this town that has held my uncle captive for these many years. Perhaps we can get together sometime over coffee when you can take a moment away from your daughter's wedding plans."

It was not a question but a statement, and Lucy couldn't miss the response her mother gave. It was just a smile, but a smile it was, and Lucy felt a tug at her own heart. Somehow going back to sorting childhood memorabilia seemed unimportant. She needed to find out more about this Dr. Levi Morsman and knew just how to do it.

12

For, lo, the winter is past,
the rain is over and gone.
Song of Solomon 2:11

"Honestly, Doc, you should've seen her smile. It was very subtle, but she smiled!" Lucy exclaimed to her old friend and mentor as he placed a sampling of his famous chili and homemade bread on the table. Her excitement and restlessness punctuated her anxiety as she struggled with the right words. She paced the kitchen floor, all the while conscious of the watchful eye of her friend.

Lovingly known as Doc Bailey, or simply Doc, Allen Bailey had an unwavering trust in God. Lucy had come to admire him as she left childhood and embarked on her "journey of life," as he had so often referred to one's spiritual growth. In the immediate years following her father's death, Lucy knew the doctor had prayed for her just as much as Wil had, but he'd never pressed her to search her heart and reacquaint herself with the God she'd turned her back on; she'd never heard him suggest even once that she suffered needlessly. Despite her coldness to spiritual matters, she had searched out her beloved friend for his wisdom and counsel during those dark months that led into her teen years. Thus, it was not unusual for her to show up on his doorstep unannounced with a load of questions or concerns, or victories.

It had been just a little over fourteen months since she'd returned from a year on the coast, working in the Brown Bean Café with the Patricks. Encouraged by Jessie and their growing friendship, Lucy had spent the year rediscovering God's love and faithfulness and returned to Thystle Creek happier and more content than she had been since her father's death. She often wondered if her contentment played a role in the improved relationship with her mother and denied attention to the fearful thoughts that it wouldn't last.

Her mentor's soft voice brought Lucy back to the present. "...and I wouldn't go getting overly excited about good manners. Your mother was just being polite. From what you've just told me, she never did accept his invitation." Allen pulled out a chair and motioned for Lucy to sit on it.

"Yeah, I know, but she never said no, either!" Lucy flopped on the kitchen chair, frustrated.

"True, and knowing your mother, she very well could have."

"But she didn't," Lucy emphasized.

"Hmm..." The doctor rubbed his chin in deep thought. "Lee *is* single."

Lucy smiled, almost reading his mind.

"From what I can understand, he has no serious ties on the coast except at the clinic and he doesn't seem to be in any hurry to return. Interesting...but...hmm..."

Lucy listened as her friend hesitated a second time. Taking a cue from his weak attempt to dissuade her line of thinking, as well as his own, Lucy pressed further.

“Dad’s been gone for almost six years, Doc,” Lucy spoke softly, almost reverently as she remembered her father. “But Mom can’t be alone for the rest of her life. I’m getting married soon and she can’t fill her days with just her job and her gardening.”

“Lucy, are you sure you’re not overreacting?” His question was gentle, but pointed.

“Maybe... No! No, I’m not!” Lucy flashed determined eyes. “The dark nights of winter are over. I’ll concede that, but winter will come again and I can’t help wondering what she’ll do all alone. It’s not that she isn’t used to looking after a big house, it’s just that it will be an empty one. There are so many memories that seem to haunt her and she cries a lot at night when she doesn’t know I can hear her.”

Lucy spent the remaining time eating in moody silence. With no solutions offered by her mentor, she left the comforts of the doctor’s kitchen feeling a little dejected, despite a full stomach. Even though she knew in her heart her mother’s future remained out of her control, she still held on to the smile that prompted her visit to the doctor’s home. After all, Levi Morsman *was* handsome, he *was* single, and he *wasn’t* committed to anyone on the coast. That much she did learn from her visit. And he *was* the perfect age for her mother. *I wonder how long he’s gonna be here?* Lucy thought to herself as she absent-mindedly kicked at some loose stones.

The small dirt path Lucy took back to town cut behind the main street and entered just east of the Emporium. Kicking the stones into the side bushes with a little more angst than necessary reminded her of the family of skunks that had emerged from the undergrowth last summer when she was returning from the same direction. She had remained frozen on the spot as the family of five crossed directly in front of her. Time seemed to stand still until the last of the young skunks disappeared into the bushes on the other side of the path. Lucy knew enough about the habits of skunks to know that it would be a couple more weeks before the offspring would be weaned and setting out on their own to establish their own dens. Lucy smiled at the memory. She could still see the adult skunk turning to look at her as though to say thank you before disappearing with her brood.

Lucy proceeded with more caution and felt it wiser to refrain from uprooting more stones.

Remembering this special moment helped abate her anxiety somewhat and she did something she had often done over the past few years: she talked to her father. "Dad, if you were here, what would you tell me to do? I miss you, but I know Mom misses you more. She's so lonely and with Wil and me getting married, she's gonna be alone even more."

Despite her resolve to leave the path undisturbed, Lucy lifted a foot full of gravel.

"You planning on doing some excavating the town doesn't know about?"

"Oh! Dr. Morsman. You startled me! I was just thinking about… I didn't notice you coming," Lucy responded quickly, shading her eyes from the late afternoon sun.

"You sure didn't," he teased gently, "and it's Lee, remember? You must have a lot on your mind with the wedding getting closer."

"That's for sure, but I was thinking about my mom. I can't help wondering how she's gonna get along when I move out. The house is already too quiet." Lucy became aware of her rambling. "I'm sorry, Lee. I shouldn't trouble you with my problems. How's the patient doing? We haven't seen Uncle Mo since the day you two dropped by. Did you get a chance to work with Doc Bailey yet? Are you making plans to go home soon?"

"Whoa, rein it in a little! That's three questions on top of each other!" Levi laughed. "Let's work backwards. No, I haven't made any plans to go back to the coast in the immediate future. Yes, I've had opportunity to work with the good doctor a few times. In fact, that's where I am headed right now. He said he had something he wanted to talk over with me and asked me to stop by for supper."

"I just left Doc less than five minutes ago. I can tell you that from sampling what's on the menu, you're in for a treat. He's certainly adjusted better than most of us thought he would after Mrs. Bailey died a couple of years ago. He loves to cook and loves having company. I guess he's not letting himself get too lonely."

Lee returned to the subject Lucy had diverted them from and unwittingly pleased her with his next question. "How's your mother doing? I've been meaning to drop by for that cup of coffee, but keeping track of my uncle and helping Doc Bailey have filled my days. I hope to connect with her real soon."

"That would be nice. By the way, you never mentioned how Uncle Mo is doing. Getting better?"

"Yes, he is. In fact he really doesn't need me around now. I'm just pleasing my mother by staying these extra few weeks." Leaning closer, Levi glanced around and then whispered, "Can I let you in on a little secret?" Without waiting for a response, he continued. "This little town has stolen my heart, and not just in a small way. I'm in no hurry to leave. And these mountains..." Levi stood tall and stretched his arms. "Having arrived on the heels of spring, I can only imagine how beautiful they are in the summer and fall."

"My dad used to say that city folk could never appreciate the beauty of the mountains and forests. He was never surprised to see frazzled, weary campers arrive for a week's vacation and go home rested and rejuvenated from living a slower pace for seven days. You'd have liked him." Lucy smiled warmly at her new friend and prayed silently that a seed had been planted, if not by her, then by the very beauty of which she had just spoken.

The remaining conversation was of no major consequence and they went their separate ways, but not before Levi turned around and called back to Lucy. "Oh, and by the way, you're welcome to share your problems with me anytime." And with a friendly wave, he disappeared around a curve in the path.

13

Trust in the Lord with all thine heart;
and lean not unto thine own understanding.
In all thy ways acknowledge him,
and he shall direct thy paths.
PROVERBS 3:5-6

Three weeks had passed since Lucy had run into Levi Morsman. She'd often thought about the secret he'd shared and wondered if that was behind his delay in returning to the coast and his life at the clinic. *He's sure making things easier for Doc. Maybe Lee will consider…* But Lucy wouldn't allow herself to speculate for very long. Rather, her thoughts reverted to the rigorous afternoon she'd just had with the Johnson children.

Poor Mrs. J., Lucy mused as she enjoyed the walk home in the late afternoon sun. *Being a mother of a new baby certainly must be demanding, but a mother of four!* Lucy had spent the afternoon helping Emilia Johnson, who seemed to be managing fine with her infant son but had little energy left for her other three children. Harry Johnson had left with his team on an extended logging job further north. As superintendent, he'd had no choice but go, and he would be away for another month. His absence added to the strain on the Johnson household, all too evident to Lucy when Emilia made a trip to the Emporium earlier in the week.

"Hi, Mrs. J. You certainly have your hands full." Lucy smiled coming out from behind the counter. She tousled the red curls of Lilly Johnson, fully aware of the child's shyness, and winked as the little girl tucked herself behind her mother's legs. "How's the little guy getting along? Is he sleeping through the night? Are the other kids adjusting?" Lucy's innocent chatter produced a threat of tears as her neighbour failed desperately to hide her frustration and weariness.

"Here, let me have him for a moment," Lucy offered as she lifted Mark gently from his mother's arms. Her comfortable hold of the infant allowed the baby to see his mother and not feel threatened that she was not holding him.

"Thanks, Lucy. I'm just so tired these days. The twins are in school for the morning, but it doesn't give me much time with Lilly while Mark is sleeping. The afternoons are so crazy with everyone home, and Lilly doesn't want to sleep anymore. She thinks she's missing out on something." This time the red curls received a motherly tousle. "When Matt and Melody were three, they napped for an hour or two. I always welcomed that time alone."

Lucy nodded sympathetically and smiled at Lilly, who was still hiding behind her mother's legs. "She's really shy, isn't she? Would you like me to come over on my day off to play with Lilly and the twins?" Bending down, Lucy directed her suggestion to the three-year-old. "What do you think, Lilly? Would you like to go to the park with your brother and sister one day this week? We could feed the geese in the pond and maybe even have a swing or two. Would you like that?"

Lilly looked up at her mother, then shyly nodded, bouncing her red curls over her eyes.

"Then that settles it, Mrs. J." Lucy stood up to face her friend. "Thursday's my day off. I'll come over after lunch. If it's not raining, we'll go to the park, and if it rains, I'll take them over to my house and give you some time to yourself. Deal?"

All Emilia Johnson could do was smile and mimic her daughter.

There had been no rain. Instead, the sun had warmed the air and the day had been perfect for mother, children, and friend.

With her volunteered babysitting complete, Lucy sauntered along Oakwood Street. She was in no hurry. Wil was planning on going to the library after his class was dismissed and with all that was going on in her head, she welcomed the solitude.

Paramount in her mind was her marriage to Wil in a couple of months. Several decisions had to be made regarding the wedding, but they had finally landed on where they would live. Just last week they'd decided to rent the Taylor house for a while until they could buy their own home. The small cottage had sat empty for seven months since old Mrs. Taylor had died last fall, and the family was not yet ready to sell it. It was a big decision, but a good one for all concerned. Lucy's mother had been thrilled to learn that they would be living just a few blocks away.

Recalling her mother's reaction, old nagging thoughts returned. *How's Mom gonna manage being alone?* Lucy shook her head, trying hard to be objective. *Of course she's going to manage. She'll be just fine!* But the concern wouldn't let go. Even though the last year had seen positive changes in their relationship, Lucy knew there were still many unresolved issues in her mother's life. She continued to submerge herself in her own world, and apart from the quiet moments with Lucy, she avoided any connection beyond her home. Lucy couldn't understand what it was that drove her mother to such depths of despair.

Lost in her reverie, she came to an abrupt halt as she turned onto Aspen Avenue. A familiar car sat parked in front of her house. She just stood there, smiling. *Again! This is getting interesting. Levi Morsman seems to be showing more interest in Mom than just a passing friendship.*

Expecting to find them in the kitchen, Lucy was surprised to see the couple enjoying the spring afternoon over a cup of coffee as they wandered about the garden examining the early growth. Undetected, she stood quietly by the screen door and listened.

"Really, Lee, you have your own garden? I'm amazed! I mean, after all, you're a doctor. When would you have time for such things as planting and pruning, let alone weeding? I can spend hours every day just fussing with the flowers and transplanting when things get overgrown."

"My hours at the clinic are very regular. I work a normal nine-to-five day, and never on weekends. Sometimes I wish I did have a change so that my life would take on some greater challenge; however, my garden is my escape and my therapy." Levi smiled at Evelyn as she bent down to move some dead leaves from a primrose trying to break through the spring soil.

Without looking up, Evelyn responded, "Escaping in the garden *can* help you get through each day." She stood while Levi steadied her, gently grasping her elbow. Locking eyes for a brief moment, Evelyn smiled, "Would you like to join Lucy and me for supper?"

When Lucy saw the look exchanged between her mother and Levi Morsman and heard her mother invite him to dinner, she knew exactly what to do. "But it has to be flawless," Lucy whispered to the empty kitchen. *And Lord, I really need you in on this with me.*

Lucy backed away from the door quietly, made a hasty phone call, and then exited her home only to come back in again, louder and more rushed. *This had better work,* she thought as she hollered for her mother.

She stumbled through the screen door with all the appearance of having just run a marathon. "Hi, Mom." Lucy smiled at Lee. "Sorry to be so loud. I've only got a minute before I'm meeting Wil at the library. We've invited ourselves for dinner at Doc Bailey's, so I'll only be here long enough to change. Those Johnson kids kept me hopping, as you can probably tell from my clothes." Lucy continued her charade by flaying her hands about in exaggeration. "But we had lots of fun and Mrs. Johnson had a chance to get some rest. Oh, and by the way, she heard from Mr. J. last night. He's getting a few days off, because of the baby, I guess, and will be home over the weekend. Well, gotta run. I won't be late, Mom. Nice seeing you again, Lee."

Lucy plotted all the way to the library, knowing Wil had already told her he was there marking exams. *Good thing I called Doc before I left the house,* Lucy smiled, proud of her attempts at playing cupid.

"What was that?" Lee exclaimed as he watched Lucy tear back into the house. "Oh, to have that much energy again. Seems like she's got enough for the two of us." Levi turned as he directed his last comment toward Evelyn and discovered her face ashen. "Evie, what is it?" Concern filled Levi's voice as he led Evelyn to the lounge chair.

"It's nothing, really."

"I'll decide that. What happened? We were out here enjoying your garden. You invited me to dinner and then Lucy appeared in a whirlwind announcing her plans, and…oh, I see." Bending down to face his friend, Levi took Evelyn's hand with one of his and lifted her chin with the other.

"Evie, you don't need to feel obligated to feed me. If being alone with me for dinner puts you in an uncomfortable position, I'll gladly take a rain check. Maybe we can do this some other time, perhaps when Lucy and Wil can join us. I don't want…"

"I'm sorry, Lee," Evelyn interjected. "I'm acting like a silly schoolgirl. Of course, you'll stay for dinner. How does leftover pot roast sound? We'll keep things simple. Deal?"

"Deal."

Evelyn stood and headed toward the kitchen, leaving Levi to wonder what was behind her reaction to being alone with him.

14

And he said unto him,
What is thy name? And he said, Jacob.
And he said, Thy name shall be called
no more Jacob, but Israel....
GENESIS 32:27-28

I'm sorry to put you in the middle of this, Wil, but I had to do something. You should've seen them. Lee has definitely got something going for my mom and I was just helping out a little. Please don't be mad at me." Lucy concluded her defence with a pitiful grin and waited for Wil to pass judgment.

"Don't be so hard on yourself. I'm sure you acted out of pure innocence, and if Lee had realized what you were doing, he'd probably be thanking you. Are you sure it's okay with Doc to have unexpected company?"

"Don't worry. He's always got an open door, and besides, I'm curious to know just what business he ran by Lee a couple of weeks ago." Lucy arched her eyebrows to emphasize her point. "Remember? I told you how Lee startled me on the dirt path behind the Emporium. He said that Doc had invited him to dinner to talk over some business. What business is Doc talking to Lee about if it didn't involve his practice?"

Wil and Lucy were walking down the front steps of the library when Wil stopped midway and turned her to face him. "Look Luce, I know you're concerned about your mother. I understand that. But you've got to stop interfering, even if it's innocently done. You can't play cupid and set up Lee and your mother." Stifling her response with a finger to her lips, Wil continued less dogmatically. "It's not your place, my sweet, nor mine, even if I do admit I've wondered if Lee and Doc have come to some kind of an understanding about Doc's practice. Now, don't go giving me that look. I have no idea what they talked about and I don't think it's your place or mine to ask. We'll just have to wait and see what happens."

Wil draped his arm over Lucy's shoulder and squeezed her close to his side, kissing the top of her head. "Come on. Lecture's over. Let's go for supper. Maybe we should stop by Mollie's and pick up some of her butter tarts. They're wickedly delicious, you know," he added with a guilty grin, and the two lifelong friends locked arms and headed for the diner.

Dinner had been perfect. The reheated pot roast had turned into a feast with salad and dessert to complement the meal. Dinner conversation had been light and Levi now found himself answering Evelyn's questions about himself over a second cup of coffee in the screened-in section of the patio. Nothing seemed to be too trivial to him, nor was he threatened by the openness with which Evelyn asked such personal questions.

"Tell me about your name, Lee."

"My name? That's a strange request."

"Just curious. Do you mind?'

"No, not at all. It's a bit of a story. Do you have time?" Levi smiled. "I suppose I should start with my mother, since she brought me into this world." Evelyn flinched slightly and Levi noticed it, but not wanting to appear too inquisitive, he continued. "Since coming to Thystle Creek and spending time with my uncle, I've learned more about my mother's childhood and early adult years than I've known my entire life. For example, she was an entertainer from the beginning—a born actress with the voice of an angel." Levi raised his eyebrows in defence of Evelyn's reaction. "It's true. She would line up her stuffed animals, her dolls, and sometimes her little friends and sing made-up songs and tell impromptu stories that had never been heard before—and probably never have since. Uncle Cliff admitted the other night as we sat looking at family pictures that he would pretend to be annoyed every time she coaxed him to listen. 'Please, Cliffy, please come and sit. Please!' she'd beg. And sit he did, among the teddy bears and dolls and little girls. I guess she was quite the little manipulator."

Evelyn laughed at the verbal picture Levi was painting and he smiled at her obvious pleasure at imagining the man she knew now as Uncle Mo sitting among stuffed animals transfixed by his little sister's theatrics. When he'd begun his story, Levi noticed a faraway look in Evelyn's eyes, and despite the laughter, he could still sense *something.* He paused in his storytelling until Evelyn turned and smiled at him, and then he continued."But each time he gave in, and each time he'd stay to the end. She would mesmerize him with her singing and storytelling. My grandparents were astonished by my mother's confidence at such a young age. They questioned themselves often as to where it came from and concluded it was just her quirky personality that touched people. She was a genuine performer who brought a smile to people's faces. It came from deep inside of her, it seems, and to this day it has never left."

Levi stretched his legs and rested his hands behind his head. "My mother was eighteen when World War I blasted its way into history. Within the first year, she convinced my grandparents to let her move to the coast." Levi placed his hand over his heart and closed his eyes in a mocking imitation of his mother: "'Where I can serve my country and bring some laughter and music to a hurting world.' Apparently it worked. They let her go, expecting her to return within weeks, if not days. But she succeeded, got a job singing in a café not far from the sights frequented by sailors."

For several minutes, Levi reiterated all that he had learned from his uncle. He told Evelyn story after story of his mother's early stage career, how she wrote weekly letters to her brother and parents telling them of her new life and adventures on the coast, the friends she had made, and the singing opportunities that filled her evenings.

"But despite my mother's bent on entertaining, she wanted more out of her life. It wasn't enough to bring a world of make-believe to a willing audience. Yes, she wanted the stage, the excitement, the challenge, all that the world of entertainment could offer, but she wanted more. Apparently, she even considered enrolling in the newly established university as a part-time student. Instead she settled for the local library where she spent hours studying in her quest to discover, to improve herself not just in the world of acting, but in academics, mathematics, and strangely enough, world religions."

"Really!"

"Yes. My mother was a deep thinker even as a child; still is, for that matter. She told me once that when she was little she would look out her bedroom window into a night sky twinkling with what she described as 'God's night lights' and wonder what was beyond the blackness. Apparently even as a youngster she had an unusual interest in God, how things came to be, what other people thought of Him and how they worshipped. Enter my father." Levi smiled privately and then turned his head toward Evelyn. "On one of the many occasions Mom spent at the library, she met my father and, as the saying goes, the rest is history. End of story."

"Lee! That's not fair."

Levi winked. "Just teasing. My father was a born teacher and held a highly respectable position in the community teaching Hebrew at a recently established synagogue. He devoured books and, like my mother, had an unexplainable yearning to understand the different religions of the world. They met in the library and over time—a very short period of time—they fell in love. My mother, twenty by that time, was sixteen years younger than my father, an age difference that society frowned upon back then. She was left with a choice: pursue her stage career or marry my father and have his children. She chose my father and married him the summer she turned twenty-one. Never once have I heard her as much as hint that she regretted her decision. It was never considered a sacrifice. She loved my father very much and wanted to spend the rest of her life with him, along with a dozen kids."

Levi sat quietly, his hands between his knees, examining the ground at his feet. When he finally spoke, his voice was lowered such that Evelyn had to lean forward to hear him.

"They had a hard time conceiving. She was twenty-nine and dad was forty-five when she finally did. Her pregnancy was so difficult that her doctor told her there could be no more babies. That was a blow to both of them, especially my mother."

Levi's voice filled the darkness that had slowly encompassed them, unaware that in sharing his mother's life he had unwittingly touched a secret part of the life of his host, had penetrated a corner of a well-guarded wall. "…and not to be left out, my dad had his own story. He had scarlet fever as a child, which left him with a heart condition. Because of that, he couldn't join his buddies overseas during the war. He was willing, but not able, so he buried himself in his passion to learn. He briefly considered becoming a rabbi, but settled as a teacher." At that comment, Levi turned to Evelyn for a reaction, but found her gazing out at her garden.

"Enter my mother."

He laughed at his own repetition, and Evelyn turned her head, her look questioning his behaviour.

"That was a long way around a question that never got answered," he said, slightly embarrassed. "Sorry, Evie. To answer your question, I'm named after my paternal grandfather, Levi Yaacov Morsman. Yaacov is translated Jacob, son of Isaac. My grandfather's family dates back to the Ashkenazi Jews from Eastern Poland. Did you know that Albert Einstein was an Ashkenazi Jew, even though his parents didn't practise the faith?" With a wave of his hand Levi continued. "Anyway, the Ashkenazi Jews have a custom of naming a child after a relative who has passed away. This keeps the name and memory alive, and in a metaphysical way forms a bond between the soul of the baby and the deceased relative. This is considered a great honour to the deceased because it's believed that the soul of the deceased can achieve an elevation based on the good deeds of the namesake, me in this case." Levi raised his eyebrows, expressing his awareness of such a responsibility, and continued. "Meanwhile, I can be inspired by the good qualities of my grandfather and make a deep connection to the past."

"Do you?"

"Do I do good deeds or do I connect with my past?"

"Do you make a deep connection to your past? *Are* you inspired by your grandfather's good qualities?"

"Yes. I never knew him personally, but from the stories I've been told, he was a wonderful man, full of stamina and spirit. He was a tailor's son who moved from a downtown Jewish community in Toronto and travelled across the country when he was just eighteen. His father had trained him well, and with a small travel bag, a hat, and very little money he set out for newer and bigger sites on the west coast. By the time he was twenty-five, he had his own tailor shop, a wife, and two small children—my father and his twin sister, Aunt Rachel, who died from polio when she was seven. My grandfather died at thirty-four from influenza. I wished I could have known him."

A great-horned owl could be heard in the distance and its screech accentuated the evening stillness, broken seconds later when Levi stretched his legs and stood, indicating it was time he should be leaving. He paused for a moment as he looked down at his host.

"Evelyn, you asked me about my name. I can't help wondering why. It's obviously a Jewish name. Does this bother you? Are you uncomfortable with me, knowing that I'm Jewish?"

Evelyn's attempt to suppress a shiver failed as her defences rose.

"I'm not uncomfortable with your Jewish heritage, Levi. I only find it surprising that you're so free with sharing it. The climate for Jews hasn't changed much since the war. You'd think that with the persecution the world witnessed in Europe people would be more sympathetic. But they don't seem to be, from what I've heard and read. And then you come along and announce to anyone who'll listen that your mother was a Gentile and became a Jew when she married your father. I find that... interesting, that's all."

Evelyn finished her thoughts on a note that raised more questions in Levi's mind than he felt ready to ask. A shy smile grew as he placed his hand over Evelyn's. "Evie, if you will allow me an old cliché...there's more to you than meets the eye. Perhaps you'll feel safe to share what's really on your mind over another dinner?"

"Perhaps."

After Levi left, Evelyn made a fresh cup of tea and wandered into her living room. A small light on the desk in the front window cast a golden glow over the room and Evelyn paused a moment, placing her cup on the coffee table. She loved this room. The pair of burgundy and grey plaid wing chairs had been Lewis's favourite spot, especially in the cold winter months when a fire burned in the hearth. Claiming one as his own, its matching footstool had often overflowed with his books and magazines and had proven useless for its intended purpose. Evelyn sighed, remembering. Efforts to reconcile with her past had helped her focus on the pleasant memories of her life with Lewis. Living with guilt and regrets had taken its toll on their relationship, but she felt she was winning the battle and moving on now that she and Lucy seemed to be on stable ground. She knew she had never dealt with all the painful memories that surfaced unexpectedly but seemed content to leave the past buried, believing in her heart that it was the best thing to do for all concerned.

"Where do I go from here?" Her words echoed in the stillness and Levi's face flashed before her—his smile, the warmth of his breath when he cupped her face in his hand, his gentle touch when he held her hand, and the story of his parents told with such love and compassion. Evelyn grabbed the throw pillow from the chair and squeezed it hard against her chest. She tried to crush the nagging ache that was slowly surfacing, threatening to choke her. She remembered looking at Levi and for a split second had felt the urge to move the curl that had fallen on his forehead. *He has nice eyes.* She squeezed the pillow harder, a groan escaping from her lips when she buried her face in the fabric. Evelyn had never considered a relationship with another man. She had loved two men and they had both died needlessly, and she was not about to open herself up for another hurt. *I couldn't bear it.* With determined steps, Evelyn placed the pillow where she had found it and unconsciously escaped into a world of denial.

Lucy's steps were soundless as she moved through the darkened house to her bedroom. Her mother had retired for the evening, and she wrestled with disappointment when she realized that her curiosity about the evening would have to be tempered until morning. She paused. A muffled sound brought her to the bottom of the staircase that led to her mother's bedroom. The sobs were all too familiar, but it had been some time since she'd heard them. Lucy strained to listen.

"What do I have to do? How much longer do I have to suffer?" Evelyn's voice filtered down the stairs.

Lucy froze.

"Oh, Lee, how can I make you understand? I can't do this again. I won't!"

Lucy slipped away from the staircase and took refuge in her own room, struggling with an overwhelming sense of guilt.

15

He shall fly away as a dream, and shall not be found:
yea, he shall be chased away as a vision of the night.
Job 20:8

Daddy, Daddy! Is that you? How... ? The fire! We had a funeral." Lucy raced through the garden and flung herself into her father's arms, throwing away any concern about soiling her wedding gown.

"Well, look at you. My little girl, all grown up. It's been quite a while." He spun her in circles as he had done so often when she was small. Her veil trailed in the breeze and her giggles were childlike. "Remember how we used to play hide 'n seek? You'd go hide and I'd come find you." The spinning and laughing continued. Seconds passed. And then it was over. The twirling ended. It had to.

"Stop, Dad. Wait. Put me down. I can't do this. I'm not a child anymore. I'm getting married today, to Wil. He's waiting for me. But there are so many questions. There's so much to tell you. It's been over seven years. Where have you been?" Lucy's words tumbled out as she stood transfixed before the man who had deserted her.

Her father's voice trailed off. His words became inaudible, his tone matter-of-fact. His stare had moved beyond her and a hush filled the air. Movement stopped and life became slow motion.

"Do you hear me, Dad?" Lucy grabbed her father's arms and shook him. "I said, I'm getting married today. And Mom's invit…" Lucy turned to follow her father's gaze and gasped as she saw her mother approaching them from the end of the garden.

"Hello, Evie girl."

Her father smiled in anticipation. Her mother stared in disbelief, her steps faltering, her whole body on the edge of a faint.

"Mom, Mom, it's Dad! He's come back!" But Lucy's voice didn't seem to register with her mother. "She's in shock, Dad. I've got to get Doc Bailey. No! Wait! He's coming to the wedding. No! No! That's not right. He's here, somewhere. Oh, Dad, the wedding! Uncle Mo's walking me down the aisle. I didn't know you were alive. They said you'd died. We had a funeral." In her confusion, Lucy repeated herself. She became irrational, racing back and forth, frantic. Tears flowed and she rubbed her eyes trying to keep her vision clear.

Unnoticed in the confusion, a thick fog had slowly enveloped the groomed garden and the aspen tree where the arbour stood, where Wil stood waiting. The mist covered the daisies and the coral bells and the satin bows, and settled on Lucy's gown, leaving large stains as each spot grew into one another. Lucy brushed at the spots, frantic to remove them, and then watched in horror as the mist turned to snow and the stains crept over her gown until it hung limp and damp on her shoulders.

In dazed silence, she turned to see her mother and father embracing. Life moved from normal to surreal. Faces merged, voices whispered into an unknown language, and the threat of blackness hovered like a menacing monster.

A man came from nowhere and separated her parents.

"Sorry, Lewis," the voice said gently but unyielding, "you must release her. She must be free to live."

Lucy's father fell backwards into the snow. Instantly an angel rose, brushing its wings free from the flakes. It winked at Lucy, paused in front of her mother, reaching to brush her hair with a gentle stroke and then disappeared before Lucy's eyes.

"Noooo! Come back. You must come back! I'm getting married. I'll play your game. Please don't go!" Lucy cried, begged, promised, but all in vain. The angel disappeared before her eyes.

The sun's rays filtered through the trees, melted the snow, and dissolved the stains on her gown and it was dry once again. Lucy screamed and ran for her mother but her mother kept fading further and further into the distance until she disappeared with the stranger. She turned and found Wil standing, waiting for her at the arbour, and she fell into his arms and sobbed.

Lucy bolted upright in her bed. Shaking uncontrollably, she brushed at her tears as she frantically smoothed out the bed sheets. There was no snow. There were no stains. There was no angel.

"It was just a dream," she whispered into the stillness of her room, yet she'd seen her father. He was as real as the racket from the birds high in the trees outside her bedroom window, and she fell back on her pillow trying to reinvent the dream before details slowly vaporized into a vague memory. But reality washed over her. *People don't become angels, and… snow in the summer!* She shook her head. *Wow! I must be really tired.*

The light chenille cover wasn't necessary, but Lucy unconsciously drew it to her chin as she snuggled down in the comfort it provided. The shaking had subsided. Her attention was drawn briefly to the screeching high in the trees outside and then her thoughts drifted to the other two who had played a large part in her nightmare—her mother and the stranger. It just took moments and then she knew. *It was Lee!*

Over two months had passed since Lucy had interrupted the evening plans that had involved her mother and Levi. She had neither asked about nor had her mother offered any information on the events of the evening. *Why should she?* Lucy thought back over her impulsive plan. *She had no idea what I was up to.* The direction her thoughts took startled her. *But what is Lee up to? Is Mom encouraging him in spite of herself?*

Levi had been back twice and each time with an obvious purpose in mind. Once, he had dropped off a new gardening book he had picked up when he had gone home for a brief meeting. It was a special edition for shade plants, he'd said, and thought her mother would like to read it. The other visit warmed Lucy's spirit as she snuggled in her blankets, relieved that her nightmare had subsided and her focus was now on pleasant things.

"Mom, Lee's here to see you." Lucy and Levi had found her mother in the back garden dividing her overgrown flowers that had all but doubled in size. Hat on to deter the deer flies, Evelyn had unknowingly left tell-tale mud streaks across her cheek and nose, evidence of the losing battle with the annoying insects.

"I–I was in the neighbourhood and just thought I'd stop by to see if the book was helpful." Levi's stammering accentuated a shyness so foreign to the man they'd come to know that Evelyn and Lucy had burst into laughter.

"Lee, you don't have to find an excuse to come by and see us." Lucy laughed as she warmly gripped his arm. "You can drop by any time, even if we do find ourselves unprepared for guests, right Mother?"

Lucy's last comment had been directed to her mother, accompanied with a motion for her mother to wipe her face, and in an attempt to remove the dirt with her apron, her mother had left a longer and dirtier streak. Levi had come to the rescue and offered to help her mother remove the evidence of her labour by wiping it away himself with his clean handkerchief.

Here, Evie, allow me. Even now his words brought a grin to Lucy, a grin that would have certainly raised questioning eyebrows had anyone witnessed it. The surprise visit had led to a cold drink in the shade at the end of the yard as the three friends discussed Wil and Lucy's upcoming garden wedding.

"Obviously we'll be limited in how many guests we invite, but the 'town fathers' have offered to have a dessert reception at the town hall." Lucy's delight had spread across her face and drew equally gratifying smiles from her audience.

"Have you given any thought to a back-up plan if it rains?"

"Actually, Wil and I have it on good authority that the sun will shine," Lucy quipped with a mischievous grin, and then more seriously: "Yes, Lee, we have. Mom is overly concerned that it will rain and spoil our plans. I've tried to reassure her that things will be just fine, but I haven't been successful, have I, Mom?" She glanced at her mother sheepishly as she revealed a worry her mother had voiced repeatedly. "We have booked our church's chapel just in case, but we're really praying that the sun will be kind to us. Not too hot. Not too cold. And besides, the way Mom's been working in this garden these past weeks, we'd better have the wedding here."

Lucy hoped her humorous, but nevertheless sincere flattery would diffuse any irritation her mother may have felt when she shared her mother's ongoing concern about the weather. "And if it does rain," Lucy went on, "we may have to contact one of those famous gardening magazines to come and feature her garden in one of its editions, just to keep her happy. Hmm, sounds like a good idea either way. If we don't have any guests to admire your handiwork, Mom, then we'd better find some other way to share your work of art."

Lucy recalled her mother's flushed cheeks as her head dropped in shyness. With no apparent need for Evelyn to respond, Levi had broken the lightheartedness.

"Ladies, forgive me if I am presumptuous, but I must confess the real purpose for my visit." Levi began to pace from the coolness of the shade of the spruce trees to the warmth of the afternoon sun. Having both women's full attention, he continued, turning to Evelyn. "I'd consider it an honour if you would allow me to escort you to Lucy's wedding."

Visions of her dream—her mother and father, and Lee—became paramount as Lucy recalled how her mother had flinched, causing Levi to continue with less bravado and more gentleness. "I understand this may take you by surprise, Evie, but your friendship, and Lucy's," he added quickly, "has come to mean a lot to me over these past few months. In fact, people in this town have been so accepting of me that I feel like I've lived here my whole life. And just so you know, my visit to the coast a couple of weeks ago has only confirmed what I've been considering for some time. I'd like to make Thystle Creek my home."

Levi Morsman in town, permanently! Lucy had pondered the idea for only a few seconds before realizing that her smile had revealed her inner feelings. Her mother, on the contrary, had just stared.

"Lucy, do you remember that day we almost collided on the path not far from the Emporium? Turned out Doc had invited me for dinner with an ulterior motive and planted the idea over his famous chili and homemade bread. By the way, thanks for the heads up; the meal was terrific." He winked before continuing. "He's concerned about his age and the growing number of patients and suggested we share his practice until he's ready to go into full retirement." He halted abruptly and turned to Evelyn. "But this is going off-topic. Evie, if you'll let me, I'd like to be with you at Lucy's wedding."

Reliving the moment again, Lucy kicked the unnecessary blanket to the bottom of the bed. She had thought about Levi's request several times since he'd asked it a few weeks earlier, recalling the painfully long silence that had followed. She remembered turning to her mother and being greeted with a confused, even scared look that was begging for an answer to her searching question, *What should I do?*

She stretched and yawned. "Well, you made your decision, Mom, and tomorrow everyone will know what it is."

The clamouring from the birds continued outside and Lucy began to feel sorry for her mother for having her bedroom on the second floor. *She's certainly got a bird's eye view.* Lucy grinned at the humour of it and dressed to face her last day as a single woman.

16

For my life is spent with grief, and my years with sighing:
my strength faileth because of mine iniquity...
PSALM 31:10

Nature's screech of alarm filtered through the quietness of Evelyn's bedroom as a battle erupted in the air just over the Sherwood home. Two large crows had descended on the neighbouring treetops and a *mother alert* filled the air. Evelyn knew the conflict would arouse others who slept along Aspen Avenue, and much like herself, they would be left wondering if the newly laid eggs would satisfy a need for breakfast, or survive and hatch.

Drawn to the window, Evelyn saw wings flapping incessantly and she heard the frantic cries of smaller birds shrieking warning calls to alert the unsuspecting. A helpless spectator to nature's law of survival of the fittest, she knew that one would win the battle; another would lose. Reluctantly, she equated what was happening outside to a memory buried deep in her past.

It had been the spring of 1950, five months after her miscarriage. Disappointment and guilt had filled Evelyn's days, yet three months later she had taken comfort in Allen Bailey's delight that she had conceived again, so quickly.

"This is wonderful news, Evelyn. Nothing will ever replace what you lost a while back, but you can look ahead to a new life, a new beginning. Louie must be strutting around like a proud peacock. Would you allow this old-timer some liberties?"

Evelyn remembered how he had continued with no intention of waiting for a reply.

"Somewhere in the book of Psalms it says that children of a man's youth are like arrows in the hand of a mighty man. He's the happiest when his quiver's full of them."

Evelyn had shifted uncomfortably while her friend spoke. She knew quoting scripture came naturally to the doctor and she'd tolerated it out of politeness, unlike most of his patients who seemed to accept his forthrightness as a means of encouragement. Then he'd taken her hands, squeezed them gently, and moved the subject into safer territory.

"Evie, it's going to be okay this time, and little Lucy will have a brother or sister to play with. If my memory serves me right, she'll be past three when the baby comes, won't she?"

Evelyn cringed as her memories paralleled the conflict in the treetops. She tried to focus her thoughts on the noise outside. She pushed back the curtains further and blinked under the bright sun. Leaves had been wrestled to the ground as attack followed attack. Soon an army of birds flailed upon the intruders to weaken their assault, but determination prevailed and the battle continued. It was all too real, and the inevitable loss of life stirred a deep pain, evoking relentless images that were threatening to invade her morning. She tried to focus on something else, anything, but the images eventually engulfed her in a vortex of pain. She shivered involuntarily, remembering.

It had been a late autumn night. Thystle Creek was threatened with its first snowfall of the season, and Evelyn had awakened from an unusually sound sleep. Sleeping had been difficult for several nights. The baby had been restless and was no respecter of time of day. All night it had stretched, poked and pressed her, and she'd welcomed the warm breath that had caressed her neck with a whisper. "Evie, are you awake?"

Evelyn closed her eyes and sighed. She remembered turning awkwardly on her back, conscious of her husband's arm across her swollen belly. She had looked into her husband's little-boy eyes and smiled.

"I am now."

"Evie, if our child is a boy, I'd like to call him Anthony William, after my grandfather. Is that okay with you?"

"And if it's a girl? Shall we call her Minnie, after your grandmother?" Evelyn countered with a sleepy laugh. "I'm only teasing you, Louie," she yawned. "That's fine with me."

She'd wanted to say, *Now, go back to sleep,* but hadn't. She knew he was excited about becoming a father again and she'd wanted to tell him how deeply she loved him. She had never been good at telling him, not even at a time like that when it would have meant so much. Predictably, the right words had failed to come, and instead she'd felt the need to speak what had been heavy on her heart for days.

"Louie, if anything should go wrong, if something should happen…"

Lewis placed his fingers on her mouth and then gently kissed her forehead, her cheeks, and then lingered on her lips. "Sh! Nothing is going to happen. We are going to have a healthy little Anthony, or Minnie," he added with a grin. "Trust me, Evie. You'll see. God wants us to fill this house with the laughter and noise of many children.

When that happens, we'll be begging for mercy."

"Lewis Sherwood, are you trying to fill your quiver?"

She'd surprised him with her quick response and had turned back on her side to avoid his questioning look.

Thinking back now, Evelyn recalled several times during her pregnancy when she had come close to asking Lewis's God for just that: a full quiver for her husband, a house full of laughter, noise and excitement, but she never did. She tightened her arms around herself. It was a summer morning, bright and fresh, and yet she continued to shiver… and the voice surfaced once again: *And he thought there was a God who loved!*

There had been no laughter. No noise. No excitement. There had been no baby. The quiver would never be full. Anthony William Sherwood had survived in the comforts of the womb but never had the chance to breathe the breath of life.

As if reliving her son's death was not enough, other memories persisted. The tears that had been shed in private. The phone calls. The visits. The confused look in a little girl's eyes. Lewis's strength that she silently resented. And the conversations he'd had with Dr. Bailey, that she learned about later, taunted her even now as she stood watching the struggle for survival outside.

"Stillborn! How? Why? A couple of nights ago, he was kicking Evie in the ribs. We'd named him Anthony William, and now he's dead."

The necessary surgery following her delivery had provided a temporary reprieve. She had been unconscious when Lewis learned that their son had died. It was only later that she screamed the same questions Lewis had sobbed. It had been on the third day that Dr. Bailey had attempted to answer their questions. She had been numb with denial and he had directed his remarks to Lewis.

"Louie, when Lucy was born, everything was fine," he reminded his friend gently. "But it was different this time." Turning to Evelyn, he softened his voice and continued. "Evie, the sudden back pain that woke you up was not the beginning of your labour as you thought. It was the result of a small tear. It's called placental abruption. A piece of the placenta tore away from the wall of the uterus. A haematoma, or a swelling filled with blood, was formed, separating your placenta from the uterine wall."

Dr. Bailey had paused before continuing. His words had sounded mechanical, hollow, professional. "When this area was compressed, the blood supply to your baby was jeopardized, and when you began having contractions, that part of your uterus which was already weakened, ruptured. You didn't do anything wrong, Evie. There's nothing you could have done differently. You just didn't know. There was a lot of bleeding and by the time you got here, well, it was all we could do to save you."

Her stare had been empty as he spoke the hardest words of all. "The little guy was caught up in it all. There wasn't anything anyone could do. We couldn't save him."

Dr. Bailey had spoken softly. The necessary surgery to stop the bleeding had meant there could be no more children, he'd said. He was terribly sorry and he'd wept with them both.

Sadness had filled their home in the early weeks following the death of their son. Dr. Bailey had said to give it time and he had been right, at least for Lewis. Repeatedly, Evelyn had seen Lewis on his knees before his God, and as time passed and healing fulfilled its role, she had witnessed an unusual peace, never the anger that should have accompanied the pain, never the anger that filled her days. She had emotionally isolated herself from Lewis and had refused his comfort, refused to weep with him, had rejected him as he had reached out for her in the night when her pain had reached an unbearable peak. She'd appeared oblivious to her husband's need to mourn with her. Rather, she'd attacked Lewis's God, hurting Lewis in the process.

Evelyn's hands slipped to her abdomen and she lowered herself to the windowsill bench. Turning from the window, she looked at her bed and relived the angry scene that had invaded the sanctuary of their bedroom.

"And you say your God is a *good* God. Can't you see, Lewis? Are you so caught up in your worship and your so-called faith that you're blind to the kind of God you worship? What is it going to take for you to realize how *wrong* you are? He's not a God of love and He's failed you again! Your all-loving God has taken another innocent life when He supposedly has the power to prevent it."

Lewis had sat on the side of their bed, head down, weeping.

Evelyn knew in her heart even now where the problem lay. Unknown to Lewis, she had struggled with guilt and blame. Once again, his God had brought judgment on her, and it was this last thought that had thrown her into an abyss of despair. Although she'd lashed out in anger at her husband and outwardly blamed his God, she held herself responsible for the pain that crossed his face in the early days following the death of their son. His arms would never hold another son or a daughter and she had blamed herself.

The smell of coffee filtered throughout the Sherwood home, helping Evelyn tear away from the clutches of the past. *Lucy's awake,* and Evelyn smiled. *There's a wedding tomorrow.* Her thoughts tarried for a moment longer. *If only I had asked Louie's God for laughter, for noise, for excitement, maybe if I had asked for forgiveness, then...* But the thought never lingered and Evelyn closed the door on her haunting past once again.

17

Casting all your care upon him;
for he careth for you.
1 PETER 5:7

The popping noise of the coffee percolator beat out a catchy rhythm that echoed an invitation throughout the house, the accompanying aroma luring the innocent to its source. Lucy sniffed the unique odour, glad she was free from her nightmare. She'd never acquired a taste for the addictive bean, but she knew her mother would appreciate waking up to a freshly brewed cup. It was one of the many perks Lucy had gleaned from working with Jessie and Garry in their café, much to her mother's delight.

The smell of muffins baking in the oven competed with the coffee and Lucy instinctively busied herself in the kitchen that had been such a major part of her life. The surroundings were pretty much the same as they had been since she was a little girl. The red and white gingham tablecloth matched the curtains, and when the cloth was not in use, red placemats with white lace trim were used in their stead. The old icebox had been replaced when she was eleven with a new fridge and freezer combination. Although Lucy had missed Mr. Bastion and his silly jokes when he delivered the block of ice, her mother was delighted to be rid of the messy job of cleaning the pools of melting water in the icebox.

The wooden highchair holding a large pot of geraniums that had been nurtured over the winter by her mother was tucked away in the corner near the front bay window. Lucy had always wondered why her mother never had any more children and had only recently learned of the losses that had followed her own birth. She now looked at the baby chair with a sensitivity that came with this new knowledge. "I can't imagine what it must have been like," Lucy spoke quietly and then let her thoughts become her own as she continued making breakfast.

Nature's battle reached her ears again and Lucy peered out the screen door. High above, the source of the noise was evident, and Lucy wondered who would win the battle. Thoughts of her dream returned and she stood for a moment looking into the garden. Images flashed randomly before her. The snow. The angel. Her father. She could not erase that part of her dream: her father's face, his smile, his laughter. "A little bizarre," Lucy whispered to the garden and closed the screen door quietly. She turned and found her mother watching her.

"Morning, Mom. Can you believe that racket?" Lucy jerked her head toward the kitchen door. "You'd think we'd be used to that by now." Her comments were loose but she was set on distracting her mother from whatever was responsible for her pained expression.

"Something will live and something will die."

Lucy did not expect a reply and when she heard what her mother said, she continued with new determination.

"Well, I suppose... the law of nature and all that. How about a cup of coffee? It's ready and the muffins and eggs won't be far behind." Lucy poured a cup and prattled on. "I wish I could get used to the taste of this stuff. It smells so good." Lucy held the cup to her nose. "But I can't seem to get it past my throat; it tastes horrible black." She forced a smile. "Maybe I should try more cream and double the sugar. That might kill the taste."

At that, Evelyn Sherwood broke into a grin.

"Here, let me fix you a cup and see if you'll like it then. By the way, what was bizarre in the garden?"

"Bizarre? Oh, just a dream I was remembering. It was nothing."

Responding to the answer with a smile, Evelyn changed the subject. "Lucy, are we ready for tomorrow?"

The question didn't surprise Lucy, but before she could respond, her mother continued.

"There must be something we've missed. I don't know how we'll manage if it rains." Resuming her fretting, she paced in front of Lucy. "This hot spell is sure to break. It'll be awful if it decides to rain in the middle of the ceremony."

"Mom, your food is getting cold. Sit. Eat. Stop worrying so much." Lucy bit a piece of her warm muffin soaked in butter. "Hmm, this is so good."

"What about the dessert reception?" Evelyn ignored Lucy's attempt to tease her into eating. "Should we have been more involved with the planning? Emilia Johnson has enough to do with four children. Why did she take this on?"

"Mom, you've got to relax. You're just confirming what I told Lee: you're a basket case. Everything's looked after. Now, eat, for goodness sake! Your eggs are getting cold. Besides, my biggest concern right now is disposing of this drink," she quipped as she gulped the rest of the coffee as quickly as possible.

A sigh of resignation escaped and her mother reluctantly gave into her own hunger, spreading some jam over her muffin.

"You're right about one thing, Mom; we have no control over the weather. We'll just have to pray...we'll just have to *hope* that the sun stays put and dark clouds don't gather. If they do," Lucy added nonchalantly, "we're all set at the church. Otherwise, the reception is looked after. All we have to do is get from there," Lucy nodded in the direction of the kitchen window that faced the garden, "to the hall. Sounds pretty simple to me," she concluded as she downed the last of her orange juice.

Of course, it wasn't that simple. Lucy had her own concern about the weather, but wasn't about to share it with her mother. *She's worrying enough for the two of us,* she thought, and proceeded with her own mental check-off list as she cleared the table. *The church has been rented. The extra flowers have been ordered for the front of the altar, just in case. Doc Bailey's ready to drive us, if necessary.* Then, as though her personal thoughts reminded her, Lucy turned to her mother, addressing an issue before her mother had a chance to voice it.

"Oh, and by the way, Doc Bailey has agreed to pick up the extra flowers at the church in the morning and drop them off at the hall on his way here, once the weather has been confirmed. So, you see Mom, there isn't much for us to do." Lucy paused. "There is one thing I'm really glad about. No one seems slighted from not being invited or exclusively chosen because they were. That sure says a lot about our friends."

Evelyn only nodded in agreement.

With that final thought discussed, Lucy and her mother left the dishes to air-dry and headed for the garden. There was last minute weeding to do, not to mention the necessary changes to convert the garden into a wedding scene. Lucy couldn't help thinking how therapeutic this activity would be for both of them.

Under the shade of the hackberry tree, Evelyn took a break from their arduous task to enjoy an iced tea. Lucy was on the phone with Emilia Johnson, who called to give a last minute report on the reception at the town hall. Evelyn welcomed the quiet moment to bask in the surroundings. Her arms snugging herself, she looked up through the branches that offered her shade and smiled. *Such a unique tree,* she thought, remembering how excited Lewis had been when he'd planted it their first summer on Aspen Avenue. Now its branching system offered refuge for nesting birds and sweet nectar for passing butterflies. Her gaze circled the garden and once again she enjoyed a smile, remembering Lucy's words, "This is the fruit of your hard work, Mom," and she'd squeezed her endearingly. It had been hard work, but Evelyn would never have used the word *work* to describe it.

White satin bows rustled in the warm breeze. Each one had a spray of rocket larkspur and baby's breath tucked in the centre knot, complemented by a variety of trailing ivy. Evelyn was glad they had elevated them on three-foot poles. *Clean, crisp and fresh, away from the ground,* she concluded. Twenty-two in all lined the edge of the garden path where Lucy would walk on the arm of Cliff Moses.

We've taken a chance putting these poles up today, Evelyn thought as she looked up at the sky, but then remembered Lucy's excitement seeing them placed so evenly along the path. She recalled Lucy commenting, rather absentmindedly, that she had seen the poles in a dream. Her look had been distant and somewhat alarming, but Mrs. Johnson's call had interrupted their conversation and she was left wondering how the dream had ended. *That was her second reference to a dream. I must remember to ask her about it,* Evelyn thought, glancing toward the back door.

They had decided to wait until the last possible moment to place the white carpet along the path. Wil had gone to Edmonton to rent it, and the two had been a pleasure to watch as they shared what it was going to look like, each from a different perspective.

In the west side of the garden, the swamp milkweed and white shasta daisies received Evelyn's approving nod. Both plants grew in abundance close to the fence to the right of the house. Various shades of blue felicia and brilliant pink coral bells and lavatera huddled at their base, adding a welcoming contrast. A luxury not normally enjoyed, Evelyn had scattered white baby's breath seeds throughout the garden edge in preparation for the wedding and was pleased at how well they had filled in along the path.

A mixture of hardy plants vied for Evelyn's attention each spring, and, as if understanding why they had to go through such a gruelling experience, they offered their limbs sacrificially in preparation for the special day. "It's not every day you have a chance to show off," Evelyn had whispered to her friends as her pruning shears clipped away heartlessly. "No pain, no gain." She'd chimed out an old cliché, trimming back dead wood and old growth from the previous year. Almost apologetically, she explained, "I need to cut some of you back quite a lot so you can show your best colours on the big day." Evelyn smiled sheepishly as she remembered her private conversations with the plants. *Silly,* she chided herself, but the memory brought her pleasure and she knew she'd do it again.

Tall ferns enjoyed the shade offered by the two forty-year-old white spruce that stood majestically in the back two corners of the yard. Like soldiers on guard duty, their height demanded the attention of anyone visiting the garden. Evelyn and Lewis had inherited the trees on the purchase of their home and Evelyn often wished she could have taken credit for planting them. On the day they moved in, Lewis had stood at the base of one of the trees and admired the home of so many creatures. "Just think of all the birds we'll get, winter or summer. Of course, we'll have to feed them once the snow comes."

Evelyn remembered how he'd grinned with delight, just like a small boy on his first day of summer vacation. She missed him terribly. *Oh, Lewis, you'd be so proud of our daughter. I wish...* but her thoughts ended there. "No sense wishing for what can never be," she spoke out loud to the tallest in her garden, having found herself standing at the base of the tree her husband had admired.

"What do you think of my decision, Louie? What will people say?"

Evelyn's reclusive life had been the centre of town gossip for several years. She knew this, yet felt helpless to change. Her buried secrets faithfully surfaced and anchored her to her past, but despite this reality, the excitement and pleasure she enjoyed with her daughter in preparing Lucy's wedding had changed something. It was during those days that Evelyn realized she stood at a crossroads, facing a life-changing question: Which path should she take? She had pondered it quietly for weeks, all during the happy times with her daughter. One path took her further into her seclusion. The other offered an opportunity to allow those who had only known her from a distance permission to bridge the gap and become part of her life.

Evelyn turned from her garden at the sound of her daughter's voice, her appeal to her husband's memory left unanswered. "I'll be right there, dear."

"Everything's all set. Seems that Garry and Jess have been a hit with the ladies and they've only been here three days. No surprise there,"

Lucy added with a grin. "Anyway, according to Mae Smytheson—our always well-informed neighbour—the preparations have gone more smoothly than anything she's ever seen done in the past."

At that, her mother smiled and leaned against the screen door, looking in the direction of the white spruce trees. "To think we actually have Mae's approval."

Her response was just what Lucy had hoped for.

"And I called Mollie," Lucy continued, on a roll. "She'll be closing at noon, as planned. She's all set and will be here by two. The ceremony will be over by then, for sure, and with the help of her husband and daughter, she'll be able to set the food up for us to be eating by three. That should be all the time we need to eat and get to the town hall by six."

Lucy's report to her mother was intended to be a checklist to help her mother relax and enjoy the rest of the day, but she soon realized that a dark cloud had settled over the moment and was reluctant to give in to it. She joined her mother by the kitchen door and put her arm around her.

"You okay?"

Evelyn sighed and turned from her garden. "I'm sorry, Lucy. I'm really pleased how well things are coming together. It's just that now that the day is almost here, I'm afraid about my decision. What will people think about Lee escorting me to the wedding? " Evelyn's voice softened to a whisper. "I hope I haven't made a mistake."

Lucy watched her mother retreat to the sanctuary of her garden, stop at the base of the white spruce, and look up.

18

Let thy fountain be blessed:
and rejoice with the wife of thy youth.
PROVERBS 5:18

The sun shone early in the morning with the promise of a dry afternoon, eliminating any fear of rain. A soft breeze rippled through the branches of the surrounding trees and provided a welcome addition to an otherwise perfect day for a garden wedding.

Guests arrived early. Warm greetings and genuine admiration of the surroundings buzzed in the air. Noticeably absent were Lewis Sherwood's parents. Having retired to Florida, Charles and Queenie Sherwood had sent a large cheque with their regrets: a Caribbean cruise had been planned months before the wedding date had been announced. They would be missed, but only by a few. In contrast, tender reference to Lewis Sherwood could be heard in the mix. "He was such a wonderful man..." "A perfect day in his memory..." "He would have been so proud..."

Conscious of the quiet references to her late husband, Evelyn struggled to stay focused.

BE STILL.

Anticipating someone behind her, Evelyn turned and found no one. As she glanced around at her guests, an unusual calm filled her and she smiled in the direction of her soon-to-be son-in-law.

Wil's family from out of town dotted the small crowd. His brother, Charles, and two sisters, Phyllis and Alice, and their families, totaling thirteen, had arrived earlier in the week from out of province and had enjoyed a small, ongoing family reunion. Four days before the wedding, Wil had learned that his older sister, Phyllis, had invested seven years into violin lessons for her now teenage daughter. To the delight of his sister, Wil and Lucy had approached Becky, asking if she would like to assist in the music for the wedding. Her squeal of delight had sealed the request.

Evelyn acknowledged Garry and Jessica Patrick when they waved from the back of the gathering, and Garry raised his thumb in approval of the garden scene. In anticipation of the dessert reception, he had volunteered to bring coffee, tea, and cold beverages for the event. As a result, the young couple from Vancouver endeared themselves to their unseen friends even before arriving. Garry's winning personality and sense of humour entertained everyone with impersonations of famous and not-so-famous people, and Jessica proved to be a willing storyteller of Wil's escapades during Teacher's College. Now they stood, enjoying this special moment with their new friends, enraptured by the beauty of nature and music that surrounded them.

Josh Graham arrived with Jennie Ralston on his arm, surprising everyone except Evelyn. A select few, including Evelyn and Vic Hanson at the post office, knew Josh had been writing to Jennie while she was in Ontario enrolled in an art college. From everyone else's observation, he appeared content in his bachelorhood. The Emporium had become the centre of his world when Josh returned from university, especially after Lewis's death. No one ever considered the thought that he would marry. Evelyn smiled. *You've certainly surprised everyone, Josh.* Much to Evelyn's amusement, it didn't take long for the predictable gossip train to chug throughout the small gathering about a second wedding sometime in the future.

Evelyn watched Emilia Johnson slip into the back row. *I hope things are under control at the hall,* Evelyn thought briefly. But it was only a brief thought that dissolved instantly when she saw Emilia squeeze her husband's arm and raise her eyebrows in the direction of the front row. Having seen the look, Evelyn's imagination left little doubt what thoughts were being shared. *Talk about a gossip train.*

"Such a beautiful day," Evelyn whispered to Levi, ignoring the stares from the curious couple. "To think I worried so much." Her smile supported her efforts to enjoy the day, for which she received an encouraging pat on her hand just as Wil's young niece began her violin solo.

The sweetness of the music filtered through the air and blended with nature's songs as *Because* travelled across the garden, beyond the hackberry tree, and into the street. Those privileged to be blessed with such sound paused, holding their breath, it seemed, for fear of missing a note. Becky Murray played flawlessly. Within the intimacy of the garden, some listened, their eyes transfixed on the young violinist. Others shut their eyes, excluding the outside world, protecting their own thoughts. Some held hands, and others smiled warmly into another's face.

It was such a smile that Evelyn received from Levi when Becky concluded her solo. Evelyn had little time to digest it before the music commenced on a lighter note, announcing the coming of the bride. A gentle touch assisted her to her feet as everyone rose, and Evelyn took one last look into Levi's eyes before turning to her daughter.

For a moment time stood still, as though a frame had frozen in the film of Evelyn's life. There stood her daughter on Cliff's arm, at the edge of the white carpet, her face beaming in anticipation and wonder. She moved slowly down the white carpeted path "like a queen," Lewis would have said. Evelyn quivered in response to the thought and felt an arm steady her. She looked up, smiled a thank you, and then stepped forward to stand with her daughter. A hush fell over the garden.

Pastor Cribbs smiled as the newly married couple embraced. The kiss was shy and the couple separated with bowed heads, beaming as only a newly married couple could do. Tears glistened in the eyes of some, but everyone grinned with pleasure as the couple turned to face their friends. Applause, handshakes, and hugs ended the formality of the moment and those present felt a special unity through the bonds of family and friendship.

Evelyn stood back from the crowd that encircled her daughter and new son-in-law and watched as they mingled with their guests, enjoying the moment and building lifelong memories. She'd awakened earlier that morning with a heavy heart, but it had evaporated when she heard her daughter's voice singing loudly and very plainly from the shower, *I love you truly, truly dear*. The two had shared a quick breakfast before they'd headed to the garden to roll out the carpet. Lucy had insisted Wil not be present to help them. Evelyn smiled, remembering her comment: "It's bad luck for a bride to see her groom on the day of their wedding. I can't believe you'd want to ask him to help us!" And, of course, they hadn't. Instead, Levi had dropped by to offer any last minute help and was quickly put to use.

Lucy's sudden embrace brought Evelyn back to her garden and

her daughter's wedding guests.

"Mom, meet my husband." Taking Wil's arm, she joined her mother's hand with his and stepped aside, grinning with pleasure in using the new title Wil had been given only moments earlier.

Wil and Evelyn shared a hug that brought pauses to everyone else's conversation.

"Well now, all my childhood and the past few years as I've courted your daughter, you've been Mrs. S. What do I do now? Shall I call you Mom? Evelyn? Certainly not *Mrs. Sherwood!*" Wil jested as he questioned his mother-in-law.

Evelyn turned to look at her friends, who were sharing this intimate moment with her daughter and new son-in-law. She blushed, and digging for a confidence that too often eluded her, she smiled. "You've already got a mother, Wil. My name is Evelyn, but I'd love it if you called me Evie."

"Then Evie it is." Another hug sealed the agreement and sparked a round of applause among those who had witnessed a breakthrough for a woman who had sheltered herself for too many years.

Evelyn smiled as the newlyweds responded to the tinkling of glasses. An uproar of laughter resulted when Wil gallantly dipped Lucy over his bent knee and granted the group a generous kiss for his new bride. She watched as her daughter seemed to float through the crowd, expressing appreciation to her guests and accepting congratulations with grace and elegance. Lucy had undergone a transformation after being on the coast, and Evelyn had reaped the benefit of it. She had listened to her daughter more in the past eighteen months than in the whole of Lucy's life, and it had brought a pleasure to Evelyn that she had never known. Even Lucy's rekindled love for her God had not hindered their time together. Many times when Lucy would slip in her conversation and indicate that she had prayed about something, Evelyn would sit silently, aware that the resentment and irritation such comments had created in the past were less irritating now. Evelyn smiled as her daughter moved among her guests, confident and happy with a regal countenance.

A movement beyond the group took Evelyn away from thoughts of her daughter. Cliff Moses stood off to the side, watching. Their eyes met and the message exchanged between the two went unheeded by those in the crowd. *Thank you.* Evelyn's eyes seemed to say it all. A smile and a gentle nod was the response and then the town patriarch moved unnoticed to a corner under the white spruce to enjoy the moment and, perhaps, remember his absent friend.

Mollie Henderson's daughter and several of Lucy's lifelong school friends offered glasses of punch to the guests as they mingled in the garden. Wil's niece continued to play in the background and Garry's laughter could be heard over the hum of the conversations. Evelyn sighed with relief as the months of planning unfolded with a grace and calmness she could only marvel at. *Is this an answer to Wil and Lucy's prayers?* The thought startled her and she shook it off as a matter of coincidence and focused her thoughts on a more pleasant memory.

Evelyn had been speechless when Lucy surprised her two weeks earlier, asking her to stand with her as her witness. There were many girls that Lucy could have asked—any one of those helping to serve the punch—thus it came as a surprise when the request had been made of her. They had embraced and several seconds passed before Evelyn released Lucy and told her it would be an honour.

Evelyn remembered being alone in her bedroom that same night, searching the darkness for an answer. *Why? After all the years I've neglected her.* Her pillow had been wet when she'd finally fallen asleep, but her smile and an unusual peace had accompanied her as she'd slipped from the real world into one of the unknown.

Laughter broke her moment of reverie as Wil teased Josh and Jennie into setting a date. Evelyn glanced through the crowd and her eyes met those of the one who had caused her such restlessness and concern days before the wedding. Evelyn knew that the implication of Levi escorting her to her daughter's wedding had not been missed by anyone, evidenced by the reaction of Emilia and Harry Johnson. Sitting to her left, Levi's presence had filled the air with questions, to be sure, but he had also brought a sense of comfort for Evelyn, an air of confidence witnessed by all through her outward composure and her seldom seen smile. She shuddered at the thought of the tantalizing rumors that would certainly filter through town over the following days and weeks. But for the moment, it appeared that her guests were focused on the two childhood friends who had stood before them, taking their vows to love, honour, and cherish.

If she could have, Evelyn would have offered a prayer of thanksgiving.

PART
THREE

19

O send out thy light and thy truth: let them lead me;
let them bring me unto thy holy hill, and to thy tabernacles.
PSALM 43:3

The late afternoon sun had slid lower in the sky and, although storm clouds loomed in the distance, the sun still warmed Evelyn as she sat at the kitchen table nursing her second cup of coffee. She stared ahead as though engrossed in a love story and relived her daughter's wedding weeks earlier.

The garden dinner had been a great success and the dessert reception had been flawless, thanks to faithful neighbours who had known Lucy since infancy. "The prettiest bride Thystle Creek's seen in a long time," Mae Smytheson had said repeatedly to anyone within hearing. Strawberry shortcake had been in abundance thanks to Ruth Norton. Mollie's apple pie and ice cream had been a big hit with several of the men folk, and her butter tarts seemed to find a home in almost everyone's stomach before the evening had ended. Coffee, iced tea, and soft drinks flowed endlessly, thanks to Garry and Jessie, who had mingled with the crowd as though they were "born and bred" northerners. And the music…it had artistically woven the warm summer evening air around the bride and groom and their friends.

Evelyn sat transfixed in her memory of watching her new son-in-law lead her daughter to the centre of the dance floor. Oblivious of those who gazed at them, their smiles had radiated their love for one another and Evelyn recalled the feeling of complete contentment she'd had, knowing how much her daughter was loved.

She knew that Lucy intended to honour her father's memory at the reception, but she hadn't known how until she'd heard the familiar voice singing, *I will spend my whole life through, loving you, just loving you*. Evelyn and Lucy had made eye contact just as Wil embraced his bride, and Evelyn had nodded slightly. Tears had glistened in both mother's and daughter's eyes, tears of happiness and some of sadness. She recalled a hand on her elbow and remembered looking up into Levi's eyes. *It was nice having him there,* Evelyn thought as she raised the warm cup to her lips and enjoyed the aroma of her hot beverage.

There had been sad moments in the days and weeks that followed the wedding, and Evelyn admitted them now with reluctance. Her darkest moments came in the evenings when she was alone and old memories haunted her, threatening to engage her in periods of regret. But Evelyn had become aware of an inner strength, a strength that had surfaced from somewhere unknown to her, a strength that had allowed her episodes of relief from the accusing voice that had gripped her for so many years. It was in those moments that she forced herself to face the truth of her life, how she had treated her husband and daughter, and she hoped that some day she would open up her past and let her daughter become part of the healing. *Perhaps some day,* Evelyn thought, as she sipped her coffee, *but not just yet.*

The calendar hanging above the highchair caught her eye and she realized that she had not turned it to the new month. *I can't believe it's been over a month.* She had seen Lucy and Wil often over the past weeks, but didn't want to overdo her visits. *Mothers-in-law can get such a reputation,* she thought, but then chided herself knowing that Wil would never view her as a meddler. Settling on a visit, she vacillated between baking a fresh batch of Lucy's favourite muffins and making Doc Bailey's chili, a recipe she'd lovingly extracted from the good doctor when she'd learned how much Wil enjoyed it. The ring of her doorbell broke her thoughts and left the decision hanging.

With the kitchen curtain pushed aside, Evelyn glanced out but found no one on the front step; instead, there was only a cardboard box. She hurried to the front hall, cautious, but strangely curious.

The box measured about two feet square and seemed to have a life of its own. It rocked gently from side to side, emitting an intermittent sound that would have been missed had the street not been so quiet. Evelyn considered closing the door and leaving the box where it sat, but with her curiosity already piqued, she carefully moved the folded lid and peered inside.

Tiny would be the best word, but *heart-stealer* seemed to resonate in Evelyn's mind. Brown eyes greeted her and tiny white paws scratched frantically at the edge of the box. It teetered slightly, bringing a yelp from its occupant as the creature fell backwards into its temporary home. Evelyn responded quickly. She bent down to lift her surprise visitor from the box only to be startled when another voice broke the quietness of the moment.

"Happy birthday, Evie." Levi Morsman stepped from behind the grove of birch trees on the front lawn, arms tightly clasped behind his back holding a bouquet that revealed itself only by its size. A mischievous grin spread across his face.

At the sight of her second surprise visitor, Evelyn burst into tears. Levi dropped the flowers, raced to her side, and lifted the white puppy from her arms.

"I'm sorry, Evie. I thought you'd like some company now that you're on your own. I had no idea it would upset you. I can take her back. It's okay. Please stop crying." Levi put a friendly arm around Evelyn in a brave effort to console her. "Here, take my handkerchief."

With the tiny intruder safely in its box, Levi escorted Evelyn back into her house and poured her a fresh cup of coffee, as well as one for himself. With Evelyn settled in the same chair she had occupied moments earlier, he spoke quietly. "I'll be right back."

Levi returned, carrying the cardboard box just as Evelyn was wiping her eyes and taking a second breath.

"Do you mind if I set this inside for a few minutes? I don't think it would be a good idea to leave her alone on the front step, especially with the threat of a storm." As he spoke, Levi lifted the little ball of fur onto his lap and attempted to calm the nervous puppy. "There's something about puppy breath," he said sheepishly. He lifted the animal to his chin and let it nuzzle him. "I've got a soft spot for dogs, I'm afraid. It goes back to my childhood when I watched our little neighbour being pulled from a creek by her German shepherd. The dog saved her life and I've had this thing for dogs ever since. But I keep forgetting that everyone doesn't share my sentiments."

Levi's chatter seemed distant to Evelyn. She had watched him step from behind the trees singing his greetings and was startled by her own reaction. Her tears were misunderstood, but her ensuing embarrassment prevented her from explaining that her tears were from delight. She watched Levi stroke the pup and restrained herself from reaching over to lift it from his lap to hers. She listened to his story of his neighbour and heard him attempt to explain why he loved dogs like he did.

"I'm really sorry, Evie, for startling you. I just wanted to surprise you with something special."

"Lee, please. You don't have to apologize. It was a wonderful gesture and I have yet to turn your gift down," Evelyn added with a tilt of her head in the direction of the object of their attention. "Here, let me hold her."

The following two hours passed quickly over an informal supper and stories about puppies, dogs and pets in general, and Levi found himself relaxing in what was becoming his favourite spot in all of Thystle Creek: Evelyn's garden.

"Nice to see the storm pass," Levi commented casually, fully aware that neither he nor Evelyn felt the need for small talk.

"Hmm," Evelyn responded and then surprised Levi with a question that broke the solitude of the garden. "Lee, do you worship in a synagogue on the coast?"

Levi turned and stared at her. Seconds passed.

"Why do you ask?"

"No real reason. I was just sitting here thinking about Lucy and Wil and the new life they've started. I've never shared Lucy's interest in church. For that matter, I never once attended a service with Louie, despite his persistence. A long time ago, I chose to reject his God." The last statement was a whisper and Levi gave no indication that he'd heard it. "Sometimes I sit here in the evening, wrap myself in my blanket now that the evenings are getting cooler, and think."

The shyness in Evelyn's confession was evident. Levi sat quietly, overwhelmed by her willingness to share so intimately.

"I sit here and think of Louie and wonder how different our life would have been had I chosen a different path in my beliefs."

Sadness filled the air as the shadows of the great white spruce grew to touch the edge of the patio stones. Seemingly undaunted by his friend's mood, Levi pressed Evelyn.

"Why was it so different? I mean, what caused you to choose so differently than your family?" The question hung in the air for a long time before Evelyn spoke.

"There's no easy answer. I wish there was. My life's very complicated. I've many skeletons, I suppose, and the memories around those skeletons haunt me. The only way I've been able to survive is to blame Louie's God." Evelyn's voice dropped to a whisper again and Levi leaned forward to hear her. "It's painful to think about it, let alone talk about it, but I can't help feeling that a time is coming when I will need to deal with it. Lucy and I had a wonderful year getting to know one another. I yearn for the years I've missed and I want so much to be a part of Lucy's and Wil's lives, and the lives of the children they'll have. I know I can't keep living like this."

They sat quietly for a moment, hearing only the music of the crickets before Evelyn broke the silence again.

"When Louie was alive, I refused to listen to him, yet he never gave up. He continually told me there was a way out of this trapped feeling I've lived with for years. He told me I had to *want* it. But, Lee, it wasn't that I didn't *want* it; I'd come to believe I didn't *deserve* it. I believed I was destined to live a life of misery, void of any happiness. I ignored the fact that I was creating the same miserable life for my family. But now, lately, I keep *hearing* something, a voice, or sensing a feeling, I don't really know what, just that *something* is telling me I need to deal with my past if I am to move on. But it's hard."

Levi stared intently at her, absorbed in her words. When he spoke, his words were soft, carefully chosen.

"Evie, I'm pretty much a stranger in your world. I've no knowledge of what your life was like before your husband died, but I do know that Louie must have loved you a great deal. From the little Lucy has shared, and the stories I've picked up from some townsfolk, he had to have been a very special person. But any freedom from the pain that you've associated with your memories of your husband can only be found by acknowledging the truth. It sounds like you're headed in the right direction. From my limited training in psychology, facing the truth is often full of anxiety, regrets, and anger—even fear, but the big step is being willing to *face* the truth. Your daughter loves you very much and I doubt there's anything you can tell her that will change her feelings for you."

"I'm not so sure, Lee."

The silence that followed found Levi lost in his thoughts of wanting to help but he feared that Evelyn preferred to run from a reality that was becoming more and more demanding each day. It was only the whimper of a small puppy that brought him back from his meditative thoughts.

"Looks like the little trickster needs to stretch her legs. I'll take her to the back of the yard and hope she'll start learning that's her area for her regular garden visits." Levi smiled at his own presumption that Evelyn would keep his gift. He winked at her and headed for the back garden with a bundle of white fur bobbing happily behind him.

"I like that name," Evelyn announced with a grin and a lighter voice than the previous conversation had provoked. "Since both of you were part of the scheme to trick me, *Trickster* is the perfect name."

"Come on, Trickster. Do you like that name, girl? Well, don't look at me like that, it wasn't my idea."

20

For thus saith the Lord God;
Behold, I, even I, will both search
my sheep, and seek them out.
EZEKIEL 34:11

The air had a bite and the well-used blanket had long since been retired for the season, no longer sufficient for an evening respite in her garden. Evelyn reluctantly acknowledged the coming winter. An early frost had touched the rows of baby's breath and their vibrant white now blended with a dirty yellow, an early colour of death for the annual flowers. Puddles of water surrounded the coral bells and lavatera, and wilted leaves floated aimlessly from the night's heavy rain.

"My garden will never look as beautiful as it did this year, Trickster. It makes me sad looking at the dying flowers." Working her way to the back of the garden through the puddles, she paused and turned to face her house. "I wonder why I feel it more this year than any other. I've always had to say goodbye to my garden for the winter, but somehow it's different this year." *Probably the wedding,* Evelyn thought, and in answering her own question, she turned back to the need at hand: Trickster. Her pet needed to have her morning outing. Evelyn laughed as the tiny creature moved precariously through the puddles until she found the suitable spot, raising each paw and shaking it like a cat caught in the aftermath of a downpour.

Glancing at the patio from the back of the garden, two prominent chairs sat side by side under the kitchen window in the screened-in porch. "Maybe it's the company that we've had lately. There seemed to be an atmosphere..." and her thoughts took her into her private world of memories as she pulled her jacket tighter, but only for a moment. Evelyn felt a tug at her shoe and laughed as she looked down at her new companion having a tug-of-war with her shoe laces.

"Come here, you little rascal." She reached down, lifted her pup up into the air, and snuggled it deep into her arms. "You must be cold, but we've got a long winter ahead of us. You'd better get used to it. Come on, I'll race you for breakfast." With that, Evelyn released her hold on the pup and jogged slowly toward the house as Trickster tumbled head over heels trying to keep up with her.

Watching her dog consume a hearty breakfast, Evelyn shook her head in disbelief, as she had done so many times in the past month since Trickster had become part of her life. "How would I have ever managed without you to keep me in line?" She tousled the pup's head and laughed as it tolerated the interruption and then continued to do what dogs do best: eat. "But I've got to get to the library. The house will be nice and quiet for your morning nap." The thought of leaving Trickster never sat well with Evelyn, and she always acknowledged the enjoyment of a quiet house as a means of feeling less guilty in leaving her pet alone.

She enjoyed her work at the library despite the fact that she had kept her distance from the many children who had come and gone over the years. It saddened her to think that. *Can't undo what's been done,* she thought as she put her sweater and purse by the front door. The thought seemed trite and she felt a pang of guilt. Her introspection months earlier had brought a cleansing, notwithstanding the anguish and regrets that were, at times, overwhelming. But there was no question that her outlook on life had changed. Quiet humming had become part of her day, and she was always pleasantly surprised when she found herself doing it. She had yet to put her finger on *why* she felt such a strange peace, for the process was subtle, but she had come to accept the idea that there *was* life beyond the wall she had built.

Part of that life was an appreciation of the opportunities she had in relating with the youngsters at the library. She had come to know some by name, with their regular visits, and it was always a delight to see the young moms bring their toddlers to *Just Evie's* story hour each Thursday morning. It had been reassuring to her a few nights ago when Wil and Lucy had stopped by for a quick visit. Evelyn had come home from the library that afternoon loaded down with books that needed repair, leaving them piled on the kitchen table.

"Mom, do you know how much you are helping Wil in the classroom?" Lucy thumbed through the stack of books and flipped the pages of one she picked from the pile.

"Wha...?" Evelyn turned, teapot in hand.

Wil chimed in. "Absolutely, Evie. You have no idea how much parents appreciate the help you give their kids. They arrive at the library, desperate—the kids, I mean—and you come up with just the right book or research material." Wil smiled at the lemon meringue pie Evelyn placed in front of him before continuing. "They actually seem to enjoy project assignments, and parents have called me, giving me the credit. Really, it's you that's made my life easier." Wil smiled as he shoved a fork-full of pie into his mouth. "I hold you in high esteem,

Madame." He bowed in mocked admiration.

Evelyn laughed. "Such nonsense. Eat your pie before I give it to Trickster."

The memory brought a grin to Evelyn as she whistled for her dog. Settling Trickster in her cage with lots of water, snacks and chew toys, Evelyn clamped the lock on the top edge, conveniently placed out of the way of overzealous paws.

"You be good, sweetie, and I'll see you at noon."

Front door locked, Evelyn headed toward the library looking forward to her morning. The summer months had always reduced the operating hours of the library, which left her free to work in her garden. Before the summer break, Evelyn had suggested that it was time for a new head librarian. She would remain on in a part-time position, but felt it was time to start training someone else. Sammy Bushby had applied for the job in June and had spent the summer months learning the "tricks of the trade," as he had so proudly acknowledged. Evelyn had known Sammy since he had moved to Thystle Creek when he was ten, and even from a distance she had become aware of his love for reading. She was quite willing to turn the reins of responsibility over to him once he was comfortable with the position, but she would stay involved simply because of her own love for books.

Evelyn found herself humming as she headed west on Aspen Avenue.

"How're the newlyweds doing, Evelyn?" Mae hollered from across the road, interrupting Evelyn's thoughts of Sammy and his enthusiasm. "Haven't seen much of them," she added with a giggle, emphasizing their noticeable absence.

"Oh, they're doing just fine, Mae. No need to worry about them." Evelyn waved to her neighbour, not daring to slow down for fear of being drawn into a lengthy conversation. Mae was notorious for prying and sharing more than she should of other people's affairs. *That poor woman has nothing better to do.* Evelyn smiled to herself at the insinuation of Mae's last comment as she hurried on down the street. *They* are *newlyweds, for goodness sake!*

With Lucy and Wil married and the warm, summer months gone, Evelyn had realized that her part-time responsibilities at the library provided a much-needed distraction. Apart from Trickster, the quietness of the house accentuated some long and lonely days. Gardening had filled the daylight hours of the summer months, and rainy days in the fall did provide time for reading, but the evening hours were another story; they were the hardest. She had found herself writing more than at any time in the past. The anger and disappointment she had struggled with in her early years of marriage to Lewis continued to haunt her and she'd found putting pen to paper therapeutic. Hours were spent writing letters to Lewis, letters of regret, letters begging for forgiveness, letters telling her husband how proud she was of him. She repeatedly apologized for ignoring him and ridiculing his spiritual walk. Tears had streamed down her cheeks, blurring her vision. She poured out her anguish for having never listened, never trusted that what he believed could possibly be true. Her love for him was penned over and over and often left her exhausted.

And there were letters to her daughter. They came easier. Evelyn smiled often, even laughing as she recorded special times they had shared of late. She wrote about how she had known Wil was the man Lucy would marry, that she had known it without a doubt when Lucy was just a young teenager. But her emotional absence had left scars. She filled many pages, begging forgiveness, confessing regrets, listing them to support her sincerity: the missed baptism, never seeing her grandmother's pearls around Lucy's neck, the visits to Miller's Mountain, the impromptu games Lewis and Lucy had played, ones she never had wanted to share. As the memories surfaced, apologies reached back to Lucy's childhood, and each time Evelyn recorded one she determined that she would speak to her daughter and voice it. Writing it was not enough.

She wrote for hours describing her watchful eye, recording unspoken questions and admitting her confusion when it was obvious that Lucy had come to terms with her God and had renewed her faith in Him. She wrote in earnest of how she envied Lucy's love for her God and the pain her lack of desire to follow in her husband's and daughter's footsteps had brought to the family. She wrote about how she longed to know her daughter better.

The hidden letters written to her parents were another matter. She would often open them in the darkness of the night, when the world was asleep. She would read and reread the years of her life, written but never shared. Each time they were laid out on her desk, she determined to share them with Lucy, but was never able to find the courage. *Let the past stay in the past,* she thought each time, and she would bundle them up and place them back in the wooden box where some had lain for years. On one occasion, Evelyn had considered sending them to her parents, but she was never able to do that either. Convinced that so much time had passed without any contact, she felt it would be pointless, and looming over her was the fear that they had moved or that one or both of them had died. This thought ate away at her like a cancer, fanning the flame of guilt unmercifully.

Evelyn thought of the second pile of letters, the ones that she had cried over while living in Halifax. The unopened letters from her parents had been handled repeatedly during those dark nights, but she could never bring herself to open one of them. The ongoing battle with the sinister voice always surfaced: *What's the point now? Reading them won't change anything.* She always lost the battle and they were always placed back in the box, unopened. No, she would never read them, not now. It was too late.

Arriving at the library, Evelyn found an overly anxious and extremely stressed young man.

"Sammy, what's wrong? You look like you're carrying the weight of the world. Whatever it is, it can't be that bad." Evelyn hung her jacket on the hook behind the door that led to the main desk and turned to her young apprentice.

"Mrs. Sherwood, there was a bad leak from the storm last night. There's an inch of water on the basement floor. I've put most of the boxes up on shelves, but when I lifted some others, the bottoms fell out."

A weary smile crossed Evelyn's face. *What a way to begin the day.* Giving her thoughts volume, Evelyn put an arm around the worried young man. "Give Ernie a call over at Maxwell's to see if he can give us a hand. It's not the first time a pipe has given us grief, but we'll need some professional help. Then call Lucy and see if she can come in and cover the front desk while we play plumber in the basement. Let's hope the damage is kept to just a few boxes." *Well, at least we're getting the bad part of the day over with early. What could beat this*? Evelyn turned to the basement door and, taking a deep breath, released the handle and headed into the dark basement. "I've done this before and I can do it again," she said as she descended the old wooden steps.

The day had turned out better than anticipated. The bottom of seven boxes had absorbed more than their share of water, but fortunately their contents were not harmed and Ernie had repaired the cracked pipe before there was further damage. Lucy had come in for a couple of hours and left at eleven-thirty to meet Wil at the school for lunch.

"I'm afraid he's still not used to me making a lunch for him," she had quipped as she'd waved goodbye to her mother.

Evelyn had volunteered to stay for the rest of day and help Sammy with the returns that had accumulated over the weekend, as well as help solve a few concerns he had with his new title of head librarian. She had not anticipated working the whole day and was glad Lucy had offered to stop by the house and let Trickster out for a few moments.

Tired and hungry, Evelyn turned the key to unlock her front door. An excited yelping welcomed her.

"Hi, Trickster, I'm home!" She chimed from the front hall, and the cage rattled as Trickster pawed at the lock, anticipating release. The bond that had grown between a lonely woman and a young puppy had ignited a love that each thrived upon and was happily witnessed by those who watched them interact.

It was just seconds later that the front door opened again, this time without the excitement previously enjoyed, and without a knock.

"Mom."

The tone of Lucy's voice brought chills to Evelyn as she scooped Trickster into her arms. *Something's very wrong.* She walked to the front hall holding her pup for security, and strength.

Lucy and Wil stood in the front hall, hands locked. Evelyn could see they were struggling to control their emotions, but at the sight of her mother, Lucy burst into tears and threw her arms around her mother's neck.

"He's gone, Mom."

All Evelyn could whisper was, "Who?"

21

To every thing there is a season,
and a time to every purpose under the heaven:
A time to be born, and a time to die;
ECCLESIASTES 3:1-2

There had been no warning. He'd said he was tired, nothing out of the ordinary, but when his uncle had said good night, Levi never knew it would be their *last* good night.

As he'd watched Cliff walk slowly to his bedroom, it had crossed his mind that sleep for some is intermittent, for others it comes with ease, and when the storm came, Levi had no reason to think his uncle would awaken. Levi had given no thought to checking on his uncle. Cliff was a sound sleeper and would've been insulted had he thought he was being fussed over. There was no way Levi could have known his uncle had quietly left this world in the middle of a storm, not until the hydro had gone out and he had taken a flashlight to his uncle's bedside table, just in case he awoke. One look at his uncle and his physician instincts told him his uncle would never wake again in this world.

The patriarch of Thystle Creek was gone and many wept. Uncle Moses. Uncle Mo. Cliff. The old hermit. He was known by many names, and loved by all. Despite the years he'd spent trying to create an air of gruffness, Cliff Moses had a heart of gold, and as a member of the small church Lucy and Wil attended, he would be duly honoured. He had been known for his love for the town's children. He was a gentle Pied Piper who had a following most adults would never understand, unless they had been on the *other* side as a child. Now many asked: Who will continue the custom? Who will deliver the first doll? Who will provide each boy with his first ball and glove? Those who'd been privileged to be a recipient of the cherished gift felt the loss in a special way. He was not just an old man. He was their friend. The grandfather many never had. As years passed, he became their neighbour who would drop anything to lend a helping hand until his stroke had limited his activities. His expressions of *fiddlesticks* or *horse feathers* when he was fussed over would only endear him to people, and he would secretly smile and be pleased. He was loved and he loved, and he would be missed.

Levi moved to the corner of the church hall with Allen Bailey, away from the crowd of friends who had gathered for refreshments following his uncle's funeral. Balancing their plates and paper cups, they conversed quietly.

"Can't tell you how sorry I am at Cliff's passing, Lee. He was a special man, one of a kind, and no one will ever be able to fill his shoes."

"Thanks, Doc. I appreciate that. I never really knew him until I came to look after him earlier this year. I was a child the only time he visited us on the coast. He kept to himself, almost frightened me."

Levi laughed with his friend, knowing how contradictory his words were since Levi's uncle had endeared himself to the children of Thystle Creek. "He'd sit in our parlour reading my dad's books on world religion and occasionally conversing with my father about what he'd read. Sometimes I'd hear them talking about Jesus as the Messiah and Paul and the disciples. Voices would rise but their debating always ended with agreeing to disagree. From what my mother told me over the years, Uncle Cliff respected Dad for his faithfulness to his religion, but kept his own personal views to himself. When I think about it now, it's too bad. He may have had an influence on my dad and things could have been different for my parents sooner than later."

Levi slipped an egg salad sandwich into his mouth and finished his last sip of coffee. "Anyway, we crossed paths only once after that. He flew with my parents back east when I graduated from medical school and greeted me with a genuinely proud spirit. I was his only nephew. He gave me a Bible for a graduation gift with some verses he'd underscored and an inscription on the inside front cover: 'This helped me through life. I'm sure it'll do the same for you, if you read it.'"

"Do you still have it?" Allen asked, carefully sliding his cup of tea onto his plate of sandwiches, celery, and butter tart square.

"Yes, I keep it on my shelf in my office at the clinic. It comes in handy sometimes when I deal with patients."

"Your uncle was a godly man, a quiet Christian that lived his life by his beliefs. He couldn't have given you a more worthy gift."

"Perhaps. I didn't appreciate it at the time. Anyway, I never saw him again until this year. From what I've witnessed over these months and the stories I've heard here today, I feel a little cheated from not knowing him better." Levi bowed his head slightly to gain his composure and then, feigning a brighter spirit, he continued. "What a patient, though!" And Allen laughed, nodding in agreement. "But I think it was more the limitations from his stroke that frustrated him. He'd just told me the day before he died that he wanted me to take him to the store to get Jackie Benson's ball and glove. He sure didn't like being dependant on anyone. And you know what I found in his things this morning?" he continued, beaming. "A parcel for Lucy. The card on it said, *Not to be opened until the right time.* I haven't opened it, but I have my suspicions of what it is." He smiled and winked at the doctor. "Did he know something I don't know?"

"Now, Lee, she's my patient and you know all about doctor-patient confidentiality!"

"I wasn't prying, really! Just curious." Lee raised his hand and crossed himself, swearing to his honesty like a child.

"What are your plans now, or am I being too insensitive by asking at this time?" The older doctor hesitated slightly.

"No, no, it's all right." Levi touched Allen's arm to reassure him. "You and I've talked before so it won't come as a surprise to you that I am making arrangements to move to Thystle Creek. I talked with Uncle Cliff about a month ago, when I got back from the coast, and he was thrilled that I was moving here, told me then that the house was mine since I was his only nephew. Apparently he had it already written in his will. Is your offer still on the table?"

"Absolutely! When you're ready, come by the office and we'll get something in writing." At that, the town's senior doctor extended his hand and the two shook with the warmth that a new friendship creates and then Levi turned to greet his uncle's neighbour who had been lingering nearby.

For another hour, Levi filtered through the crowd, receiving kind words and condolences, and by the end of the afternoon he was ready to head to Mollie's to accept her dinner offer. He walked Jim and

Helen Broughton to the coat rack and found Evelyn waiting at the bottom of the stairs leading to the back door of the church. He was taken aback somewhat knowing that Evelyn never attended church and was instantly warmed by her presence.

"Evelyn! Thank you so much for coming. I didn't see you at the reception." He squeezed her gloved hand gently.

"Well, actually, I left right after the service and then changed my mind. I just came back for a moment. I felt better waiting here to speak to you rather than mingling."

"I appreciate your coming back."

"I wanted to let you know how much Cliff meant to me, Lee. His love for Lucy... well, I know you know all about that." Evelyn's voice broke and she bowed her head.

"It was hard for you to come, wasn't it, Evie?"

"The last time I was here was when Lewis died..." Evelyn's voice trailed off into a whisper. Then she held her head up and continued. "Lee, your uncle filled in for my husband on Lucy's wedding day and I will be forever grateful for his love and sensitivity. It's time I put aside my own feelings and think beyond myself. If I'd had the courage, I would have stood up in that service and told the whole town what I thought of that man!"

Evelyn's fortitude surprised Levi. Others turned and conversations paused as those close by listened to a voice they seldom heard.

"Cliff did more for the children of this town than... than, well, he just did. He was a great man, gentle and kind despite his tough veneer. We'll be hard pressed to find another man like him. I just wanted to tell you how much I'll miss him." Ending her speech in a whisper, Evelyn turned to leave, but not before a soft applause reached her ears. She turned and found several townsfolk smiling at her, some wiping tears, all of them nodding in agreement with her. Levi reached for her arm and whispered a "thank you" and watched her slip quietly back up the stairs to the exit doors. Admiration filled the faces of those who watched her leave, especially one.

Evelyn made her way home again, glad that she had changed her mind to speak with Levi and glad that Lucy and Wil were staying behind to be a support for him. Christina Morsman had flown in from the coast for her brother's funeral and Evelyn had enjoyed a brief conversation with her while she was waiting to speak to Levi. *I must have her over for tea before she heads back,* Evelyn considered, with more bravado than she felt. *She reminds me a lot of Cliff, the smile, I think, but Levi certainly looks like her.*

As she settled into bed later that night with Trickster happily on her mat under the bedroom window, Evelyn thought back to the conversation she'd had with Levi earlier in the summer. Her thoughts turned to the many letters she had written, especially to her daughter. "Perhaps it's time I spoke with Lucy, Trickster," she said as she reached for the bedside light. Her faithful companion raised its sleepy head only high enough to stretch a wide yawn before flopping back on its blanket, obviously content to have been spoken to, but too tired to do anything about it. The little creature fell back to sleep, but not before hearing its mistress speak a word which had no meaning in the animal language: "Soon."

22

And ye shall know the truth,
and the truth shall make you free.
JOHN 8:32

"It was so kind of you to have me in for tea, Evelyn." Christina Morsman sipped her tea with a satisfying but polite slurp and a shy grin. "Excuse my manners, but I guess at my age, it's allowed."

Evelyn laughed, thoroughly enjoying this elderly woman whose charm had stolen her heart. She proved to be all that Levi had shared months earlier. *Entertaining, enchanting, and energetic with a dash of mystery*, Evelyn thought as she smiled inwardly at her choice of words.

"Please, call me Evie. I feel as though we've been friends for years. Perhaps it's your smile. I thought about that last night and even said so to Trickster."

At the mention of her name, Trickster raised her head and toddled over to the one who had presumably called her.

"I can see she's got you trained. What a delightful dog. How long have you had her?" Christina laughed watching Trickster prance in circles at Evelyn's feet as she lifted a box of dog bones down from the cupboard.

"Haven't you heard the story?" Evelyn asked, but was quickly distracted by Trickster's demanding yelp. "She's allowed one of these a day, but when I break it in half, I'm sure she thinks she's getting two." Trickster tried to sit up on her hind end, but toppled over, much to the amusement of the two women. Delighted by the show, they applauded until the young dog settled down on its mat to enjoy a well-earned biscuit.

"Can I pour you some more tea? I can't remember when I enjoyed a cup so much. Whenever Lee visits, we seem to settle for coffee. I've forgotten how gratifying a hot cup of tea can be."

At the mention of Levi's name, Christina paused, her cup in mid-air as Evelyn topped up the contents. "I'm happy to see that Lee has found a good friend in you. He seems to love this little town, and from my understanding during his last visit back home, he intends to stay on here." Christina's eyes filled despite her smile, and Evelyn waited as they tarried in their conversation for just a moment. "Levi's a wonderful son, Evelyn. As much as I enjoy having him nearby, I'd never want him to feel he had to stay somewhere because of me. I'm reasonably content in my tiny apartment, so he has no need to worry about me."

"You *are* his mother, Christina, and Thystle Creek is a long way from the coast. It's only natural that Lee would worry a little about you. After all, he's been used to having you nearby and it will seem strange to him not seeing you whenever he feels like it."

"I suppose you're right, dear. I just don't want him to tie himself down on account of me." Another polite slurp and Christina smiled up at Evelyn. "He really is a wonderful son, you know."

"Christina, if Lee is as wonderful a son to you as he has been a friend to me, you have been truly blessed. Take Trickster, for example. You asked me a moment ago how long I've had her. Only two months, although she is almost four months old. Your son gave her to me for my birthday."

"Really! How quaint. How did he manage that?" Christina wiped the corners of her mouth, removing biscuit crumbs and a small speck of strawberry jam.

"Well, he tricked me into opening a box on the front step before he stepped from behind my white birch singing *Happy Birthday*. Hence Trickster's name." Evelyn turned to look at the sleeping dog, unaware of the smile on her guest's face. Turning back, she continued. "Lee said he knew I'd be lonely with Lucy gone, and I was, as much or more than I thought I would be. Your son came to the rescue with this bundle of white fur and brown eyes. How could anyone resist that cute little ball of fluff?" Evelyn acknowledged her sleeping pet with a nod of pride and contentment. "He confessed his love for dogs and was full of apology when he thought I didn't want her. I'm sorry to admit my reaction was unexpected, and unacceptable," Evelyn added reluctantly. "He took me by surprise and I burst into tears."

"Like father, like son. Jacob was notorious for surprising me. I do believe he got more pleasure out of my reaction than he did out of what it was he was surprising me with." Christina's youthful giggle matched her coy look.

Evelyn welcomed the opportunity to change the subject, feeling embarrassed for her actions, but more for having admitted them to Levi's mother. "Lee has shared how you and his father met, but I'm sure you have your own story. Tell me about your husband." The gentleness of her request and the genuine expression brought a beam to Christina's face.

"My Jacob?"

"Yes."

"Ah, where to begin. Perhaps at the beginning—that's always the safest place, wouldn't you say?" Christina's face glowed and her snow white hair sparkled from the sunlight as she sat near the window. Fascinated by this unique woman, Evelyn smiled in anticipation of hearing her love story.

"I was going to do so much in my corner of the world. The First World War had changed everything. Smiles were gone. Music had ceased to be, at least for most, and those who did sing struggled with guilt. How could one be happy when people were dying? But I thought I could make a difference. I thought I could provide some distraction, some happiness, if only temporarily, to a hurting world."

Evelyn nodded at Christina's choice of words, remembering Levi's account of how his mother had convinced her parents to let her move to the coast.

"When I left Thystle Creek for Vancouver, little did I know my life would change in the first year. As you know, I met Jacob—or *Yaacov* in Hebrew—at the local library. My, he was handsome! Not terribly tall, not like Levi—he must get his height from my side of the family—no, Jacob was not tall by the measure-stick, but he stood tall, shining like a beacon in a storm. He was my beacon, anyway." Her eyes glistened, and once again Evelyn waited quietly.

"I found living on the coast very difficult—something I never admitted to my family back here in Thystle Creek. I was a small town girl with high ideals and great ambitions. I loved the theatre, the stage, and the excitement that came with it; but I was lonely. I'd go home to a one-room flat late at night and sleep most of the day until the clubs opened in the evening. Then I'd sing and entertain until my voice tired and my body ached. Night after night. Week after week. The next thing I knew, I'd been on the coast for six months and had seen only a dozen or so sunrises. I decided I needed more for my life so I cut back on my acting and singing career and spent long hours studying at the library: music and drama for sure, but mathematics, science, even religion, anything that struck my fancy. I wasn't in school, so I felt no pressure to prove myself to anyone other than myself. I had no deadlines and was accountable to no one."

Evelyn laughed at her new friend's obvious rebellion.

"Jacob seemed to be at the library each time I went. I'd watch him interact with university students when they became bogged down with research for an assignment. He always had a suggestion, some advice; and his wit, my, he was captivating. Professors were never known to darken the door of a library, but Jacob was just a humble Hebrew teacher who loved life and loved to challenge young minds. He was a master at what he knew. I'd watch from a distance, but we'd often nod to one another, and then one day he spoke and we talked for hours. He became intrigued with my interest in religion, and I was drawn to his uncanny knowledge of life in general."

Christina closed her eyes and then opened them wide, leaned forward and whispered rather mischievously, "Actually, it was his smile that caught my attention first."

Evelyn giggled at Christina's engaging secret with the enthusiasm of a teenage girl hearing about the thrill of a first kiss.

"It was a magnet and I was helpless in its magnetic field. The day he introduced himself to me was the day I knew."

"You knew? What did you know?"

"He was the one for me." Christina embraced herself and her childlike snickers filled the room. "Silly, now when I think about it—a well-respected Hebrew teacher and a small town girl, several years younger—but it was meant to be. After our first exchange, it seemed we'd meet by accident and then we'd meet on purpose. He'd listen to my heart when I spoke of my passion to learn, and I'd listen to him when he shared his understanding of the many religions he had studied. Because I was a Gentile, he encouraged me to read books written about great preachers like John Calvin. During one of our quiet visits at the library, I remember sharing a quote from Charles Spurgeon: 'Our anxiety does not empty tomorrow of its sorrow, but only empties today of its strength.' He was quite impressed."

Christina rubbed her eyes. "Oh, how I enjoyed reading. My eyes give me trouble now, so I don't read as much anymore." She placed her napkin on the empty plate in front of her, leaned forward again and whispered, "But don't tell Levi. He worries too much about me already."

Settling back in her chair, her teacup empty, Christina confessed in a voice filled with pride, "I fell in love with Jacob before our first meeting was over, and, I found out later, he with me."

Trickster twitched in her sleep and yelped quietly. Christina gazed out the kitchen window, oblivious to the young dog's fitful sleep, and Evelyn watched her face. Her eyes would open, then close, and then she would sigh, and Evelyn wondered what was behind such a pensive look. Christina finally spoke. "We married the following summer and I never looked back." Another faraway look in the older woman's eyes brought a second pause in her story before Evelyn broke the silence.

"Did becoming a Jew create problems for you?"

"Of course. I'd be lying if I said it didn't." Christina gave no indication of surprise at Evelyn's directness; she just continued her story. "We were in it together, Jacob and me. We knew that most people would never understand and a lot would never accept us, but our love didn't allow for any other choice."

Evelyn rose from the table and carried the dishes to the sink. She stood with her back to her guest for several minutes before turning. "I don't understand how you could survive that kind of cruelty. Why didn't you just move?" Evelyn's voice rose slightly in her frustration to understand.

Christina smiled. "I suppose that would have been the easy thing to do, Evie. But Jacob loved his work. Besides, living a life of secrecy can be very harmful. No, we decided to be open about it and trusted our love for each other to see us through the hard times. It was like cement in a brick wall, our love. It held us together when things got tough, when unkind words were thrown our way, especially when the Second World War began."

"That doesn't make sense, knowing what was going on under Hitler's rule," Evelyn challenged as she returned to her place at the table, a little more settled.

"You are quite right. It doesn't make sense. Jews were being persecuted in Europe, murdered by the hundreds of thousands, and yet back home here we were being attacked and ridiculed for our way of life and mocked for our way of worship. The God Jacob and I worshipped was the same God that those who criticized us worshiped, for goodness sake. I could never understand it. I just could never understand it." Christina repeated herself and then fell silent.

"People can be cruel."

"Yes, my dear, they can." Christina patted Evelyn's hand and smiled. "But it's really up to us as to how much others offend us, isn't it? Sometimes we are our own worst enemy, you know. Often we can do more harm to ourselves than the words of others. There's a passage in the scriptures that speaks on that very thing. Let me see, I think it's in Mark, maybe Chapter Five, or Six—my mind's not as sharp as it used to be—it's the story of Jesus teaching in the synagogue in His own town and the people were offended. He was just the carpenter's son, they said. Unfortunately, their offence turned into hostility and anger, and they ended up suffering because of it when Jesus left and went to other villages instead." Christina paused for a moment before continuing. "Many people said unkind things about us and we were offended. Unlike the people in Nazareth, we learned that it was up to us not to nurse that offence and cultivate it. If we'd done that, our spiritual lives would have become cold, much like the people back in Jesus' day."

The turn in the conversation to spiritual matters made Evelyn uneasy. She rose from her chair to put Trickster outside, but turned first to her guest.

"You mentioned Jesus and His teachings, but Jewish people don't believe the New Testament. How can you… how could Jacob ever get guidance from One whom he didn't recognize as the Messiah?" Evelyn opened the door and stood by it, waiting for Trickster to visit the end of the yard. An awkward feeling had surfaced that Evelyn could not shake. She took the opportunity to wait for her dog to return, hoping her question would be left hanging and they could return to the less threatening conversation they had been enjoying.

"You are right, again, my dear, except for one thing," Christina responded, and Evelyn turned to face her new friend with a growing uneasiness. "Over time, my dear Jacob came to understand that Jesus Christ *was* the long-awaited Messiah, revealed through the Old Testament prophets. When he realized this, he became more engrossed in his readings than ever before. He had already retired from teaching and was often overcome with regret that he had missed years of opportunity to direct his students to the truth."

"The truth? Can one ever be sure of the truth?"

"Oh, yes, very much so. I heard somewhere that truth and time go hand in hand."

Christina's confident response amazed Evelyn. This soft-spoken woman had breached a wall that even Lewis had been unable to scale. Excitement replaced her anxiety and Evelyn excused herself for a moment. She left Christina enjoying the playful tumbling of Trickster as the young dog chased and overshot her rubber toy.

With a determination that would prove to take her down a path that had long been avoided, Evelyn went to her bedroom, opened her bottom dresser drawer, unlocked a wooden box, and ceremoniously lifted something out. When she rejoined her friend, a tiny felt jewellery bag was clutched in her right hand.

"I'd like to show you something." Evelyn's hands trembled as the contents tumbled into Christina's outstretched hand. "My grandmother gave this to me on my fifth birthday. I've hidden it for over twenty-five years."

The two women stared at the small piece of jewellery. Neither spoke, only to have the moment broken as Evelyn's doorbell chimed. A voice called from a partially opened front door and the jewellery was quietly returned to its bag and then slipped into Evelyn's apron pocket.

"You ladies having a good visit?" Levi's voice boomed through the front hallway.

Christina whispered to her host just before her son appeared in the kitchen doorway, "Although I'm not the least bit tired, Levi will insist that I have an afternoon nap. You'll see."

"Hi there, you two. From the smiles on your faces, I can only guess how much has been shared in this room. If only walls could talk. Better still, maybe Trickster can tell all."

At the sound of her name, Trickster bounded over to Levi and automatically rolled on her back to receive her usual greeting. Scratching her furry tummy, Levi continued on a more serious note. "I hate to be a spoil sport, Mother, but I believe it's time for you to have your rest."

With the last comment, the two women chuckled openly.

"And hello to you too, son." Christina stood and turned her cheek to accept her son's kiss as he greeted her. "You are correct about one thing: we've had a wonderful journey down memory lane. At least I have."

Taking Evelyn's arm, the elderly woman squeezed it gently as they walked to the front door. "You have a delightful friend here in Evelyn." She kept her eyes on Evelyn as she spoke to her son. "She has been a wonderful audience for my reminiscing. We will do it again soon, won't we, dear?" Her pause was only momentary as she questioned her friend. "Perhaps we could pick up where we left off over your delicious biscuits and another cup of tea."

"It would be more than my pleasure," Evelyn responded, hugging Christina tenderly. The two friends looked at one another, aware that a bond had grown in the last couple of hours, one that would be treasured as it matured.

"Goodbye, Evie." Christina patted Evelyn's cheek and left on the arm of her son.

Night had fallen when Evelyn stood in front of her dressing table mirror holding the felt jewellery bag, trembling.

"What happened this morning?" Evelyn spoke to the image before her. "What was said that was so different from anything Louie ever said?"

In her heart she knew the answer to her questions. The answer lay in her hand, in a brown felt bag. Slipping its contents carefully into her hands, she trembled again as she raised her arms to secure the clasp around her neck. A Star of David hung from a gold chain in the vee of her neck.

23

Blessed is he whose transgression is forgiven,
whose sin is covered.
PSALM 32:1

"Do you understand, Lee? Before your mother went back to the coast, she encouraged me to share this with you. She said you would understand. Do you?" Evelyn whispered.

He wanted to, but Levi remained silent for a long time watching the snow fall on the front lawn. He leaned forward, his arms on his knees, watching the Christmas lights blinking off and on from beneath the mounds of snow on the front bushes. For just a moment he appeared mesmerized by the winter wonderland being birthed before him. When he finally spoke, his words were slow, his voice soft.

"Yes, I do, Evie, but I find it amazing that you've kept it a secret all these years." Shaking his head, he turned to Evelyn. "You never told Lewis?"

"No." Evelyn sat quite still on the couch beside Levi, not looking at him. Her hands opened and closed as her fingers twisted in her lap.

Levi turned away. Unprepared for such deep feelings, his reaction to her answer surprised him. Was it pity? No, it went far deeper than pity, but he could not be distracted right now. For the moment at least, he had to remain focused on what Evelyn had just shared.

"I remember a while back when you asked me about my name. I thought it strange, but there never seemed to be the right time to talk about it again. I can understand now why you asked." He smiled, hoping to dissipate the tension that had developed.

"Lee, I know I've done something terrible. While I was in the middle of it, I never allowed myself to think about anyone else. Now all I can think about is Lucy. Will she ever forgive me?"

Levi attempted to speak, but Evelyn shook her head. "You and I have been friends now for several months. Not long ago, you told me you were pretty much a stranger in my life, and you were right. We met at a time when I was just beginning to admit how wrong I've been for so many years, but you never knew me before. You never knew me as a woman who struggled just to exist from one day to the next. You never saw a wife who all but destroyed her marriage by her selfish, self-centred pity, by her constant ridiculing of her husband's faith in his God. You never knew the mother who neglected her daughter and missed years of her life. I was not nice to be around." Her raised voice revealed her turmoil. "My own neighbours felt sorry for Lewis and I'm sure they pitied him for having married me. And Lucy…Oh, Lee, what have I done?"

Evelyn buried her face in her hands and wept.

"Evie, listen to me." Levi took her hands from her face. Cupping her chin in the palms of his hands, he wiped Evelyn's tears away with his thumbs. "You did what you believed was the right thing at the time. No one knew and it was easy for you to leave it in the past. But the time has come for you to right it. You need to talk to Lucy. She's your daughter and she loves you. Don't assume the worst. Just remember who she is and all that she believes in." With that, Levi slipped his arm around Evelyn's shoulder and drew her to him.

He sat for a long time in an emotional tunnel, watching the snowflakes drift silently to the frozen ground.

A few moments passed before Evelyn rose and went to the kitchen. As he watched her leave, Levi hoped Evelyn would receive some encouragement from what he'd said. He could only imagine that her thoughts would be scattered, and all he could do was pray that she would find some peace in having shared her story with him. He followed her to the kitchen and watched her open the oven door, ease the rack toward her, and raise the lid of the roasting pan. The aroma of pot roast drifted through the kitchen. "Smells familiar in here." Levi smiled, remembering their first dinner together. "Expecting company?"

Evelyn smiled at Levi's attempt at humour and he welcomed it as a sign of the peace he had just prayed for.

"I've made an assumption that you'd stay for dinner, Lee. Are you open for a free meal now that your mother's returned to the coast?" Evelyn stepped aside as Lee lifted the pan from the oven, placed it on the counter, and then moved out of the way. "Actually, there's more than enough for two. Perhaps I should call Lucy and Wil."

The uncertainty in her voice was not missed on Levi.

"I think that would be a great idea. And, if that invitation is still open, I'd be happy to join the three of you for dinner. But I have something I'd like to say before you call Lucy."

Levi crossed the kitchen floor, took Evelyn's hands, and drew her closer to himself.

"Evie, there's no doubt that you need to talk to Lucy. She has a right to know and I can be here for moral support, but you need to tell her for your own sake."

"Lee, I can't..."

"Yes, you can. You owe it to your daughter, but more importantly, you owe it to yourself. You've carried this for too long and it's time to let it go. Besides, you shouldn't shortchange your daughter. She comes from tough stock and she loves you very much."

"I want to be honest with her, Lee. I just don't think... there's so much pain. I... there's still more you don't know." Evelyn dropped her head and a tear fell on Levi's hand. He lifted her chin and smiled into her eyes.

"Then just tell her what you can. The rest can wait until later. But you'll see. Lucy will be just fine with all of it and you'll find yourself sharing the rest sooner than you think."

Evelyn sighed and let her forehead fall against Levi's chest. Levi closed his eyes and relished the moment. It felt right for her to be in his arms. He warmed to an idea that had been simmering for weeks, and his courage mounted.

The kiss was gentle, so gentle that at first Levi wondered if he had actually kissed her. He embraced Evelyn a second time, stirring a breathless passion, one he feared would surprise Evelyn but one he hoped she'd welcome.

"I think I'd better make that call." Evelyn eased herself from Levi's embrace and absentmindedly smoothed the front of her apron.

Again Levi lifted her chin to look into her eyes.

"I'll set the table," he offered, and winked as Evelyn lifted the receiver to call her daughter.

"That was a great dinner, Mom, and your invitation couldn't have been more timely. Wil was late getting home from basketball practice, and I've come to the conclusion that I might as well wait until I see the whites of his eyes before I start supper. Your call came just as he walked in the front door."

Lucy's presence relaxed Evelyn as they busied themselves in the kitchen after supper. She loved having her daughter visit and she enjoyed the humorous stories of "playing house," as Lucy had so often described her life with Wil.

"...and it was so good it knocked Wil's socks off." Evelyn grinned as her daughter went on about the roasted chicken dinner she had cooked two nights earlier, complete with all the trimmings, dessert, and even candles. Lucy's unbridled chatter seemed to lessen the anxiety Evelyn had felt earlier in the evening when she had decided to tell Lucy of her Jewish heritage.

The men had gone to the basement to check out the plumbing for Evelyn's new washing machine, and Evelyn and Lucy caught up with the latest town news. Evelyn was amazed at how well she and her daughter could talk about the simple things in life. They shared recipes, discussed plans for Christmas dinner, suggested what gifts to buy for whom, and buzzed with pleasure over the news that Christina Morsman planned a return visit at Christmas.

"I'm glad you had a chance to spend some time with her before she returned to the coast. She seems like an awfully nice lady." Lucy paused for a moment and turned from the warm soapy dishwater to face her mother. "We had quite a chat at the church after Uncle Mo's funeral. I wouldn't be surprised if she's throwing around the idea of moving back to Thystle Creek. Uncle Mo's house was left to Lee, but it's the family homestead and she had this faraway look in her eyes when she started to tell me stories of her childhood. I think she has quite a story hidden inside."

Lucy turned back to focus on washing the dishes, but was stopped by her mother's silence. "Mom, what is it? Has something happened to her?"

"No, no, Christina's fine. In fact, she called Lee earlier today. She got home safely and is glad to be settling in before the wet weather arrives, although she did say she was looking forward to her Christmas visit. I'm sorry if I seem preoccupied. I was remembering a conversation she and I had a few days before she went home. I'd like to share it with you and Wil when the men finish in the basement."

"Okay. As soon as I'm done here, I'll make some tea. Wil is trying to stay off coffee and Doc Bailey has suggested it would be a good thing for both of us, me especially."

"Why *you* especially? You never seem to be bothered by it now that you've grown to enjoy the flavour."

Lucy grinned at her mother, acknowledging the time when Lucy had no use for the beverage. She opened her mouth to say something just as the men joined them in the kitchen.

"Well, Evie, it looks like you're all set for your new washing machine." Wil towered over his mother-in-law as he reached over her head for a glass from the cupboard. "Sure could use a cold drink, though. That basement's like an oven. You don't need to worry about your furnace," Wil added as he ran the cold water tap.

Evelyn smiled at her son-in-law's complaining. "My new machine arrives in three days and it'll be a real treat to get rid of that old wringer." Turning toward the kitchen door that led to the front hall, she added. "Lucy's just put on the kettle for some tea. Let's go into the living room while we wait for the kettle to boil."

"The living room? Why so formal? Oh, oh Luce! We're in trouble." Wil teased his mother-in-law in his usual way and plunked himself down on a kitchen chair. "We'd rather take whatever you've got to give us right here in our comfort zone." He pulled his wife to his knee, grinning. "Okay, we're ready. What have we done?"

With a cursory glance in Levi's direction, Evelyn turned to the young couple. They sat giggling at one another, so in love, so happy, that she lost her nerve. With her inner defeat covered by an old familiar mask, she shook her head and waved her hand in the air. "Nothing important, Wil, it can wait," and abruptly changed the subject to a more congenial topic: Christmas.

The warmth of their living room fire had beckoned the young couple. Wil was content to sit quietly enjoying the fire, listening while his wife examined every tone, expression, and word shared during the evening they had just enjoyed with her mother and Levi.

"It was good to see Mom interacting with Lee, tonight. She seemed more relaxed than she has been in a long time, and Trickster has certainly brought a new dimension into her life. Lee sure did her a favour when he gave her that dog."

"Yep, Trickster's quite the little pup."

"When you guys were checking out the plumbing in the basement, we talked about Lee's mother. Mom had her over for tea a couple of times. She really likes Christina."

Following a lengthy pause, Wil squeezed his wife gently. "Hey, where'd you go?"

"I was just thinking about Dad." The soberness of her comment alerted Wil, but he waited for his wife to continue.

"Dad and Mom never entertained. I can't remember even one time when Mom prepared a meal and invited someone over. Occasionally Doc Bailey or Uncle Mo would drop in and end up staying for supper, but that's not the same thing as a planned evening. It was just never done. But tonight, well, it was really nice. I just can't help thinking what Dad missed out on all those years."

Wil remained silent. It was all true. The Sherwoods never had people over. The way he was raised, a week never went by that someone wasn't invited for dinner. It was just the thing to do. He snuggled his wife closer in his arms.

"Luce, there's nothing you can do about that. Your dad is gone and thinking about all the things that may have been missed in his life will drive you crazy. Focus on the positive. Remember how happy he was despite the hardship at home. He was the light that shone for this town. His social life *was* this town. He didn't need a formal dinner in his home to feel happy or wanted. He knew your mother loved him in her own way, and for him, that's all that mattered."

A prolonged silence followed. Wil finally stretched and stood to put another log on the hot coals, thinking how glad he was that he'd stocked up on their wood supply early. "Winter's arrived sooner than expected."

Lucy ignored Wil's comment as he stoked the fire. "Did you notice the way Lee was looking at Mom tonight? It was almost as though he knew something that we didn't know."

Wil simply nodded and smiled, cautious not to answer. He knew his wife, and he feared that whatever he said, Lucy would embellish it.

"Wil! Are you listening to me? Didn't you notice the change in Mom just before we had our tea? She was acting strange, almost nervous. She said she wanted to talk to us about something, something she'd talked to Christina about, and when you teased her, she seemed to skirt around it and it never came up again." Suddenly, Lucy sat upright, excitement written all over her face. "Wil, do you think she and Lee are..."

Wil stoked the fire one more time before returning to the comfort of the couch. "Don't do this to yourself. You know..."

"Listen to me!" Lucy's interruption silenced Wil. "Lee *did* seem to be more attentive. They *are* seeing one another a lot. It's only logical that Lee may be more interested than a casual friendship."

"All true. But I'm not so sure about your mom. She's pretty private. It's hard to know what she's thinking. We'll just have to watch whatever's there to unfold. By the way, did you get a chance to tell her about…?"

Lucy turned and kissed her husband, silencing him for a second time before turning back to the fold of his arm. "Nope, but I almost did."

"What stopped you?

"You."

"Me? When did I do that?"

"When you and Lee came up from the basement. But it turned out for the best. She seemed preoccupied with whatever was on her mind. Besides, I wanted you there with me."

Lucy snuggled further into Wil's arm and sighed with a contentment that seemed to fill the room. "I wonder how she's going to feel when I tell her she's going to be a grandmother." Lucy's words were pensive.

Wil moved his wife sideways to look at him. "Ecstatic! She's going to be a doting grandma and *you* are going to be a *wonderful* mother." His words were slow and pointed, and then, taking advantage of his wife's position, he kissed her and added, "Have I told you lately how much I love you?"

Wil kissed his wife again with a gentleness that came from a deep well of pride and love, but as Lucy molded her body to his, Wil's passion heightened and his breathing became rapid. The willingness in his wife's response stirred a fervor that accelerated with each kiss that followed. Releasing his wife, Wil stood, lifted Lucy into his arms, and turned toward their bedroom.

24

Thou hast set all the borders of the earth:
thou hast made summer and winter.
Psalm 74:17

Winter settled over the community of Thystle Creek. Snow had begun falling early in October and Aspen Avenue, picture perfect throughout the year, was bewitching. Life seemed to come to a halt when winter worked its magic.

"It's a winter wonderland, Evie," Levi hollered over the wind to Evelyn as she stuck her head out the back door.

"Yes, Lee, it's beautiful, but you've been shovelling that path from the back door to the end of the yard for over half an hour. Don't be so fussy. Trickster will make it to the end of the yard just fine. There's a storm coming and you need to get home." Evelyn returned his wave and shut the kitchen door, but not before a cold wind blew across the top of the roof, sending a gust of snow across Evelyn's feet and onto the kitchen floor.

"I'll never get used to this," Evelyn muttered good-naturedly to an empty kitchen. A quick wipe cleaned the floor, but only for a moment.

With a second gust of wind, the back door flew open and Levi and Trickster rushed in. Levi was covered with snow from hat to boots. His newly grown beard was speckled with icicles, and his toque had been pulled down over his thick black hair to the edge of his eyes, touching his frozen eyebrows and resting on the rims of his steamed-over glasses. Trickster stood beside him, completely enveloped in fresh snow that gave her the appearance of being twice the size she really was. Only a small amount of blue plaid could be seen confirming that her little coat had protected her from a greater deluge.

"The abominable snowman and friend," Evelyn chuckled, keeping her distance until Trickster had finished shaking herself free from her temporary snow-coat. "So much for my clean floor. You guys are a sight to behold."

Trickster bounded toward Evelyn, wiggling and spinning in anticipation of having her second coat removed.

"It's cold out there. I'm afraid I've been spoiled from living on the west coast. I forgot what winter could be like," Levi laughed as he watched his furry companion prance impatiently around Evelyn's feet.

Wrapping her dog in a large woollen blanket, Evelyn sat on the floor vigorously rubbing Trickster's ears and fur. She wrestled with her pet until Trickster finally squirmed from her arms and raced around the kitchen floor looking for her favourite squeaky toy.

"Let me dry your jacket by the fire, Lee." Evelyn rose with Levi's help, reacting slightly to his cold hands, and headed toward the fireplace. "You need to warm yourself, too, but just for a few minutes. There's a storm heading... sorry, I guess I already said that, but you need to be going before you see your newly shovelled path filled in again." Her warning repeated, Evelyn turned toward the living room.

Levi's groan stopped even Trickster from playing. "I'll just have to come by tomorrow and redo it for you, girl; can't have you sinking out of sight on us." Levi tousled Trickster's damp fur, enticing her to drop her toy, but to no avail.

The fire was inviting and Levi rubbed his own hair dry as Evelyn draped his jacket and scarf over a chair by the fire. "Mother's been looking forward to this Christmas shopping trip for days. In fact, that's all she's been talking about since I picked her up at the bus station last week. You two must have really hit it off. Her decision to move back to Thystle Creek still has my head spinning, it happened so fast, but apparently Mother had her mind made up before she returned to the coast last month. I can't help wondering how much of her return is centred on her friendship with you." Levi raised his eyebrows.

Evelyn remained silent, but smiled.

"Anyway, what time would you like me to come by in the morning?"

Evelyn shook her head. "Didn't you just admit how you have forgotten…or maybe you never really knew what winter storms can do, especially to a little town. We can't go to Edmonton tomorrow, Lee. We'll be shut down for days. If it's clear enough for you to bring your mother over for a visit, that may be all we can do for now." As an afterthought to his earlier comment, she paused, hand on hip, a coy look in her eye, "By the way, have I told you how happy I am that Christina has returned to live with you?"

"Only a dozen times since I arrived this morning." The teasing came naturally to Levi, and Evelyn had come to enjoy his warmheartedness. "But Mother will be disappointed in the changed plans. Let's just see what the morning brings," he added optimistically.

Only a short time passed before Levi donned his partially dry coat, scooped up his mitts and toque, and headed for the door. Trickster followed at his heels, her body language indicating her anticipation of another romp in the snow. But Evelyn lifted her safely into her arms as she walked Levi to the front door. "Be careful, Lee. The wind can play mean tricks on you. It looks like it's coming from the north, and that's a bad sign. That usually means we're in for…"

A kiss firmly planted on her lips silenced Evelyn.

"You worry too much, Evie. See you in the morning." Levi walked carefully to his car. "And close the door; there's a storm coming," he joked as he waved goodbye without looking back at a flustered woman standing in the doorway.

With no surprise to Levi, the next morning proved Evelyn correct. Not unusual for that part of the country, a blanket of snow brought most of Thystle Creek to a halt. Levi marvelled at how generations past had managed to navigate horse-drawn wagons through such unforgiving mounds of snow, concluding that they had probably hibernated with the bears. Today, most vehicles were left buried in their driveways, or at best, parked on the road waiting out the storm. Most vehicles, but not his.

Over an hour had passed before he reappeared at his front door, proud of his accomplishment and pleased that his perseverance had paid off. "You can put away your snowshoes, Mother. The car has been dug from its grave," he quipped as he banged the snow from his boots and brushed off his jacket before stepping inside the front door.

"And to think I almost had them on."

His mother's sharp wit was not lost on Levi. There she stood, coat in hand, holding a foil-covered plate of fresh biscuits, waiting for him to close the door. "Are you about ready to drop me off at Evelyn's? We have lots of planning to do, even if we can't go shopping."

Levi smiled at her feigned impatience and obvious eagerness. His mother's decision to move back to Thystle Creek after so many years away surprised him. Her life had changed when she'd met and married his father, and she had never made a return visit to her hometown. Levi wondered if her conversion to Judaism played a big part in her never coming back. *I must ask her someday if that was why she never returned.* It was a fleeting thought, but one that made enough noise to grab his attention. His father had never visited his mother's birthplace either, and he himself had only made one visit in his senior teen years when he went on a week-long camping expedition with the Scouts to the foothills in central Alberta. Now that Thystle Creek was his home, he couldn't help thinking how much his father would have enjoyed the slower pace, especially in his retirement years when his health had failed and all he had were his Bible and his regrets.

Levi had graduated from medical school and was working in a downtown clinic in North Vancouver when his father came to an awareness of Jesus Christ as the Messiah. Levi had witnessed his father's despondency at failing to see the truth before, but he eventually resigned the past to the past and directed his energy to sharing the Good News with his family and friends.

And now, here his mother stood, thriving on being "back home," as she had told him a few days earlier. The apartment in Vancouver had been quite adequate, he never doubted that, but he had seen a new energy in his mother during her visit a few months earlier. *Could it be Evelyn*? A bond had grown between them, much to his delight. *They are so much alike,* he mused as he hung up his wet jacket on a hook near the back door. Reaching behind for a dry one in the front closet where his mother stood, he paused. "You enjoy Evelyn, don't you, Mother?"

"Indeed, such a treasure at my age. One often concludes that the need to make new friends dwindles the older one gets." Her eyes sparkled with her own wisdom. "Life has given me many people to call 'friend,' Levi, but the older I get, the less time and energy I seem to have to develop new friendships. But Evelyn, she's a blessing, a special person with a special need. Wouldn't you agree, son?"

"She is certainly that."

His mother's comments unnerved him. Her look had been gentle and for a fleeting moment Levi considered sharing his feelings for Evelyn. He knew he could trust his mother, but he wasn't sure where Evelyn stood. And there was the matter of Evelyn's indifference and coolness to spiritual things. *Perhaps I've just wanted to ignore that,* he admitted silently, and realized he wasn't ready to reveal the depth of his feelings just yet, even to his wise and godly mother.

Holding his mother's coat as she slipped it on, he thought of the woman he was about to see and wondered how he could break down a wall that had been part of her life for so many years. *I can only wait on You, Lord, for direction. So, lead on. I'm right behind You.* His prayer was heartfelt and filled with wonder at his daring to accomplish what one before him had failed to do.

Levi pulled his car up in front of Evelyn's home and recognized Wil and Lucy's pickup angle-parked in front. Wil stood in knee-high banks of snow, shovelling a path to the front of the house.

"You'd better sit for a minute or two, Mother. I think Wil could use some help." Levi pulled the hood to his parka tighter around his face, left his car running, and stepped into the wind.

"Glad I came prepared," he hollered as the wind blew his first shovel-full back in his direction, submerging him in the invasive white powder. Wil laughed at the sight and waved in appreciation of his help.

An hour later, five adults shared hot chocolate and winter stories, each trying to outdo the other.

"Lee, you should've seen the snow fourteen years ago. Now, that was a winter you'd never forget! In fact, all winters I've ever known have been measured by that one." Lucy sat on the kitchen floor resting her back against the cupboard, Trickster curled up asleep on her lap. Her exaggeration amused everyone. "I remember Dad telling me that seven-year-olds would get lost in the seven foot snow banks, never to be found until the snow melted in the spring." Laughter filled the room, arousing Trickster, who circled several times on Lucy's lap before settling back to sleep. "For awhile I believed him, but if the truth were known, he was afraid I wouldn't be seen if a truck went by, and so I could never help dig his car out until I was older and taller."

Evelyn continued the story.

"Driveways were always a problem—still are, for that matter. Those who had a car left it at the end of their driveway figuring it would be easier to dig it out there rather than shovel the whole driveway. Louie was one of them and it took him most of the morning to get our car out from under."

At the mention of Lewis's name, a silence fell on the group.

"I can vouch for that," Levi jumped in, determined to prevent a downward spiral of emotions at the mention of Lewis's name. "I couldn't believe how much of that stuff fell in one night." He stepped over Lucy and Trickster, smiling as he did, and put the kettle on, grateful that Wil continued with his own rendition of the historical winter report with genuine fervor.

"Each year we started out with renewed vigour to keep the path in front of our house clear, but it soon became a losing battle. Energy depleted quickly. We settled for a narrow footpath from our house to the front walk, even to this day."

"And how thankful I am for that! I'm afraid this short, old gal would get lost right up there with all the seven-year-olds," Christina chimed in, adding to the excitement and enthusiasm that the latest storm had created. She raised her cup of hot chocolate and toasted the efforts of the two young men who had come to the rescue and saved them from a day of isolation.

Laughter filled the room and sent Trickster hunting for her new ball, only to be interrupted by the front doorbell. When Wil opened the door, he found his pastor brushing off his coat and stomping his boots to rid them of excess snow. Stepping inside from the blustering wind, Pastor Cribbs stood hat in hand with any remaining snow melting in a puddle at his feet.

"I'm sorry to interrupt, folks, but Lee, there's been an accident. Josh Graham's car left the road sometime in the night. Seems his wipers froze up on him and he missed the curve down by County Road 12. Hit a snow bank and spun into the ditch. He was knocked out and Jennie Ralston hit the dash with her shoulder. Broke her right arm. Doc Bailey could use your help. Seems a man pulling a small travel trailer, and his little boy, stopped and helped them—crazy to be pulling one of those on a night like last night, come to think of it—anyway, the two may have saved Josh's and Jennie's lives."

"You head on home, Pastor, and I'll go right over to the office. Evelyn, call Doc and tell him I'm on my way. Wil, could you see that Mother gets home? I don't know how long I'll be."

"Don't worry about me," Christina interjected. "You just be careful getting out to Doc's. This storm seems to be gaining new life. Evelyn, if it's all right with you, I'll stay put right here."

Evelyn nodded affectionately as she handed Levi his parka, hat and gloves. "Be careful, Lee. It's nasty out there."

Levi bent down and kissed Evelyn on the cheek.

"I'll be fine. I'll check in when things settle down. Wil, maybe you and Pastor here could find out about the stranger. He needs to be thanked."

Lucy stood speechless in the background, still digesting the kiss that had been exchanged between Levi and her mother.

25

Take my yoke upon you, and learn of me;
for I am meek and lowly in heart:
and ye shall find rest unto your souls.
MATTHEW 11:29

Evelyn relived the excitement generated in her kitchen three days ago, tempered somewhat by Josh and Jennie's accident. She grinned at the memory of Christina's comment of "hibernating until spring." *She certainly has lots to hibernate with now,* Evelyn thought, looking at a fresh snowfall that had filled in old footprints on the front path. The laughter of Tuesday evening continued to echo in her mind as she sat looking from her kitchen window. She sipped her hot chocolate, a drink she rarely enjoyed so early in the day, and smiled. The warm companionship and the presence of those she had come to value as dear friends filled her with a new wonder. *How long has it been since I've felt this good inside? Have I ever?* The disturbing questions erased her moments of pleasure and her thoughts turned to her husband.

Evelyn watched the rising sun stretch its multi-coloured arms across the freshly fallen snow and she struggled with the old accusing voice threatening to surface. "Louie, I'm so ashamed," Evelyn whispered in the early morning light. *Every day I fight the guilt about how I neglected you.* She had long since discovered the ugliness of guilt: it was always there. Sometimes it would sit quietly in a corner, as it were, almost out of sight, and just when she thought she'd mastered it, it would raise its head and pounce. She sighed heavily, slowly circling the rim of her mug with her fingers. Her hot mug warmed her hands as she stared into its contents. "I loved you, Louie, but I couldn't show you." She spoke as though Lewis sat across from her. "The weight of my past smothered me, and even though you tried to help me, I ignored you, even ridiculed you. Maybe I didn't want release or freedom. I don't know, but I'm different now. Somehow, I've changed. I don't understand it. I can't even think when it happened. I just know I'm different. You'd be proud of me. Lucy and I have grown closer and I've met someone, someone you'd like. But am I free to love again, Louie? Do I dare?"

Trickster had settled herself in her bed by the back door, oblivious to the one-way conversation, oblivious to Evelyn's voice as it permeated the quietness of her kitchen.

Is this what prayer is like? Evelyn wondered. It never occurred to her that these quiet moments with the memory of her husband were part of her spiritual journey. She just knew she felt better each time she talked to Lewis. And there were many times. Again, the concept of prayer crossed her mind. She knew Lewis had talked to his God. She knew Lucy and Wil prayed. She even overheard Christina and Levi share a recent "answer to prayer." But she didn't pray. It was that simple.

Evelyn rested her forehead on her folded arms as the morning sun rose higher, casting warm rays through the kitchen window. It warmed her and she raised her head to see diamond-shaped stars sparkling on the snow banks by the road. She shook her head in amazement when she realized that overnight the banks, formed as remnants of ploughed roads, had grown to the height of the lower branches of the trees lining her street. It was still too early for children to be up, but Evelyn knew it would only be a matter of time before the sleds would be tracking paths from the top of those mounds to the sidewalk. School was out for the Christmas holidays and parents would be drilling their children about staying clear of the road. Each mother took on the task of watching the children play safely. *One day it'll be Lucy's turn to stand guard.* She smiled at the idea, realizing the implications it had for her becoming a grandmother.

Her moments of solitude over, Evelyn carried her mug to the kitchen sink. Her thoughts turned to Josh and Jennie and the accident they had endured. There was still no word on who the stranger was that had helped them, but Evelyn was very happy to hear from Levi that Jennie's arm, though badly broken, had been set with relative ease.

"She'll be courting a cast over the holidays and for the next several weeks, but someone is obviously courting her." He'd laughed. "She's got a diamond on her left hand, Evie. Looks like Josh has gone and got himself a gal."

Evelyn had been thrilled to hear that Josh and Jennie were going to be married. Her suspicions had been raised at Lucy's wedding, but nothing had been confirmed. She had kept her thoughts to herself, but was fully aware that she was not the only one who had noted the new couple. Gossip in a small town was like a lizard's tongue, always active, always searching. She thought of Mae, and smiled.

Her response to Levi rang in her ears as she turned and stared out at the awakening dawn. "Josh really needs someone in his life, Lee.

He's carried a lot of guilt these past few years over Louie's death. He needs to be freed from it."

At first, they had just been words, spoken in sincerity but never intended to be taken personally. But as soon as they had echoed in her head, they'd left Evelyn numb. Levi had broken the silence.

"Well, I suppose all of us need to be freed from the things that haunt us, don't we?"

Thinking back on the conversation that had followed and where her thoughts had been just now with Lewis, Evelyn knew the time had come for Lucy to know the truth. She had delayed talking with her, justifying her procrastination with the excuse that the time had never been right. Too many interruptions. Too late at night. Too early in the day. The truth was that she was afraid. Yet she realized there would be no freedom from her past until she spoke with her daughter.

"Snowstorm or not, today's the day, Tricks. I need to talk to Lucy and Wil today." Her dog rose from its bed and ambled toward Evelyn. She rubbed against Evelyn's leg and Evelyn reached down to scratch her pet's head. "You seem to know just what I need, don't ya girl. But first things first. I need to have a shower."

Evelyn rose and her dog raced toward the back door.

"What? You little monkey. Do you need to go outside? Haven't you seen what's out there? Well, never mind, when you have to, you have to." With that, Evelyn opened the kitchen door. Trickster bounded outside and was immediately lost in a mound of snow that had built up against the screen door. "Hang in there, Tricksie, spring's coming," Evelyn laughed as she watched through the window of her closed door. "You'll make it!"

It was only moments before the job was done and Trickster came barrelling through the narrow tunnel her little body had created moments ago. The new path had become user-friendly, but it was evident that the young dog was glad to be in where a gentle hand greeted her and dried her and fed her and loved her.

Evelyn's thoughts jostled about in her head as she dressed. The warm shower had relaxed her somewhat, but in anticipation of her conversation with Lucy, she still struggled with the right words. *How will I begin?* she thought, and rehearsed possibilities before her mirror. "Lucy, there's something I want to tell you." *No. That's not it.* "Lucy, there's something I *have* to tell you." She spun from the mirror, frustrated. She tried again looking out the bedroom window. "Maybe, 'Lucy, I've kept something from you your whole life and now it's time to tell you.'" Every effort sounded so academic to Evelyn and she could feel her anxiety mounting. It was only a slight noise downstairs that distracted her from going down the path of avoiding telling Lucy altogether. Trickster was nowhere to be seen and Evelyn concluded it was her dog until Trickster crawled out from under her bed with a long-lost toy clutched in her mouth.

A half-hearted smiled crossed Evelyn's face, distracted momentarily from what she had heard earlier. And then the noise came again. Caution preceded bravery and Evelyn walked slowly down the stairs. Boots sat in a puddle of water on the tray by the front door and Evelyn smiled at her own apprehensions. *Good thing no one could read my thoughts.* She squeezed her eyes shut, embarrassed at her unwarranted fears. "Lucy, is that you?" Her question seemed redundant as she headed toward the basement door and called down the stairwell. "Lucy?"

"Yep, just me, Mom. Hope I didn't startle you. The shower was on when I got here so I just made myself at home." Lucy appeared at the bottom of the stairs, paintbrushes in one hand and a bag of rags in the other. "Wil's out front digging you out again. Looks like he'll be there for a while. I helped out for a bit, but decided I'd let Wil be the gallant one." Lucy laughed at her obvious cowardice and her mother's look of disapproval. "He'll be fine. He's in his element. Do you mind if I look through some of your painting stuff? We've decided to freshen up some of our rooms and thought we might borrow some things. I know it's still winter, but we should be able to paint, don't ya think?"

"I'm not sure, that was your father's department, but go ahead and look through whatever's down there and take it home. If it's too soon, at least you'll be ready when the spirit moves you." Remembering how much she enjoyed her morning beverage, she added, "I'll make some hot chocolate to warm you up. Better put your jacket and other paraphernalia in the dryer for a few minutes." Evelyn tossed her daughter's belongings down the stairs into Lucy's arms. "We'll have to remember to do this when Wil comes in."

In a matter of moments, Lucy arrived in the kitchen and placed a box of paint trays, brushes, rollers and rags inside the doorway. Trickster immediately sauntered over and sniffed all that her little nose could reach.

"Sure you don't mind?" Lucy's question accompanied a loving tousle of Trickster's head. "Hi ya, girl."

"By all means, help yourself. I've no intention of getting involved in that kind of work anytime in the near future, if ever." Evelyn smiled as Trickster rolled over for her usual belly rub.

With the kind deed done and a contented dog chewing a treat Lucy had unearthed from her pocket, Evelyn and Lucy settled themselves at the kitchen table to enjoy their hot chocolate. Lucy tapped on the front window and raised her hot drink to her husband and laughed. "It's here when you get finished," she hollered through the glass. Wil just nodded and continued his "task of love," as Evelyn had tagged his willingness to dig her out with each snowfall.

"Quite the guy you've got there, Lucy."

Her daughter turned from the window and Evelyn caught an unusual look in her eye before Lucy bowed her head slightly. *Is that a tear?*

"Lucy, what is it? What's wrong? Are *you* sick? Have you seen Doc Bailey? I'm sure he'll help." Anxiety mounted with each question and Evelyn could only stare at her daughter and wait.

"Mom, I've…we…you're right. Doc Bailey can help me. I've been to him twice now and I do feel a lot better."

The words moved over Evelyn like a black cloud on a sunny day. "You've been to see Al? How sick are you?" Evelyn's heartbeat pounded in her ears, imagining the worst.

"I'm not sick, Mom. I…we're…" Lucy raised her head, eyes sparkling, face beaming. "Mom, we're going to have a baby."

Evelyn gaped.

"A baby! You're going to have a baby? You're going to have a *baby*!" With each sentence, Evelyn's eyes grew larger until she rose from her chair and walked in circles in the middle of the kitchen. "You're going to be a mother!" Reality hit Evelyn with an urgency and she reached down for Trickster. Scooping up her pet, she spun around. "Do you hear that, Tricksie? Lucy's going to be a mommy. What will that make you, an aunt?" Trickster's yelping reached ear-piercing volume as Evelyn spun her high overhead. Stopping abruptly, she turned to Lucy. "That means I'm going to be a grandmother. How about that, Tricks? I'm going to be a *grand*mother! Maybe I'll be a *grandma*, or *granny*, or *nana*." Once again Evelyn spun around, holding her dog tightly as her sheer pleasure was witnessed by daughter and pet.

"What did you call your grandmother?" Lucy asked, smiling as she enjoyed her mother's reaction to her news.

"Bubi."

And the moment was broken. At the sound of her grandmother's name, Evelyn stopped her spinning, stopped her laughing and lowered her pet to the floor.

"Bubi?" Lucy questioned, her curiosity piqued.

"Yes, Bubi, B-u-b-i. The "u" sounds like *ah*." Evelyn's weak smile accompanied a long sigh and she joined her daughter at the table. "Sometimes I'd call her *Grandmama* when I got older, into my teens." For a long while both women sat quietly, watching the mound of snow grow as Wil continued to unearth the path from the front door to the sidewalk.

Lucy spoke first. "Mom, did she own the pearls I wore?"

"Yes, yes she did."

"That's the first time you've ever spoken of your family, apart from the pearls."

A moment in history had been made in her home, and only Evelyn knew what the next moment would bring.

PART FOUR

26

Truth shall spring out of the earth;
and righteousness shall look down from heaven.
PSALM 85:11

Evelyn lowered her head and took comfort in the warm mug between her hands. "I'd like to say I've thought about this moment for many years, but in truth, I've hoped it would never come. It's only been in the last few months that I've been burdened with an unexplainable need to tell you." Evelyn moved to reach for her daughter's hand, but instead folded her own hands deep within her apron. She looked out the window and absorbed Wil's efforts for a moment and then turned back to face her daughter.

"Lucy, what I'm about to tell you may have an influence on our relationship, you as my daughter, me as your mother and grandmother of your child." Evelyn shut her eyes again, willing her courage not to leave. "You are right to say I have never spoken of my family. I'm not proud of that. I should have been honest with you and your father, but..." Evelyn sighed again before continuing, "...it was too difficult. I just hope you will understand and not be bitter toward me.

One of my many regrets is not having told your father." The thought of Lewis almost shook her resolve. "He above anyone else would have understood."

Evelyn paused and the sound of Trickster snoring distracted her. Looking at the calm, trusting dog, she drew strength to continue. "I grew up in Toronto, a big city compared to Thystle Creek. Actually, there's no comparison. The noise. The traffic. The busyness. People from all walks of life were my neighbours. My father owned a bakery. His specialty breads and biscuits earned him the reputation as the best baker for blocks in all directions. We lived above the store, my father, my mother and Bubi." Evelyn smiled again at the mention of her grandmother. "There were other shops on our street that specialized in different foods, small markets that displayed their fruits and vegetables on tables in front of their stores in the warm seasons along with buckets of fresh flowers. I remember a butcher shop down the street from our bakery. I didn't like going there because of the bloody aprons the men wore. I didn't like to think what they were doing in the back room, but I was often sent with a note that told Mr. MacIntosh what my mother wanted. There were numbered plastic cards hanging on a hook inside the door that determined when you would be waited on. I could barely reach one, even when I stood on my tip toes. I played in the sawdust on the floor while I waited for my number to be called. I never did understand why they put it there—the sawdust on the floor—but it helped me pass the time while I waited. They were always busy."

Another sigh, another memory, and Evelyn continued.

"There were several clothing stores on our street. My mother haunted the yard goods store almost weekly. She loved to sew and made most of my clothes when I was a little girl. I was her pride and joy and she loved to make frilly dresses. We never took family pictures. It was a luxury we couldn't afford, but I do remember one being taken when I was five." Evelyn dared to look at her daughter as she unveiled her childhood, trying to determine Lucy's thoughts. "It was my birthday and my mother surprised me with this beautiful, blue taffeta dress she'd made, with three inches of crinoline at the hemline. I remember twirling round and round and then falling against the table and bumping my head. I cried a lot, but my father knew how to make my tears go away. He took my picture. 'Let's smile those tears away,' he'd said. That picture used to sit on top of the piano."

The clock ticked. Trickster continued to snore gently on the mat in front of the kitchen sink and Evelyn slipped into another world. She could hear her grandmother playing the piano with the constant rick-racking of her mother's sewing machine treadle in the background. She could smell the baking that filtered up the back stairs from the store kitchen. She could hear the laughter from customers—longtime friends—chatting with her father in the lower level. Time stood still as she stared out the window into the winter morning, seeing a little girl spinning and falling and her father jumping to her aid. A pain swelled up in her chest and Evelyn sat quietly for a few moments, living in the past.

"I had many friends," she continued with renewed energy, "special friends that would often come home with me after school to have a piece of my mother's baking. Like my father, she excelled in the kitchen and challenged him to be the best baker on Queen Street." Lucy laughed and Evelyn felt a spark of hope. "I had a happy life. No siblings, but I was content. I loved school. I enjoyed reading. I probably read too much—perhaps that's where my love for books came from—and I played less than I should have.

"Tell me about Bu… Bubi," Lucy corrected herself, and her interest encouraged Evelyn to dig deeper into the secluded memories.

"Bubi was special. She had given birth to my mother when she was in her early twenties and soon after that became a widow when my grandfather was killed in a mining accident in Hungary. She immigrated to Canada in 1906 when my mother was two. She's a strong one, my Bubi. Determined, yet compassionate at the same time. Alone in a strange country, but she survived."

Evelyn paused.

"We were a happy family, the four of us, and then things changed."

Evelyn stopped talking for several minutes.

"What changed?" Lucy whispered.

"When I was thirteen, I became aware of an unusual quietness about my parents. They had been going out every evening for a week and returning when I was already in bed. Whenever I came upon them talking quietly, their words became whispers until they finally stopped talking altogether." Evelyn's voice quickened. "I found Bubi crying one evening shortly after she'd been alone with my parents. I thought there was something wrong with her or my mother or father. Over the next couple of weeks it became obvious that there was nothing wrong with anyone, physically speaking; neither Bubi nor my parents were sick. But things were different, something had changed. Happiness had left our house. My grandmother stopped humming as she sat in her knitting chair. There were sidelong glances, sad ones, at my parents and she would often reach for her handkerchief in her apron pocket. I knew she was wiping her eyes, but she always pretended to be blowing her nose.

"Several months passed, and then one day I came home from school and discovered we were moving. Overnight, my father had sold his business at a great financial loss and we were moving the very next day to a small town north of Lake Ontario in the eastern part of the province. I can't begin to tell you how I felt other than confused and scared, and very angry."

The release Evelyn was beginning to feel suddenly overwhelmed her. A surge of courage replaced the haunting fears she'd lived with for so long. She stood slowly, looked with determination at her daughter, and glanced out the window at her son-in-law. "I just…I'll be right back." Evelyn turned and left the room. When she rejoined Lucy in the kitchen, she was holding a felt jewellery pouch.

Resisting the urge to lean against the counter, Evelyn returned to her kitchen chair. In her absence, Lucy had poured fresh hot chocolate into each of their cups. Again, Evelyn held the sides of her warm mug, but this time to steady her shaking hands.

"When we moved, my parents insisted we change our names. Our old ones were to remain a family secret, never to be shared under any circumstance. My young mind was convinced we were hiding from the police."

Evelyn looked up at her daughter and caught a faint smile, which slowly disappeared when Evelyn resumed her story. "But, again, I was wrong. I was given the name Evelyn. We took the surname Crawford. I was never to be called by my real name—Evlyna Chava Cohen—ever again. Chava is another name for Eve. It means life. *V'haadam yada et chava vatahar vateled et qain vatomer qaniti ish et HaShem.* That's the Hebrew translation of Genesis 4:1: 'And Adam knew Eve his wife; and she conceived, and bare Cain, and said, I have gotten a man from the Lord.'" Evelyn paused before resuming. "Lucy. I'm Jewish, and by Jewish law, so are you."

"Wha…?"

Evelyn did not look up at her daughter. Instead, she stared into her hot drink, overwhelmed at how easily and quickly she recalled the verse she had learned as a child. She forced herself to continue.

"Turned out we weren't moving by choice; we were forced to move. Lifelong friends had stopped acknowledging us, let alone talking to us. Our neighbours ignored my parents. My father's customers refused to do business with him. Overnight we had become outcasts." Evelyn raised her eyes and looked into her daughter's. "You see, Lucy, when my parents had gone out those many nights months earlier, they had been secretly going to special church meetings. It was there they claimed they had found their Messiah, that the Jesus Christ in the New Testament was *the* Messiah. They became Hebrew Christians. The night I found Bubi crying was the night they told her of their decision. I was told several weeks later, after thinking for weeks that someone was dying. At first, my grandmother and I were not terribly upset. Perhaps Grandmama more than I, but we both thought my parents would come to their senses and that this new life they were living would pass before anyone learned of their decision. We'd hoped my parents would see they were wrong and our lives would pick up where they'd left off. But that never happened. It soon became public knowledge, since my parents never hid their new belief. It was almost as if they wanted the whole world to know. They talked about it openly, all the time, to anyone who came into the bakery. Within days, my father's business suffered. His regular customers, his Jewish customers, stopped buying their bread from him. We received hate phone calls. My parents were called traitors, turncoats, even rats, and then one day my mother found a dead one nailed to the front door of our shop with a note on it, 'This will happen to you.'"

"Mom!" It was a whisper and Evelyn looked up at her daughter and saw her shudder as she wrapped her arms around herself.

Evelyn continued.

"My parent's decision to accept Jesus Christ as the Messiah forced us to move. World War II was raging in Europe, and even as

Jews were being hunted down and annihilated at the hand of Hitler, discrimination against Jews continued to grow on this side of the ocean. As a Jewish community in downtown Toronto, we'd stuck together, but when my parents accepted Jesus Christ as their Messiah, everything changed. We lost all our friends. No one at school would talk to me. Most Gentiles didn't trust us, and our Jewish neighbours avoided us as though we had the plague.

"My anger at my parents, especially my father, took root then and I never forgave them. I began to think of them as traitors myself and I refused to accept their decision. Despite my objections, the embarrassment I'd endured at school, and the painful look in Bubi's eyes, they never wavered in their belief. In their minds, they had no choice but to start over again, begin a new life somewhere else where no one would know them, where the stigma of being an Orthodox Jew was gone with a simple name change. As far as I could see it, they had turned their backs on their Jewish heritage and I never forgave them for it. I was too young to understand the hostility that had grown toward the Jewish culture and religion over the years before the war. I had lived a sheltered life. All I knew was that my parents had rejected all that they'd taught me, all that they'd believed, and how they'd lived for years. I wanted nothing to do with their new religion or their new God."

Twenty minutes later, Wil pushed open the back door, head down against the wind. He'd banged his boots against the outside wall after shovelling a path to the end of the yard for Trickster, and was welcoming a reprieve from the inclement weather.

"Well, I've finally got that job done. We'll see how long it lasts this time." Stepping inside, still covered in snow and wanting desperately to have a warm drink, he stared at the scene before him.

Lucy held something in her hands with such a sacredness that Wil stood in silence, watching, snow dripping to the floor around him. Evelyn sat with her arm around Lucy's shoulders, each woman smiling as they looked at the chain that had fallen loose from Lucy's hands.

"Look, Wil, this is my mother's," she said, and then added, "My great grandmother gave it to her when Mom was five years old." Lucy raised the necklace and let it dangle in front of her.

Wil stared in bewilderment. Mother and daughter embraced each other through their tears, each trying to talk first, while emotions ran high. Unable to make out exactly what Lucy was holding, he started to disrobe from his snowy boots and jacket, turning to the only one who was paying attention to him.

"Well Trickster, looks like mother and daughter are riding high on something very profound." At that, Lucy and Evelyn laughed, assuring him most emphatically that it was more than just profound.

The importance of Lucy's reference to a great grandmother had not missed its mark, but Wil had failed to see the shining star on the end of the gold chain.

27

For if they fall, the one will lift up his fellow:
but woe to him that is alone when he falleth;
for he hath not another to help him up.
ECCLESIASTES 4:10

"What a day! I don't know about you, but I'm exhausted." Lucy turned out the bedside light and snuggled under the eiderdown comforter. She muffled a giggle when Wil fanned his arms and legs like a child making a snow angel.

"Hey, I'm making it warm for you."

"Can you believe it, Wil? I'm Jewish! Me, Lucille Jacqueline Sherwood Douglas. I'm one of God's chosen people!"

Wil didn't respond.

Lucy smiled in the darkness as she contemplated the full impact of the news her mother had shared. Then, with restlessness winning the battle to relax, she rose from the comfort of Wil's arms, switched on the light, and wrapped a comforter around her shoulders. Cross-legged at the bottom of the bed, she nudged her husband. "Wil, talk to me. This has been a very memorable day. You can't just go to sleep and leave me *thinking*." Lucy's exasperation accelerated and Wil surrendered to his wife's poking, and yawned.

"You're right. That wasn't very sensitive of me. I mean, why would anyone want to be sleeping when they're in bed, eyes shut with the lights out? How thoughtless of me," Wil teased. He propped himself up against the headboard and ran his fingers through his hair. "You never did tell me what your mom had to say about the baby. Was she pleased about it, becoming a grandmother, I mean?"

"Pleased? You should have seen her. She was dancing around the kitchen floor with Trickster, trying to decide if Tricks was going to become an aunt when I became a mother. Can you believe that? My mother, the quiet, unemotional, private person I have known my whole life, putting on a display of such…illogical, unnatural behaviour." The way Lucy embellished her mother's reaction to her pregnancy only added to the excitement of her memory. "Sure, we used to dance in the kitchen when I was a kid, but this! You should have seen her." Lucy grabbed her knees and rocked on the end of the bed, laughing as she related the scene to her husband. "Even Trickster was yelping when Mom was twirling around. It was only when I asked her what she called her grandmother that things changed."

Lucy stopped rocking. "She's really happy about the baby, Wil, but when I asked about her grandmother's name, our conversation changed and we never got back to the baby. I'm sure we will. It was just such a tangent to go off on…but for good reasons, though," Lucy added as an afterthought and then drifted off into her own private thoughts.

"Wil, Mom told me all about her family, her parents, where she lived, and about her being Jewish. Right?"

"Right."

"She even talked about her anger at God and how she doesn't

want to have anything to do with Him. Right?

"Right again."

"Then don't you think it strange she didn't explain about Bobby and the torn two dollar bill?"

"It would never occur to her to tell you. She doesn't know you know about it. "

"True. But if Dad thought it was all right to tell me when I was just twelve, why wouldn't she tell me now that I'm an adult? While she was telling me all the things that happened, why didn't she include that story? I can't help feeling there's more. Something's missing. I can feel it."

"Be patient, Luce. If there's more, and I'm saying *if,* it's got to be up to your mother to tell you. You can't tell her you've known all these years. I think that would do more harm than good. Just leave it. All you can do is pray that… "

"And that's the other thing," Lucy interrupted, her eyes large with excitement as her thoughts tumbled out. "Look at how she quoted that verse in Genesis without blinking an eye. And look at her anger at God. That proves she believes in Him. I told her that it's hard to be angry at someone you don't believe exists, but all she did was just close her eyes and shake her head."

Lucy stood and paced across the bedroom floor pulling her comforter over her shoulders like a cape. She paused and turned to her husband before continuing.

"Don't misunderstand what I'm about to say, but I can almost understand why she'd be angry: the forced secrecy, her changed name, the whole Bobby Jenkins scene, then the loss of her babies and Dad's sudden death. She's never learned to trust God for all that comes into her life, so what can you expect? I remember the anger I had at God when Dad died, only too well. But all along, I *knew* God was there. I *knew* He existed. Mom's got nothing to fall back on. She's so determined to hate God that she's blind to any reasoning. Somehow she's got to be reached, someway." Lucy yawned.

"Come to bed, Luce. You can't solve your mother's problem overnight."

Reluctantly, Lucy put the folded comforter on the chair under the window, crawled into bed beside her husband, and turned out the light once again. "You're right, but there *is* more, Wil. I can feel it. There must be something we can do."

The sleepy grunt from her husband signaled an end to their conversation, but it was a long time before Lucy finally gave into her weariness and fell asleep.

With the dinner dishes washed and air-drying, Evelyn curled up by the fire in her semi-dark living room, wishing for company. Trickster joined her in their favourite chair by the fire and Evelyn instinctively scratched her pet's ears. Being alone had always been difficult for her, and in the years following Lewis's death, the problem had only grown worse. However, tonight was different. A restlessness, a longing had been building over the months and tonight it seemed paramount. She wondered if her friendship with Levi was part of the problem. He continued to confuse and frighten her. He floated in and out of her life like a dandelion's puffball in a spring breeze. Evelyn touched the side of her face and, despite her inner turmoil, smiled. Trying to keep up with his visits and the motives behind them often left her head spinning, and after each visit her aloneness heightened.

Considering her downcast spirit, she chided herself. "Tricks, you'd think I'd feel better after talking with Lucy." She stroked her pet absentmindedly. "And I've got a grandchild to look forward to, for goodness sake." But she didn't feel relief. There was more and Evelyn wouldn't allow the missing piece an audience. "Life's such a puzzle, Tricks. So many pieces make up the picture, but knowing where each one belongs is a big struggle. Sometimes it would be easier if we'd just leave the pieces in the box and forget about trying to figure it all out." Trickster raised her head and cocked it to one side. Evelyn laughed at her attempt to philosophize and made another effort to concentrate on a book that was fighting with Trickster for space on her lap.

In a few moments, her efforts proved hopeless. Her thoughts continued to evolve around the past several hours with her daughter and son-in-law. Lucy and Wil had left mid-afternoon, shortly after Evelyn had repeated her story to Wil. She wasn't sure how he'd taken the news, and looking back on it now, she was sorry things had turned so abruptly away from their news about the baby. "I never even heard when the baby is due, Tricks. We need to call first thing in the morning."

Trickster wagged her tail at the mention of her name, but didn't move her head until the front doorbell rang, startling them both.

"Who on earth...?" Evelyn glanced at the clock and noted the late hour: eight-fifteen.

28

Hope deferred maketh the heart sick:
but when the desire cometh, it is a tree of life.
PROVERBS 13:12

My goodness, what brings you two out on such a night?" The delight in Evelyn's voice echoed through the wind as she opened her front door. Christina and Levi stood there, smiling childlike grins. Huddled together against the wind, they pulled bags from behind their backs.

"We've been shopping," Christina exclaimed, enthusiasm oozing from each word. "I can't wait to show you what I've bought."

"What? You've been out *shopping* on a night like tonight? Lee, I'm surprised..."

"Don't look at me. You obviously don't know my mother. When her mind's set on something, nothing will budge it. Good thing the Emporium keeps late hours at Christmas time."

"Well, don't just stand there. Come in, come in."

Banging their boots on the front mat, the two shoppers stepped into the front foyer. "Are we interrupting?" Levi asked.

"Goodness no! Trickster and I were just curled up by the fire listening to the special music this season brings. Lucy and Wil were here earlier, and just a few minutes ago I found myself talking to this creature you gave me." Evelyn reached down and scratched Trickster's furry head. "You didn't mind, did you girl!" As though on cue, Evelyn's dog jumped up against her leg and welcomed the affectionate scratch.

Levi smiled as he helped Christina take her coat off. "Then you won't mind the intrusion? Mother insisted we stop."

"Really! I did?" Christina smiled up at her son's eyes and winked at Evelyn. "Well, I suppose I did, although he's not being entirely truthful. Nevertheless, I'm very happy to be the instrument by which he can tell his half-truth." Christina bowed in mock humility.

Evelyn felt her cheeks flush. Remembering her thoughts earlier in the evening, she imagined a dandelion's puffball brushing her face. To cover her embarrassment, she laughed at her friend's unique sense of humour. "You two go on in by the fire. I'll heat up the cider. I've got lots to tell you."

Evelyn saw the look exchanged between mother and son as she turned toward the closet to hang up her guests' coats. Stopping midway, she turned back to Levi, his jacket in hand. "On second thought, Lee, would you mind putting Trickster out the back for a moment? She hasn't been too excited about going out in this weather, but she has to make a visit to the backyard."

"No problem. Come on, girl, let's get this *has-to* over with."

Evelyn slipped her arm through Christina's and the two women headed for the living room already lost in a conversation that excluded Levi. "There's not much opportunity to do serious shopping in Thystle Creek, but I did manage to find some interesting things at the Emporium." Christina settled in her favourite chair by the fire. "That's quite a store your husband developed. I just love the slogan, *Why look elsewhere when SHE's got it.*" Evelyn laughed at Christina's exaggeration of the words and told her the story about Josh and how he'd won Lewis's heart, and the town's respect, as a youngster.

"Sounds like quite a young man. I hear he and Jennifer Ralston are engaged. Any word on the wedding date?

"No, but I'm sure it'll be this spring sometime. It's always beautiful here when the spring flowers are at their fullest, but then I suppose you know that, having grown up here."

Both women looked up as Levi joined them, but continued in their conversation. "I understand you sold your shares of the Emporium to Josh a few years ago."

"Yes, I felt it was the best thing to do. I found it too difficult to be involved in the store after Louie died and I knew that Louie would have gladly entrusted his business to Josh. It's turned out to be the best move for everyone. I'm still involved in the annual July picnic, but other than that, Josh has full control."

"Lee, has there been any word on the man who stopped to help Josh and Jennie?" Evelyn had been thinking of that for days, but had heard nothing.

"Yes, as a matter of fact, there is. We ran into Doc Bailey at the Emporium tonight and he mentioned they've finally tracked down the man and his son. Turns out he's moving here from out east. Quebec, I think. Widowed a couple of years back, he wants to start fresh. His name's Robert Adams—goes by Rob. His six-year-old son is B.J., short for Bradley James. They're staying in one of Mrs. Granton's guest rooms until they can find something permanent. He's a teacher and intends to approach the school board after the Christmas break for a position, even if it's just part-time to start."

The conversation continued. Nothing serious, nothing profound, and Evelyn welcomed the company. In watching Levi interact with his mother, she began to feel the same longing she had experienced earlier in the evening. Images of her own parents flashed before her competing with the sinister voice: *Don't waste your time thinking of them. Look what they did to you. You owe them nothing.*

FORGIVE!

"Evie?" Evelyn jerked her head at the sound of Levi's voice.

"Sorry, Lee." She struggled for inner composure and forced herself to focus on her own daughter. "I haven't had a chance to tell you, but Lucy and I talked today. She'd just told me... Oh, my goodness! How could I forget this? I'm going to be a grandmother! Lucy told me this morning."

"A baby!" The exclamation came in unison. Evelyn nodded and continued on a lighter note, sharing the excitement of the morning. "I was dancing around the kitchen with Trickster yelping in my arms, but before I could get any more details, the conversation took a turn and we never got back to it. So I can't even give you her due date."

"What wonderful news, but what did you mean, *it took a turn*?" Christina had been dozing under the influence of the fire. Evelyn's announcement brought her upright in the chair, causing the afghan that had been draped across her legs to slip to the floor.

Over fresh hot cider, Evelyn recounted the details of her visit with Lucy and Wil, right down to the startled look on Wil's face as he stood watching them inside the back door.

"I'm sure we must have been quite a spectacle, that poor man, walking in on two rather emotional women. He must have wondered... well, it doesn't matter. He would never have guessed what was going on."

"How did he respond?" Levi asked, concern etched in his voice.

"Not sure. He was quiet. But it was Lucy's words that have left me a little confused."

"What did she say, Evie?" The gentleness of Christina's voice encouraged Evelyn to continue.

"She said, 'I can't believe it, Wil. I've got the best of both worlds.' That's all. But she didn't direct her remarks to me and I didn't feel comfortable enough to ask what she meant. It was almost as though they were sharing something private, something special, and I didn't want to intrude."

Silence filled the room. Seconds stretched into long minutes and only the crackle of the fire broke the stillness. Even Trickster remained quiet, content to curl up on the afghan at Christina's feet. Finally, Levi stood and stretched. "Well, Mother, I think we need to be getting home. It's been a long day and tomorrow will be here all too soon. You need to ... "

"Please, Levi, stop mothering me. I've managed quite nicely to get to be my age without you doting over me. If I get tired, I'll just follow Trickster's example and curl up and go to sleep." Turning to Evelyn, her voice softened. "Evie, would you let me help you understand Lucy's remarks? It's important you give me permission, because without it, I would be intruding on your privacy and I would never want to be guilty of that. I value you as a friend and wouldn't want to put a barrier between us. But I think I can shed some light, some hope, and I don't doubt Lee could as well." Christina reached for her son's hand and squeezed it. Her eyes glistened under Levi's understanding smile. "Sorry, dear. Didn't mean to be so sharp."

The clock on the mantel chimed ten o'clock.

29

And Jesus said, For judgment I am come into this world, that they which see not might see; and that they which see might be made blind.
JOHN 9:39

Evelyn's willingness to listen had been given through a simple smile. Her desire to understand Lucy overcame the fear of further conversation.

Christina turned from her curled position and faced her friend. "Evie, are you familiar with prayer?"

Evelyn squirmed inwardly. She wasn't sure where this would take her. "Yes. I'm aware of the concept. Lewis often told me he was praying for me. Sometimes I would hear him through the closed door to the den. I never believed in it; I still don't."

Christina smiled at Evelyn's honesty. "Lucy said she had the best of both worlds. Correct?"

Evelyn nodded.

"One of the *worlds* Lucy was referring to involves prayer. You see, dear, when Lewis prayed, or when anyone of us prays, we are daring to approach the Creator of all beings, Holy God. But He *is* holy and can't look on us because of the sin that fills this world. It says in Habakkuk, a book in the Old Testament, that God has pure eyes and cannot look on evil, cannot look on iniquity, what the Bible calls *sin*. But out of His unconditional love, he provided a way for us to go to Him in prayer, through His Son, Jesus Christ. Knowing *this* is one of Lucy's worlds."

Evelyn stirred, noticeably this time. She glanced over at Levi, who was watching his mother. Evelyn tried to understand. *Unconditional love?* She only knew of a God who judged. Who demanded. Who punished. Who allowed killing of the innocent. But a God who loved, unconditionally? Her attention was drawn back to Christina when a second question was put to her.

"Have you ever read the Bible, Evie?" Christina paused while Evelyn shook her head.

"No, I'm only familiar with the Talmud. I saw my father read it when I was a child. That was before he ... changed."

"If you were to read the Bible as a whole book, you would read in the New Testament that Jesus Christ was born to a Jewish family which was in a direct line from Abraham, Isaac and Jacob, men who make up a very important part of the Torah. When you told Lucy she was Jewish, she immediately understood that she was part of *that* family, that she was one of God's chosen people, the Jews."

Evelyn stared at Christina, her confusion mounting; but with a growing desire to learn more, her silence gave Christina freedom to continue.

"Until today, Lucy has lived a life as a Gentile, but a Christian Gentile who accepted Jesus Christ as God's Son when she was a little girl. In her Gentile world, He is her Saviour. She has learned today that she is fully Jewish through you, and in her new Jewish world, Jesus Christ is her Messiah. She is a Hebrew Christian."

Evelyn listened. The logic was there, she reasoned, but it was all too much, too fast. *Gentile. Saviour. Hebrew Christian. Messiah.* She found it difficult to comprehend. Was Christina saying that a person could be both Gentile and Jew? Weren't all Gentiles Christian?

Her own memories of Jewish life surfaced. The holy days that made their holidays different from the Gentiles', the special food blessed by the Rabbi, the many laws that proved impossible to keep. She remembered the mindless persecution against Jews that increased as a result of the war and the fear that someone would eventually find out she was Jewish. As Christina talked, for a fleeting moment Evelyn had a glimmer of understanding of what her parents had chosen to believe, but it became lost among everything else she was hearing. *What could all of this mean for Lucy?* It all seemed so contradictory, so wrong.

"Are you saying it's like Lucy is living in two worlds of two different beliefs?" Her question came quite simply, much like a child wanting desperately to know what was right and what was wrong.

Levi took her hands. "Yes and no." He smiled. "Lucy has lived most of her life as a Gentile Christian, going to a small church, worshipping God in a simple yet satisfying and meaningful way. That will never change for her. But now she's learned that she's Jewish. Will her worship change? Not likely. No doubt she will remain who she is, but to know she is one of God's *chosen people*... beyond the shock and no doubt some confusion, she must feel very honoured."

Evelyn withdrew her hands from Levi's, not because she didn't feel comfortable, but because she didn't want him to feel her trembling. She stood and walked to the fireplace, head down, and quoted her daughter. "The best of both worlds." She turned to her friends, eyes filling with tears. "I'd never have thought she would react this way. I honestly believed she would hate me. For me to tell her she was Jewish, well, in my mind it was the same thing as receiving a sentence for a crime she never committed. I truly thought she would hate me."

Levi went to where Evelyn stood and turned her to face him. "Evelyn, the last thing we want to do is confuse you. Perhaps it will help if we took a more neutral ground. Come, sit down and let me tell you more about my father."

Christina patted the seat beside her, but Evelyn sat alone, with Trickster. The comfort and warmth of the dog on her lap relaxed her somewhat, and Trickster gave Evelyn an opportunity to mask her shaky hands as she stroked her dog.

"My father used to say, 'I'm only here for a short while, so I have to make my time count for something.'" Levi smiled at his mother as he quoted his father and then turned back to Evelyn. "I used to think he meant being a teacher. But when he became a Hebrew Christian, his expression took on new meaning."

There's that phrase again, Hebrew Christian, Evelyn thought, twisting slightly in her chair.

"My father struggled with the years he'd spent denying Jesus Christ as the long-awaited Messiah for the Jews and believed in his heart that he had to make up for lost time. The testimony of his faith in Jesus became his obsession in life, a good obsession."

Despite her mounting turmoil, Evelyn smiled weakly at his choice of words.

"Both he and Mother opened their home and welcomed anyone who wanted to hear their story." He paused before he said the word. "*Haimishe*. It's Hebrew for *hominess* or *comfort*."

"Yes, I know," Evelyn whispered. It had been many years since she'd heard that word and hearing it calmed her.

"Of course you would." Levi's look was gentle as he hesitated for a moment. "Anyway, that's what our home was, *haimishe*." He laughed at the memory and smiled in his mother's direction. "Mom and Dad openly shared their belief with anyone who showed an interest, certainly to any Jewish person, over *challah* and *rugulach* or *schnecken*. Remember the potato *latkes* you'd make, Mother? You still love to get into the kitchen and work the braid on the *challah*." He winked at his mother, who smiled at his teasing. "Before my father died, a small group of Hebrew Christians formed a church that is thriving today. The effects of his faith in the true Messiah are still evident long after my father's death."

Evelyn listened as Levi continued to reminisce in the presence of his mother. She thought at times he had forgotten his mother was there, but then he would turn to her with a smile, warm and loving, or a nod in her direction. His stories helped, but Evelyn continued to struggle with the change in his father's beliefs and wrestled with the understanding of *Hebrew Christian*.

Evelyn rose, easing Trickster aside in the chair. "Didn't people look at you both differently? I mean, your husband, your father was such a recognized man in the community. Surely there was some reaction when he turned his back on all that he had believed...and taught," Evelyn added with growing frustration. "One day he believed one way and the next day he believed entirely the opposite." Evelyn turned to the quiet woman sitting by the fire, seemingly engrossed in the beauty of the flickering flames. "Christina? He was your husband. You knew his beliefs when you married him. You even relinquished anything you had believed in before and became a Jew yourself. How did you just walk away from all that you had come to believe simply because your husband had changed his mind? Were you willing to sacrifice your friends, your *life*? And what is this *faith* you speak of?" The pleading in her voice matched her desire to understand, but her confusion was taking hold and Evelyn sank again in her chair, this time putting Trickster on the floor.

"A quick answer is, yes, we lost friends, many friends, and it's not enough just to say it was *difficult* to walk away from our Jewish beliefs, but we knew in our hearts that we had to make a sacrifice in order to follow the teachings of Jesus. As to your question regarding faith, it certainly is hard to explain faith, but faith is what it takes to receive understanding. 'In the beginning, God…'" Christina quoted the first words of the Bible. "Evie, it takes a God-given faith to accept these words. If you can't believe these and accept that the God in the beginning is the same God today who encompasses love and mercy, judgement and worship all at once, it's impossible to believe anything beyond them." Christina's words were soft.

"Perhaps this will help," she continued. "There's a story in the New Testament about a blind man who had been blind his whole life. He was known by the people in his town as a beggar, sitting by the city gates with his hand outstretched, waiting for someone to put food in it. One day Jesus came by and made a paste of mud and put it on the man's eyes and then told him to go and bathe in a certain pool. When the man did, he came out of the water *seeing*." Christina paused and leaned forward slightly. "It took a God-given faith for this blind man to obey, but when he did, he recognized who Jesus really was." Leaning back in her seat, Christina closed her eyes for a moment.

"My Jacob was young when he found this story. Feeding his passion to learn of the world's religions, he exposed himself to beliefs and foundational truths of many other religions, and certainly many things he would never have believed in, such as this story. He was intrigued, at first. After rereading it several times, he had many questions, but he was the teacher who was supposed to have all the answers." At that remark, Christina extended her chest, a pantomime of a pompous person, puffed up and arrogant, but not for a moment negating her love for her husband. "He shared the story with me and when I questioned what he was going to do about it he said, 'Nothing. I'm just going to forget about it.' And he did. He didn't know how to explain this miracle, so he shut it from his mind and never returned to it, not until after he had retired."

Levi rose and stood behind his mother, his hand on her shoulder.

"One night, shortly after he'd packed up all his books from his library at the synagogue and brought them home, I found him sitting in the middle of our little den, reading. It was late at night. I'd already gone to bed and had awakened to discover he was still up. When I approached him, he looked up at me with tears falling down his face. Alarmed, I bent down, thinking he was ill. He just looked at me and said, 'I've missed it. All these years, I've missed it,' and he broke down and wept."

Evelyn watched Christina reach for her hanky and dry her eyes. Levi stood motionless. The fire crackled. The mantel clock ticked.

"What had he missed?" Evelyn whispered.

Christina recited the verse with her eyes closed. "'And Jesus said, For judgment I am come into this world, that they which see not might see; and that they which see might be made blind.'" Opening her eyes, she looked at Evelyn. "It's found in the New Testament, the book of John."

Evelyn lowered her head. It was full and she couldn't imagine hearing more, yet some unknown Spirit prompted her. "What does it mean?"

Christina turned to Levi, who continued for her. "The first part of the verse means that Jesus came to this world to bring clarity to everything. He brought light, or sight, just like he did for the blind man. That man received physical sight and then as he began to recognize

Jesus for who He was, he received spiritual sight. Jesus came to help those who had never had their eyes opened, to help them understand the truth of God and His Word. The second part of the verse tore my father apart. 'They which see might be made blind.' It told him that Jesus came to expose the arrogance, pride, and ignorance of the self-righteous Pharisees, and for the first time my father saw himself for what he was: in his own words, 'a conceited Pharisee.' He thought he had all the answers and after reading this verse and those that surrounded it, he was terrified. His discovery of Jesus as the Messiah, the Promised One of Israel was not long after that and Mom and I were not far behind.

"Dad used to quote another verse, in his own way: 'The eyes of my understanding have been enlightened.' He asked to have it shared at his funeral and to be sure to add that he was born a Jew and died a *complete* one, one who had found the true Messiah.

"And now we come full circle, back to Lucy. Indeed, she does have the best of both worlds." Levi's remark brought a silence, interrupted only by the chiming of the mantel clock on the midnight hour.

The evening ended with hugs and promises. Christina invited Evelyn to join them for the Christmas Eve service. Out of politeness, Evelyn promised she would consider it, but felt she needed to have some time to think. She promised Levi that if she became burdened with more questions, she would talk to him or his mother. "But I need to tell Lucy about our conversation," Evelyn said with more courage than she felt. Christina and Levi agreed, but Evelyn struggled inwardly with how to tell her and what to say about the invitation.

30

The Lord hath appeared of old unto me, saying,
Yea, I have loved thee with an everlasting love:
therefore with lovingkindness have I drawn thee.
Jeremiah 31:3

The buzz of greetings and best wishes for the season filled the air like an orchestra warming up before a performance. Voices escalated in volume, demanding to be heard, each with its own story of importance. Muffled in the background of this growing orchestration, the organ played softly, a stark contrast to its environment.

Evelyn sat with her daughter and watched people congratulate Lucy and Wil on their news of a coming child, and some turned in stunned silence when they saw Evelyn sitting beside her daughter. If she hadn't been so nervous, Evelyn would have laughed at people's reactions. "They look at me as though I have two heads," she whispered to her daughter. Lucy hugged her mother and smiled.

There was no way Evelyn could explain to her daughter her inner fears, the uncomfortable feeling that was growing by the minute. The only time she'd been in a church was for Lewis's funeral, apart from slipping into the back pew when Cliff Moses died. When it came to worshipping, all she could relate to was the synagogue she attended as a child, and that was a long time ago.

Evelyn watched as people mingled, chatted, laughed and hugged one another. Contrary to her known tradition, men sat with women and the children seemed to be right in the middle of everything. Some were even in pyjamas, ready to be tucked into bed "before Santa can come," she heard some parents say.

"Hello, Evie."

Evelyn turned abruptly and almost bumped into Levi as he bent forward to greet her. "Hi."

"Nervous?"

"You have no idea!" Her lips quivered as she tried to smile, but she found Levi's look gentle and reassuring.

"You'll be fine."

"Hello, Evelyn, nice to see you." Evelyn turned to face Helen Broughton, but not before acknowledging Levi's mother who sat beside Levi.

More smiles were directed her way and then another voice drew Evelyn's attention to the side aisle.

"Evelyn Sherwood! Well, I'll be. I'd never have thought..."

"Hello, Mae." Evelyn smiled at her neighbour, imagining Mae's phone call to her daughter that afternoon reporting that "Evelyn Sherwood was in church for the first time since she moved to Thystle Creek. Can you believe that?" Or something to that effect.

The booming voice brought everyone's attention to the front as Pastor Cribbs welcomed friends, families and any visitors. Lucy nudged her mother under the watchful eye of many in the surrounding pews.

The singing was pleasant, non-threatening, and Evelyn began to relax. Levi's presence sitting behind her helped, and the comfort she felt as his voice boomed over her shoulder when the congregation sang surprised her. But the comfort was short-lived. As the pastor led the congregation in a prayer of celebration over the birth of Jesus, her thoughts raced back to a childhood memory long forgotten, and the voice of her father filled her head, drowning out everything around her. *Adonai, Adonai El rachum v'chanun, erech apayim, v'rav chesed v'emet, notzer chesed la'lafim, noseh avon vafesha v'chata'ah v'nakeh.* Evelyn suppressed a shudder as the memory raced through her mind. *The Lord, the Lord of compassion, Who offers grace and is slow to anger, Who is full of loving kindness and trustworthiness, Who assures love for a thousand generations, Who forgives iniquity, transgression, and misdeed and Who grants pardon.*

Loving kindness…forgives…pardon, reverberated in Evelyn's head. *Can this be the same God Lewis had talked about, prayed to?* Evelyn squeezed her eyes tightly. The words of her father speaking of a loving God echoed relentlessly in her head. She'd forgotten! In her anger she'd forgotten about the God her father had prayed to. She'd forgotten the words he'd used. *Compassionate. Loving. Trusting. Forgiving.* She'd been blaming God for so long that a precious childhood memory had been lost. Anger had absorbed her, and now she sat in a church for the first time and came face-to-face with what she'd turned her back on.

It was too much. Evelyn pressed her hand against Lucy's arm and whispered. With Lucy's house key in her hand, she slipped out of the row and quietly walked toward the back door. Concerned eyes followed her, none the least of which were Levi's and Christina's. The last thing she heard as she opened the church door was a startling declaration from the pastor as he began his message: "Not many of us can trace our heritage back to God's chosen people, the Jewish nation, but as Gentiles we can also receive the blessing that was offered first to the Jews and then to the Gentiles through the gift of the Messiah."

Now, weeks later, long after the holiday season had come and gone, the minister's words still echoed in Evelyn's head. Looking back, she thought the decision to go to church with her daughter on Christmas Eve would be difficult, but possible. She had not been prepared for what she'd heard. Evelyn shuddered, remembering... *the blessing that was offered first to the Jews and then to the Gentiles through the gift of the Messiah.* She'd repeated the words for days, and even now she was unable to bring closure to the emotional impact they'd had on her.

Retiring for the evening, she stumbled over three boxes of Christmas decorations in the darkened hallway. *Hope Wil can put this stuff in the attic for me soon. In my state of mind, I could break a leg.* She laughed at her near-accident and foolish thinking, glad of the momentary distraction. Thinking of Wil, Evelyn's thoughts turned to her daughter and she recalled the evening following the Christmas Eve service. *It had been nice to get out and meet with people,* Evelyn thought as she straightened the pile of boxes.

Levi and his mother had been invited back to Lucy and Wil's home, along with Allen Bailey and the Broughtons. Evelyn had gone ahead of them when she unexpectedly left the service, and by the time they had arrived, she had relaxed with a warm cup of tea and was able to enjoy the rest of the evening. And it had been a nice evening. No one had mentioned Evelyn's early departure; rather, stories had been shared about past Christmases and family traditions. Everyone roared with laughter when Wil had dramatized the family tradition of waiting at the top of the stairs for his father to be dressed *and* shaven before anyone could go downstairs on Christmas morning.

"Just picture this. Here we are, all four of us sitting at the top of the stairs like high-strung horses waiting at the gate to bolt at the sound of the gun. Still in our pyjamas—I was probably still in diapers—waiting for our father to shave." Wil's mocking disgust fuelled the story and added to the humour for his captive audience. "Can you imagine doing that to your children? My mother had no part of it. In fact, she sat with us, waiting impatiently. What treachery! But it was done every year and... " turning to his wife, he crossed his heart and promised, "Lucy, I swear I will never do that to our children."

Everyone had applauded and then broke into hysteria when Wil had slyly added, "Besides, we don't have any stairs in this house."

She chuckled out loud remembering the scene with her son-in-law, aware that Trickster had raised her head from her bed under the window in response to the noise. She looked at her pet and sighed a feeling of gratitude to Levi for giving her Trickster. She considered going over and giving her pet an affectionate hug, but knew that it would mean a trip downstairs and a visit to the back of the yard. "Better let sleeping dogs lie," she whispered, grinning at how perfectly the old saying fit the scene before her, grateful her pet had fallen back to sleep.

Evelyn reached for the Bible lying on her bedside table. Much to her amazement, Levi had given it to her as a Christmas gift. He'd included a letter indicating that he'd marked certain passages in the Old Testament, passages that his father had discovered and had been amazed that they'd never been shared in any readings at the synagogue. "Jeremiah 31:3 speaks of God's everlasting love," he'd written, and had included a notation he'd copied from his father's Bible: *A breath of fresh air*. Psalm 22 had a marker in it, as well as Isaiah 53. In his note he'd encouraged her to read these chapters when she was ready to learn more about Jesus Christ as the Messiah for the nation of Israel.

Evelyn leaned further over her night table and picked up the notebook that had accompanied her gift. "For your thoughts," Levi had said, and as she scanned the pages, she was amazed at the thoughts that had accumulated over the past few weeks.

> December 25. Christmas Day. Lee gave me a Bible tonight. It terrifies me. Just holding it seems overwhelming, intimidating. Does he really expect me to read it? Why would he give it to me in front of Lucy and Wil and Christina?
>
> December 31. Can't seem to open the Bible. It just lies by my bed. I look at it and feel guilty. Where did this guilt come from? Perhaps in the New Year.
>
> January 1. Christina asked if I had any questions about what I've read. I didn't have the heart to tell her I haven't read anything. I hope she doesn't keep asking me, although she was very gentle. Not surprising. She's a very gracious woman.
>
> January 2. Where is God when it hurts? A new year and I'm still struggling. I've tried to read what Lucy suggested. I don't think of God as my shepherd, yet the thought of having him on my side... At times the pain is so deep, I don't think I can see past it.
>
> January 5. Genesis 1:1. *In the beginning God...* Christina said I needed to believe in this before I could go any further. I'm having a hard time with it.
>
> January 9. John 3:16. Lee said in his note at Christmas that this verse would help me get started, but I don't understand how a God of love could give up his only son

> and then just let him die. But then again, he let Bobby die... and my babies... and Louie. Is that what a God of love does? Is that how he shows his love, by letting people die? I can't believe in that kind of God.
>
> January 12. I'm just opening the Bible and letting the pages fall where they will. Another verse. Acts 13:38, and more confusion. "Through this man is preached the forgiveness of sin." What man? Jesus? Will he forgive me? Can I trust him for my future? Do I have a future with Lee? Would he love me despite my doubts, my fears, my... secrets? Do I dare love again?

Dare to love again? Did I really write that? Deep in thought, Evelyn reached for the light and clicked the switch. Darkness settled around her. Her eyes adjusted. Despite all that she had read in her journal, despite the questioning thoughts centred around Levi, in the quietness of her room she could still hear the pastor's voice: "The blessing offered first to the Jews and then to the Gentiles through the gift of the Messiah." Sitting up, she turned on the light and lifted her Bible from the table. Trickster stirred but plunked down, disinterested. Evelyn looked for the note Levi had given her and scanned the pages until she found what she was looking for. Checking the contents page in the front of her Bible, she turned to Isaiah 53, and snuggled down into her pillows to read.

An hour passed before the covers of the Bible were closed and it was placed back on the table. Reaching for the light once again, Evelyn mentally repeated the verse that had leapt off the page: *"Surely he hath borne our grief and carried our sorrows." I wish Lewis was here.* The thought surprised her, but she nodded her head in the dark at the next thought. *He'd have the answers for me. He'd be so happy knowing I was at least curious about his Jesus. I'll look for his Bible tomorrow. Maybe he wrote notes in it like Levi's father.*

Evelyn fell asleep refusing to acknowledge the face of one who remained in the shadows. She had fought and won the battle to forget, unaware a new battle hovered in the wings.

PART FIVE

31

Then I will give you rain in due season,
and the land shall yield her increase,
and the trees of the field shall yield their fruit.
LEVITICUS 26:4

The serious threat of further winter storms diminished. The east-facing side of Aspen Avenue benefited from the warmth of the morning sun, and mud puddles grew next to homes where spring flowers, waiting like restless giants, were anxious to break the surface. When the melting accompanied the spring rains, it was difficult to appreciate the promise of warmer, drier weather, yet the folk of Thystle Creek recognized that it was all part of the seasonal change and they welcomed the reprieve from a long winter, despite the dampness.

The steady dripping from the eaves may have been annoying to some, but for Evelyn the *thump, thump, thump* of water dripping from the edges of her rooftop held promise for warmer weather. She knew it meant being in her garden soon and implementing the new ideas she had envisioned over the winter. Levi had laughed when she'd insisted he listen and look at her makeshift drawings. Indeed, she had plans, and even though Lucy's wedding last summer had prompted Evelyn to be overzealous in her gardening, this year's changes would only be an asset. She could foresee long hours in her garden, a welcome diversion from the struggles and thoughts that had been haunting her for months, and focusing on the beauty that surrounded her would also be a good distraction from the voice that threatened her all too often.

With the anticipation growing, Evelyn found it difficult waiting for the weather to break and winter to say its final goodbye. And she knew she wasn't alone in her restlessness. Trickster was anxious to romp in the yard again, unhampered by mounds of snow. Her good-natured temperament had taken a back seat of late and Evelyn felt sorry for her. "Short-legged dogs and five foot snow drifts certainly don't get along very well, do they Tricks?" Evelyn chuckled as Trickster stuck her head out the back door only to receive a large drop of cold water from the eaves above the door. Braving the elements, she edged out further into the yard, cautiously exploring the familiar pathway that was growing wider with each passing day. Evelyn watched from the kitchen window, keeping her hands free from touching her clothing. Covered in flour, she had been in the middle of making pastry when Trickster had demanded an immediate exit. "You won't last long out there, no matter how much you want to stay outdoors." And, almost in response to her words, Trickster did an about-face and trotted most decidedly back to the warmth and dryness of the kitchen, her necessary job completed.

The phone rang just as Evelyn finished wiping Trickster's feet and hanging the soiled dog-towel on the hook by the back door.

"Hi Mom, it's me, Luce."

"And so it is. Who else would be calling me 'Mom'?" Evelyn

teased and smiled, remembering how healthy her daughter looked in her sixth month of pregnancy. "How are you feeling?"

"Not bad. Have to admit the first few months weren't the greatest, though. Glad they're over with. I really do feel good now. Baby's not too big yet, so I am fairly comfortable, although from what I've been told—leave it to Mae to give me the full details—the last month is not so great."

Evelyn shook her head at the mention of their neighbour. "Mae means well, Lucy, but sometimes her mouth forgets to listen to her brain and she doesn't think before she speaks. Just remember, when all is said and done, you'll forget any pain and discomfort you may experience when you hold that precious baby in your arms."

"I know. It's just that people give you too much information thinking they're doing you a favour. The other day Patsy Dunford told me all about her labour. Thirty-two hours! All grunt work, and Jimmy was her fourth! I suppose it's only natural that people think they have to tell me all the possible problems that can happen when you deliver. Mom... you still there?"

"I'm sorry, dear. What were you saying?"

"I was just saying that Patsy was talking about the many problems people have giving birth, that sometimes... oh, Mom, I'm so sorry! Talk about not thinking before speaking."

"Don't worry about it, dear." Evelyn tried to sound undaunted, despite her inner struggle. "How are plans coming for the party?"

"Pretty good. Actually that's why I called, to find out if you're still coming tonight. I've been planning this party for so long that Josh and Jennie's rescue is almost old news. No more threatening storms according to the weatherman, so we shouldn't have to postpone it anymore. Thought I should let you know there's about a dozen people gonna be here, but you know most of them. You okay with that?"

Lucy's question was simply put, but Evelyn recognized her daughter's unspoken concern and her desperate attempt to undo any harm her earlier comment may have caused.

"I'll be fine, Lucy. I'm looking forward to meeting the man who saved Josh and Jennie from serious harm. Have you heard if he was able to get on at the school?"

"Actually, he's filling in for Nora Davidge, maybe for the rest of the school year. Seems her twin sister in the States is facing some major surgery and Miss Davidge is needed to help with her sister's three children until their mother is on her feet again."

"That's good news for our Good Samaritan. Not so sure about Nora's family."

"Let's hope it's not serious. Well, I'd better go. We'll keep the evening simple—cups and saucers and small plates for some snacking food and crunchies. Jennie is bringing a tray of cheese and crackers. I've made some great meatballs and sauce. Doc Bailey is bringing some of his famous bread, Christina is baking some Jewish cinnamon sticks, and I'm counting on a couple of pies from you." Lucy added.

"They're almost ready to go into the oven. Apple and raisin, is that okay? But I need to get back to them before the day gets away from me."

Lucy's parting words echoed in the quiet kitchen. *You'll be fine, tonight, Mom. They're all your friends.* Evelyn smiled at her daughter's genuine care for her well-being. Lucy's innocent reference to the difficulties some face with childbirth had all but choked Evelyn, and she felt sorry for her daughter, knowing how upset Lucy would be feeling long after she'd hung up the phone. Evelyn forced herself to focus on her pies, humming an old tune to keep the long-silent voice from making its presence known. If it managed to do that, she would not be going to a welcoming party for Rob Adams and his son B.J., even if those attending *were* her friends.

"I'm sure Mom's okay, Lee, but maybe you could call and offer to pick her up just to make sure she'll be here. I don't like doing this sort of thing, but I think I may have upset her earlier when I was talking about... well never mind *what*. She tried to mask her feelings, but she didn't succeed. Do you mind calling her?"

Levi had just returned from a day with Allen Bailey, meeting his patients, and being introduced to them by Allen as their new doctor. It had been a long day, but he was looking forward to a party at the Douglas's for Rob and his son, and assured Lucy that he would look after her mother and get her to the party. Levi welcomed any opportunity to spend with Evelyn. *I wonder what was said that triggered this sudden concern from Lucy*?

Levi listened to the phone ringing and smiled when the voice at the other end greeted him warmly. "Thought you might need a lift to the party tonight."

"Did Lucy send in the cavalry, thinking I would chicken out?"

Levi thought he was being subtle, but felt rather sheepish at Evelyn's response. "Was I that obvious? Sorry, Evie, just responding to a concerned daughter. You okay? Anything I can do to help?

"Yes, you were. Yes, I am. And no, I'll be fine."

Levi appreciated Evelyn's attempt at humour, especially when he was convinced she was covering up something.

"Great. Nothing more to be said then. But can I still pick you up? Seven o'clock sound okay?"

"I'll be ready, with bells on."

Levi hung up the phone and stood with his hand resting on the receiver, staring at his reflection in the mirror over the mantel. *What is it about that woman that brings my heart to my throat and turns my face the colour of burning coals?* He turned and found his mother grinning at him like a young schoolgirl who's bursting to tell a secret.

"What!" Levi exclaimed, defensively.

"What? You're asking me? You can see the colour of your face. Don't you think that explains my grin? How's she doing?"

"Who?"

"Oh, really, Levi, I may be old, but I ain't blind. I know love when I see it."

The twinkle in his mother's eye weakened Levi's resolve so much that he laughed out loud.

"Mother, you are so right! Am I that obvious?"

"Certainly to this mother; not so sure about Lucy's. Now, as I asked a moment ago, how is Evelyn? I'm looking forward to seeing her at Lucy's party tonight."

"Well, Lucy just called and asked me to drop by and pick up her mother. Something was said earlier today that caused Lucy some concern. She wondered if her mother was all right or if she might be looking for a reason not to come. Seems she's fine. At least she sounded fine over the phone and I... we'll be picking her up around seven."

"Why don't you drop me off early so I can help Lucy? Then you can go on over and get her without me. You know the old saying, 'Two's company, three's a crowd.' You two never seem to have much time alone. Besides, I hate being the fifth wheel, or in this case, the third."

Levi laughed at his mother's attempt at playing cupid, and he loved her even more for it. But she was right, as usual. He seldom had time alone with Evelyn and he often wished that they could just have a date, the two of them. He knew how much his mother enjoyed Evelyn's company, though, and hated the thought of leaving her home alone while he visited Evelyn. On the other hand, he knew that if a friendship with Evelyn was to develop into something more, they needed to spend time together as a couple.

"Mother, have you seen any change in Evie's interest in spiritual matters? I mean, has she asked you to help her understand anything she might have read?" The question sobered the moment, and before his mother had an opportunity to answer him, Levi withdrew it. "I'm sorry. That's not fair. Besides, Evie's got to be the one to broach the subject. We've pointed her in the right direction. I suppose all we can do is keep praying and wait until she's ready."

"Levi, Evelyn is on a journey. There are a lot of hills and valleys ahead for her and it's just as well she doesn't know about them. It may take months of reading, questioning, maybe even denying, but if she knows all that is ahead of her, she may regress..." Levi opened his mouth to interrupt his mother, but Christina raised her hand to silence him. "Yes, Levi, she may regress behind her wall, in her protected space where, if she feels any love for you, it will remain hidden and any secrets she has will remain secure. But, to answer your question, no, she has never spoken to me about receiving the Bible from you or about anything she may have read in it, but that doesn't mean she isn't reading it or that she won't eventually ask questions. Just be a good friend. Don't press her and don't expect from her what she is unable to give. In her own time and in her own way, she'll come around. While God takes her on her journey of discovery, she will need a good friend in you, a sounding board, if you will, someone who will not judge her and bring further guilt on her already guilty conscience. Be patient, son. God has His own timetable for Evelyn and He will work it out when He's ready. Just keep praying."

Christina left Levi standing by the phone looking at his watch.

32

And thou shalt rejoice in thy feast, thou,
and thy son, and thy daughter, and thy manservant,
and thy maidservant, and... the stranger...
DEUTERONOMY 16:14

I'd like to propose a toast," Josh Graham said, raising his glass, "to my new friend and guardian angel, Rob Adams. Thank you for stopping, for caring, for looking after us in a time of great need." Josh reached for Jennie and drew her to his side. "You truly personified a Good Samaritan, and we'll be forever grateful. Here's to a brave man and his son, B.J. Thank you from the bottom of our hearts for possibly saving our lives."

Evelyn quivered slightly. For a moment, no one moved. The depth of sincerity with which Josh had spoken penetrated those who knew the sacrifice her husband had made to save Josh years earlier, but her husband's name was not spoken. No one volunteered to share the story, not even for the benefit of Rob Adams.

"Hear, hear!" Allen Bailey lifted his glass and broke the silence, bringing a quiet sigh from Evelyn. He touched Josh's glass and then turned to reach for Evelyn's hand, tenderness written all over his face. The camaraderie that followed eased any discomfort that may have been felt as everyone followed suit, clinking glasses, patting Rob on the back, and shaking hands with six-year-old B.J. The atmosphere lifted from somber silence to hearty thanks.

"Tell us again, Rob—for the benefit of those not knowing—what made you stop?" It was obvious to Evelyn that Josh was not about to let his new friend off the hook.

"Well, actually, it was my son here, B.J." Rob acknowledged his son with obvious pride. "He'd been sleeping in the backseat, slept through most of the storm. When he woke up, we were passing the four-corners intersection and he noticed a light blinking in the snow mound just off the road."

Jennie Ralston slipped her once-injured arm under Josh's.

"...and I said he must have been imagining something or maybe it was some kind of a reflection. But B.J. insisted, so I stopped the car. I couldn't turn around with the trailer attached; the snow had left some pretty big ruts. I was worried that someone would plow into the back of us, but I knew I had to take a chance and look, even if it turned out to be nothing."

Rob's audience had stopped eating. Some leaned against a wall. Others sat while Rob's voice penetrated an unnatural silence. Evelyn listened from an armchair in the living room.

"I walked back to the intersection, telling B.J. to stay put, and found Josh's car turned on its side—the passenger side—and partially buried in a snow mound. I couldn't open the driver's door until I cleared away the snow. When I looked in the window, I saw two people—Josh and Jennie, as it turned out—unconscious. The car was still running so I made sure the exhaust pipe was clear of snow and then ran back to my car to get B.J. and a shovel. I knew I was taking a chance exposing him to the storm, but I didn't like the idea of leaving him alone in the car. Besides, I knew I couldn't dig them out alone.

"The storm had blown for hours, but it had started to let up just before we came upon the accident, and the full moon provided enough light for us to dig. It took us a long time. I knew I was cold and I didn't want to think about how cold B.J. was." At that, Rob jostled his son's head and gave him a big hug. His audience remained fully engrossed in his story, especially Evelyn, who watched B.J. with motherly affection.

"I heard moaning coming from the car. Jennie was awake and in a lot of pain. Josh was still unconscious and all B.J. and I could do was keep digging. Finally, we got the door open and the cold air helped wake up Josh. He wasn't noticeably hurt. Some bruises, but no broken bones, just really groggy; but Jennie was in trouble. We managed to get her to our car and then I drove as fast as the weather and the tow-behind trailer let me to Dr. Bailey's house. Fortunately, Josh was conscious and able to give me directions. And, well, the rest you know."

Quiet *wows* and *whews* filtered through the house in a domino effect as person after person released their breath until Lucy broke the tension by offering coffee and tea and homemade pie.

Jennie walked over to B.J. and planted a kiss right on the top of his head, and everyone roared with laughter when B.J. ducked under the table, taking refuge behind the edges of the tablecloth. "That's for saving my life, big guy." The laughter heightened when the adults heard an audible *yuk* coming from beneath the table.

Evelyn smiled at the bantering between Jennie and B.J. and appreciated the ease with which everyone interacted, inwardly acknowledging that this evening represented her first social event in many months. *I don't think I've been to a party since Lucy's wedding, apart from coming here on Christmas Eve.* She looked around and realized how fortunate she was to have friends who had stuck by her, despite her obvious preference to be alone.

Helen Broughton was one of them. She had been so kind on Christmas Eve at church and then later at Lucy's. Evelyn smiled, remembering Helen's comment: "Evelyn, I heard Lee call you Evie. Would you mind if I did, too? It seems... less formal than Evelyn. After all, we've known each other for years." Evelyn had nodded in agreement. She'd enjoyed the conversation she'd had with Helen and determined to know her better. Sitting across the room balancing a cup and saucer and a luncheon plate, Helen glanced up and nodded. Evelyn smiled, mouthing back a silent, *Nice to see you!*

As the evening progressed, Evelyn realized how much she was enjoying herself. Pastor Cribbs, who had been gracious at Lucy's on Christmas Eve by not mentioning her early departure, took great pleasure in introducing his wife Bessie, who promptly invited Evelyn over for coffee the following Tuesday.

Abby Waters, a young woman from Lucy's church introduced herself and Evelyn learned that Abby and her husband Jake had moved to Thystle Creek the weekend of Thanksgiving. Over coffee and pie, Evelyn listened as Abby shared how she and Jake had lived in the same community as Rob Adams and his wife Holly.

"We grew up in Madison, a small English-speaking town just across the Quebec border. We've known each other all our lives. We were just kids, the four of us, when we all decided to get married the summer we were eighteen." Abby's faced beamed with the memory. "One big wedding. Two brides. Two grooms. And everyone came who lived in the area. My parents were a little worried. Jake's so reserved. But Rob's parents seemed okay with the whole idea. They were in their early forties when Rob was born, so I guess they were glad to see Rob settle down since they were getting on in years."

Evelyn smiled at the refreshing honesty of her new friend.

"We were all great friends..." Abby continued after a cursory glance at her husband.

"Holly got pregnant while Rob was at Teacher's College, and when B.J. was born, they moved to a larger nearby town where Rob got his first teaching job. They rented a small flat above the local post office and were thrilled to set up house. New baby. New town. New job. The works. Then Holly got sick. She died when B.J. was three." Another glance over her shoulder, and Abby lowered her head in silence. When she continued her story, she shared that there had been some rivalry between Jake and Rob, but that they had remained buddies. A final glance toward Jake and Abby abruptly changed the subject. She went on to talk about her love for reading and attempts at writing short stories, and took great lengths to share her favourite authors.

Not missing the altered conversation or the nervous glances toward Jake, Evelyn obliged her young friend and responded in like manner. "You need to stop by the library, if you haven't already. They have a wonderful selection of historical fiction, surprising for such a small town as Thystle Creek," Evelyn added with a shy wink. Moments later, Abby nodded slightly at Jake and apologizing, she excused herself to join her husband.

Evelyn found Abby quite inspiring. She had been thrilled at Evelyn's suggestion to visit the library and even invited Evelyn to join her on her quest for good reading material. Jake, on the other hand, remained strangely aloof, and Evelyn watched as he placed a firm hand on Abby's elbow. Having heard the history of the young couple and their relationship with Rob, Evelyn couldn't help wondering if there was more behind Jake Waters moving his wife to Thystle Creek. But rather than disturb her evening with such questioning thoughts, she focused on Allen Bailey as he sat discussing some medical procedure with Levi.

Evelyn warmed with the knowledge of Allen's friendship. *Such a true friend, that man.* When he'd felt the need to come to her rescue earlier in the evening at the indirect reference to Lewis saving Josh in the fire, Evelyn was reminded once again of the kind of person the town doctor was. *It'll be hard filling his shoes, but I'm sure Lee will do just fine.*

In digesting the earlier moment, Evelyn remembered the surprising effect the reference to her husband had had on her. There had been a time when any mention of the day Lewis had died would have forced her behind her wall of self-preservation. Anger would have erupted within. *But not this time,* Evelyn thought, sensing a small victory.

Who are you kidding? These people are so insensitive! Don't they realize your pain? For a moment, Evelyn felt herself slipping into a familiar trap, but in looking around the room, she found her daughter and smiled. She looked around again until she found Wil, down on his hands and knees coaxing B.J. to come out from under the table for some hot chocolate and special cinnamon sticks Christina had made. Her grin broadened when a small hand reached out from under the table and was greeted by her son-in-law's as he helped the shy young boy crawl out from his hiding place.

There would be no slipping backwards, not this time. She won the battle by looking to the two most important people in her life—soon to be three.

Watching Wil tease B.J., an unexpected memory surfaced and reinforced her victory.

"Daddy, Daddy, come find me!" Lucy's voice filled the room while her little body snuggled tightly under the dining room table. "Bet you can't find

me." Her little voice giggled in anticipation of being proven wrong.

Evelyn had watched, unseen, from the doorway as Lewis feigned difficulty, looking behind the curtains in the living room, under the coffee table, beside the piano, all the time ignoring the faint giggles coming from the dining room.

"Let me see, where can she be? I guess I'm going to have to give up."

"Here I am!" Lucy jumped out from under the table and the two rolled with laughter, all the while Lucy coaxing her father, "Your turn, Daddy. Let me find you!"

"Where are you?" A soft whisper brushed her ear.

"Lee! You startled me."

"I can see that. Are your thoughts worth more than a penny?"

"Just a memory of Lucy playing hide 'n seek with Louie when she was a little girl, a little younger than B.J." Evelyn nodded in B.J.'s direction. "I remember Lucy playing under the dining room table, begging her daddy to come find her. It was a nice memory." Her smile stretched across her face. It felt good to remember.

The evening ended on a high note. Evelyn stood back, watching as gracious thank yous from the Broughtons and the Cribbs were extended to Lucy and Wil for opening their home; and she noticed that it was just Abby who expressed appreciation for having been included in the evening, Jake having already left the house. Everyone smiled as Jennie hugged Rob and Allen again for their role in her rescue and ultimate healing, and cheered when Josh and Jennie announced their plans for a spring wedding.

With B.J. fast asleep in his arms, Rob paused at the front door. "Thanks so much, you guys. Can't tell you how much I appreciate your kindness. It's been overwhelming."

"On the contrary, Rob, the appreciation belongs to us," Josh said, reaching over B.J. to embrace his new friend. "No one's missed what could have happened if you hadn't stopped." It was evident to all that as Rob and Josh said goodnight, a special bond and new friendship had been established.

Evelyn insisted on helping Lucy and Wil clear the dishes scattered throughout the living and dining rooms. Levi and Christina remained behind too, and it was over hot, sudsy dishwater and several busy tea towels that the evening was discussed, dissected and digested, the five adults agreeing it had been a success.

Only one troubling spot remained for Evelyn: There was something distant, almost disturbing about Jake. She made a mental note to stay in touch with Abby.

33

Ointment and perfume rejoice the heart:
so doth the sweetness of a man's
friend by hearty counsel.
PROVERBS 27:9

"Hi Mrs. Sherwood, this is Abby Waters. We met a few weeks ago at the party for Rob and B.J." The voice rang familiar even before Abby had introduced herself. Evelyn smiled, but felt a pang of guilt for not having called Abby as she had promised herself she would.

"How nice to hear from you, Abby. I'm so glad you called. Are you and Jake getting settled out at Ruth Norton's?"

"I…we like it, all right. Mrs. Norton has given us the small bunkhouse and it's very cozy. She even brought out some curtains. Said she was glad someone was staying in it. She seems to like the company." Abby paused. "It's just that Jake gets restless when there's nothing to do."

"You tell Jake he'll be busy enough in a few weeks. It's a good thing for Ruth that he's handy on the farm. She can always use extra help come strawberry time. I don't know anything about strawberry plants, but Ruth works from sunup to sundown once the land dries from the winter snowfall."

"That's good to know. I'll be sure to tell Jake. Mrs. Sherwood, I..."

"Please, Abby, call me Evelyn or Evie."

"Evie's nice. Thanks, I'd like that. Evie, I was wondering if you would like to go to the library some day this week. I'd need to know what day so I can ask Jake for the truck. Oh, and are you familiar with the Emporium?"

Evelyn smiled at her enthusiasm and directness. "Yes, dear, my husband Lewis owned it before he died. Josh has full ownership now. Why do you ask?"

"Well, we could use the money and I was going to stop by and see if there's an opening for me. For work, I mean," Abby added in a softer voice.

"I understand. Leave it with me for a day. Lucy's been working there all through her pregnancy, but she's due in six weeks. This might be good timing. In the meantime, why don't I come out and pick you up. I'd enjoy the drive and we can leave Jake with the truck in case he needs it for something. How does the day after tomorrow sound?"

When there was no response, Evelyn wasn't sure if the connection had failed; and then she heard voices. The words were not discernible, despite the volume, but Evelyn heard enough to know that an argument had ensued in the Waters's home. The silence stretched for some time before Abby spoke again. This time, the enthusiasm that Evelyn had been enjoying just moments earlier was gone.

"Sorry, Mrs.... Evie. I had to ask Jake about my working. He's okay with it until he can get something permanent, more than strawberry picking. He's a proud man. He doesn't want me working and I have to quit when he says so." The tone of Abby's voice in her last remark startled Evelyn, and her previous feelings about Jake Waters surfaced.

"I'll come out just after lunch on Wednesday."

"That's a great idea, Mom." Lucy's response relieved Evelyn's anxiety in asking about a position for Abby. "Wil's been after me for a few weeks to quit working. I wasn't ready, but now that you've suggested this, I think it's time. Besides, Wil needs some persuasive influence on getting the living room painted before the baby comes. All that stuff I brought home months ago is still sitting unused. I'll mention Abby to Josh when I go in tomorrow. I'm only working four hours in the afternoon but I'll talk to him and see what he thinks. I'm sure the connection Abby and Jake have with Rob will help."

"Abby's quite an outgoing young lady, Lucy, but I'm not sure about Jake. He seemed almost withdrawn at your party."

"I think he's just quiet, at least that's what Abby says. She comes to church alone and apologizes for Jake's absence. Seems he doesn't do the church scene. Too many people, she says. I don't know what to think." Lucy's voice trailed off into silence.

"Honey, I've lived most of my life hiding behind a wall not to notice when someone else is doing the same thing. I can't help wondering if there's a serious problem in their home."

Evelyn surprised herself at her openness with her daughter. It actually felt good to be honest about how she had shielded herself for so long, but she felt a twinge of awkwardness in saying so to Lucy. "Well, will you listen to me?" Evelyn laughed to mask her embarrassment. "Confession time, wouldn't you say, daughter of mine!" Evelyn laughed again, only this time she noted the lengthy silence at the other end of the phone. "Maybe it's all the reading I've been doing lately, Luce. I suppose there's some truth to the old expression, 'Confession is good for the soul.'"

"You've been reading your Bible?"

"Let's just say lots of questions have landed in my journal. But that's another topic for another day. You get back to me with Josh's response about Abby, and I'll encourage her in whichever way I need to."

Confession is good for the soul. Evelyn repeated those words for the hundredth time since talking with her daughter. Each time she wondered how it applied to her. What had prompted her to say such a thing to Lucy in the first place? *Was* she confessing? Was she acknowledging the *need* to confess? Evelyn sat at her desk in the quietness of the late evening, writing. Question after question flowed onto the pages of her journal. Several weeks earlier, she had found Romans 3:23, "For all have sinned and come short of the glory of God." For some reason she had been avoiding her reading and when she discovered this verse, it seemed to jump off the page. She turned the pages of her journal back to the day when she had defined the verse in her own way, in her limited understanding.

> February 28. It seems that everyone has been sinning pretty much all their life and there's nothing anyone, especially me, can do about it. I suppose there's some comfort in knowing I'm not alone. I can't believe this verse applies to Lee or Christina, though, and certainly not Lucy or Wil. But it does say 'all.' So it looks like God, this loving and merciful God, took pity on us and gave us an escape route: Jesus. Did I just write 'us'?

Staring out into the night, Evelyn closed her journal. The questions confused her, but she couldn't deny that she had thought them and thus written them down. She picked up Lewis's Bible and stroked the leather cover before opening it. She had removed his Bible from the bottom drawer of the bedside table in late January. She knew where it was all along: on his side of the bed. There had been too many nights that she had watched her husband read from it before putting it in the drawer and turning out the light. Her hands had trembled as she'd lifted it out and laid it on the dresser. It sat there for days before she turned the cover. When she did, pages of single sheets had fallen to the floor. What she read left her weeping for hours.

> Lord, I can't reach Evie. Only you can. I know you are in control of all things, including when Evie will come to understand how much you love her, but my heart breaks for her, Lord. Give me your grace to wait for your timing.

Another read,

> Father, Lucy is just a little girl yet she loves you so much. I pray that her love for you will grow. I pray for the man you have set aside to be her husband. Seems like such a long time yet before I can walk her down the aisle, but I take great joy in knowing YOU know who it is. I pray for him and ask your blessing on his life, even now.

And another…

> Lord, what if something should happen to me before Evie finds you? What if your time for me comes before she understands you are an all-forgiving God? Who will show her? Who will help her? She suffers so much. The wall between us is too high for me and only you know what's on the other side. Everyday I see the pain in her

> face and my heart aches. I love her so much. Forgive me, Lord, but I am so afraid sometimes for her lost soul.

Evelyn had taken the notes and slipped them into the pages of the Bible Levi had given her, pausing for a moment in thought. *I still can't call this* my *Bible. It's just Levi's gift to me, not* my *Bible.* It lay on the night table by her bed. Tonight, she chose to read at her desk and to read from Lewis's Bible. She found the notes disturbing, so much so that it distracted from her attempt at daily reading. Yet she found that reading from Lewis's Bible brought a measure of peace, and she was grateful for it amidst the confusion that often came when trying to understand what was so foreign to her.

Her cup of hot chocolate sat cold by her arm as she read deep into the night. Her voice, though whispered, echoed in the quiet room. Trickster lifted her head every now and then, looking to see if the spoken words were directed at her, then stretched, circled, and finally flopped at Evelyn's feet with a sigh, all unnoticed by Evelyn.

"For I delivered unto you first of all that which I also received, how that Christ died for our sins according to the scriptures; And that He was buried, and that He rose again the third day according to the scriptures." Evelyn reached for her journal and wrote:

> May 2. I'm curious to know who 'our' is referring to in First Corinthians, Chapter 15. Is there any connection between the 'all' I read about in...

Evelyn stopped and reached for the journal she had just read from to check the reference.

> ...Romans, Chapter 3? I wonder what part of scriptures this verse is referring to.

Laying down her pen, she picked up her red marker and, as so often in the past, underscored the words *all* and *scriptures.* She had long since established a pattern: each red underscore was a question for Levi.

Closing the Bible, Evelyn rose and awakened Trickster. "Come on, girl, I need to put you out before morning comes. And from the look of the sky, it's not too far off."

Waiting at the back door enjoying the fresh nip of spring air, Evelyn surprised herself by thinking of Abby and Jake. *I need to call Josh myself tomorrow. I can't help thinking Abby needs that job for more reasons than what she's told me.*

Trickster's scratching at the back door ended her thoughts and she opened the door to usher in her pet, both now very anxious to call the day a day and head for bed. "I'll call Josh in the morning, Tricks," Evelyn spoke to her dog as they climbed the stairs, believing in her heart that her dog understood her intentions exactly.

34

Be not hasty in thy spirit to be angry:
for anger resteth in the bosom of fools.
ECCLESIASTES 7:9

The spring waters of Miller's Creek flowed down from Miller's Mountain fast and cold. Pregnant with winter runoff, it defied its own name and showed no mercy for broken branches or loose earth on the shore. Just north of town, it divided into two branches: Miller's Creek, continuing further west and deeper into the Rockies, and Thystle Creek, moving south to the more civilized part of the province. In the early weeks of spring, chunks of ice had floated down both creeks midstream, after crisscrossing and dislodging any remains of trees along the shore that had the misfortune of falling dead after a summer drought. Now the water moved more freely at most points along the river's route, but its speed and ensuing current were still a menace.

Fortunately, there were no rapids in the section of the river that flowed under the bridge at the east end of town, yet every year parents warned their children about the spring waters. It was a boy's playground, no doubt, and fathers openly admitted facing the same temptations in their youth as their sons now faced. But at the urging of their wives, fathers had reinforced the dangers of the swollen creek. "The summer heat will change it, make it safe," boys were told, "but spring is a dangerous time to be playing near the creek." Everyone knew to stay away until the spring runoff had subsided and Thystle Creek, living up to its name, had once more become a slow meandering body of water.

Jake Waters had just driven past the bridge on his way to pick up Abby at the Emporium when he saw Bradley Adams trying to dislodge a large tree branch from the shore. He grinned as B.J. leaned precariously over the water, poking and prodding his target to no avail. Heavy with debris that had travelled downstream, the shoreline resisted any efforts B.J. made for the branch to give up its resting place. Jake knew B.J. was no stranger to cold weather and fast moving water. Living in a town where skiing was a recreation as well as a popular means of travel across frozen water, he was very aware of the unpredictability of spring waters. But Jake also knew B.J. was the son of a man who had taken the woman Jake had once loved and Jake resented the youngster for not being his son. Jake parked his truck on the far side of the bridge and watched, hands on his hips and a smirk on his face. "Stupid kid. *Someone* has to teach him a lesson."

In the half year he'd lived in Thystle Creek, Jake had yet to earn a reputation for being gentle. It seemed apparent to most that he didn't seem to understand the meaning of the word. He approached B.J. as silently as he was slow and slid down the embankment. B.J. continued to splash and jab at the branch, distorting any opportunity to hear Jake's approach.

"What are ya doing there? Trying to get drowned?"

B.J. jumped up, lost his balance, and slipped into the edge of the water. Jake moved quickly and pulled B.J. to safety with a rough grab at his jacket. Flying through the air—albeit only a little, but nevertheless airborne—B.J. landed facedown in the wet leaves and mud. A boot had remained behind when one of his legs had sunk into the muck up to his knee.

"Need to be more careful, boy." Jake threw the soggy boot to the ground beside B.J. "Water can be a dangerous place to be playing," he added, towering over B.J., making no effort to assist the youngster upright. "Shouldn't you be somewheres else by now? School's been out for over an hour."

Wet and shaking, B.J. crawled from his supposed rescuer, grabbed his boot, and scampered up the embankment.

"That's right, now. Git yourself on outta here, and tell your father... ah, never mind, I'll tell him myself." Jake hollered at B.J.'s back as B.J. made his way further from the water and further from Jake, whose voice and actions did anything but instill friendliness.

"Lousy father ... " Jake muttered and fed the festering thought that Rob Adams didn't deserve to be B.J.'s father.

On her way to Lucy's for dinner, Evelyn spotted B.J. walking down the street in the same direction she was going. This didn't surprise her, since Lucy looked after B.J. until Rob finished at the school each day; however, what did surprise her was the lateness of the day. *Wonder where he's been?* Lucy often brought B.J. to the library in the afternoon when school was out and the quiet lad had long since endeared himself to her. But Evelyn hadn't seen him in a couple of days and she'd missed him. Alarmed by his slight limp, Evelyn pulled up beside the youngster and rolled down the passenger window. "Hey, there stranger, I'm going your way and can give you a ... " She halted mid sentence when B.J. turned his tear-stained face in her direction.

Two hours later over coffee and homemade cranberry loaf, four thankful adults appeared satisfied that the young child they had listened to—and then scolded—understood the seriousness of his actions and that he did not appear to suffer unduly from his unfortunate experience with Jake Waters.

"Rob, are you surprised by Jake's behaviour," Evelyn had asked over dinner, "why he frightened B.J.?"

"Not really," was all Rob had offered, and his evasive answer had disturbed Evelyn. Yet she'd respected his choice to go no further in his opinion of Jake, choosing rather to express further appreciation to Lucy and Wil in having them for dinner. But with his son asleep in Wil's armchair, Rob finally shared some light on why Jake seemed distant, even unfriendly.

"Evelyn, in answer to your question earlier, no, I'm not surprised, just really disappointed. I'm afraid Jake is getting back at me through my son. You see, Jake had loved Holly for years, all through grade school. He'd smothered her with attention and thrived on the teasing he took for wanting to marry her someday. Holly never felt the same way, but despite her rejection, Jake talked about her day and night.

"As we grew into teens, Holly took a liking to me. Jake and I had been friends since Kindergarten, but once Holly looked at me in a different light than just a friend, Jake never treated me the same. Abby, on the other hand, had it as bad for Jake as he did for Holly, and just waited it out. Seems that once it was obvious that Holly and I were getting married, Jake focused his attention on Abby.

"Didn't Abby ever think that Jake was on the rebound?' Evelyn asked, sympathy for Abby growing by the minute.

"Probably, but she was willing to settle for second place, as long as she got Jake. When Holly and I moved out of town, Jake seemed to settle down. Abby had told Holly that she'd wanted a baby, too, once she found out Holly was expecting, but Jake had said no way. He wasn't ready to be a father. I think he was too busy nursing his anger with me to think of being a father.

"We lost touch for a while. Then, when Holly got sick and died a couple of years later, Jake appeared at my door in a rage, totally irrational, blaming me for Holly's death. He also said that B.J. should have been his child and that I was an unfit parent."

Wil and Lucy exchanged looks of horror while Evelyn stared at Rob in disbelief. "No one would believe that for a minute, Rob," she assured her friend.

"Thanks," Rob smiled his appreciation of Evelyn's support. "But back then, I knew that if B.J. and I were ever going to have a fresh start, I had to put distance between us and Jake. I figured I could keep in touch with Holly's parents by mail and the occasional visit, and since my parents were gone and the farm was sold and I was an only child, nothing was keeping me out east. Unfortunately, Jake heard I was looking for work here in Thystle Creek—doesn't take much for that kind of news to spread between small towns. He got a head start without my knowing it."

"And to think that I invited him to your welcoming party. I thought because you all grew up together, it would be the most natural thing to do. I sure messed up on that," Lucy sighed, her regret very evident.

"Actually, he was quite civil at your party and I felt really hopeful that things had changed, but when we ran into each other two weeks later, I knew they hadn't. But, you know, in truth, I feel sorry for him. He could have a great life with Abby if he would just let go of his anger."

Evelyn heard the words spoken by a young man who truly

seemed to care about his friend. She knew anger, intimately. She knew how destructive it could be. As much as she understood the entrapment Jake faced, she promised herself, for the second time, that she would connect with Abby more regularly.

35

I will praise thee; for I am fearfully
and wonderfully made: marvellous are thy works;
and that my soul knoweth right well.
PSALM 139:14

The Audubon Society had announced the arrival of the migrating birds heading north to the Arctic for mating. The Horticultural Society had enthusiastically filled the planters hanging from the lamp posts with a profusion of red and white in anticipation of Canada's birthday. Banners, strung across the main street, boasted of the annual First of July picnic. The forest fire alert sign posted *Red*.

Moving aside the pillow that had provided some additional support, Lucy slid to the edge of her bed. She twitched as she tried to stretch her cramped legs, conscious of a dull ache in her lower back. "Looks like Daddy let us sleep in, Little Lu," Lucy remarked lazily to her unborn child. She had combined her name with her father's, and in many ways, it made her happy, thinking of her dad and using part of his name. She felt closer to him, sometimes talking about him to his unborn grandchild. Other times she was overcome with sadness as she realized how much she missed her father and what a wonderful grandfather he would have been.

Yawning, Lucy shifted her weight and stood up, stirring her child within and receiving a jab to her ribs. "I know, I know. It must be crowded in there." Lucy stretched again, trying to relax some of the muscles in her lower back. "I don't think it will be much longer, Lu." Lucy smiled wistfully as she smoothed her tummy and slipped her feet into her slippers. Her smile grew into a wide grin when she looked over at the wall that housed two narrow windows. A pair of old floral drapes her mother had given her as throws to protect the furniture from any paint splatters still hung where their sheer curtains belonged. Wil had finished painting the window frame three days ago and, as yet, the makeshift drapes still hung from a cord he had anchored to the edges of the window frame. He'd put them up after she'd gone to bed two nights earlier, but not before admonishing her about her need for sleep.

"It's been a long day, Luce, and you've been on your feet since sunup. We need to keep daylight out as much as we can in the morning." Thinking he had been planning on sleeping in as well, Lucy had crawled into bed and fallen asleep without noticing what he had used.

Lucy just shook her head and smiled as she tied each curtain back with two of Wil's old ties. *What a guy!* she thought.

A shimmering heat wave rising from the asphalt driveway welcomed her. "It's like a mirage in the Sahara Desert, Lu. Looks like we're in for another scorcher. You're better off where you are until this heat passes."

The morning sun had filled the cloudless sky, confirming that the heat wave of the past seven days had not let up during the night. Lucy sighed, no doubt echoing the sentiments of most of the residents of

Thystle Creek. Everyone had been complaining about the unusually hot June, but there was little anyone could do about it except to dress accordingly and stay out of the sun. Heeding the advice given on the morning newscast every day that week, Lucy slipped into a thin white top. She stopped abruptly in front of the mirror.

"Hey, will ya look at us, Lu!" Turning sideways, she frowned at how snug her top was. "Good thing we haven't got much longer to wait or we'd have to go shopping, you and me." As an afterthought, Lucy's mind drifted. "You're getting pretty big. You keep putting the weight on and I'll start worrying." She let the thought go unfinished as she studied her image in the mirror, allowing herself to go down another path.

Early in her pregnancy, she had asked Wil if he preferred a son or a daughter. She'd been a little worried, but continued on a lighter note. "Someday a machine will confirm the sex of an unborn child for curious parents, if they ever want to know—and I could never imagine why they would."

Wil had hugged her and laughed. "Well, then we wouldn't have to paint the baby's room yellow," he'd teased with a squeeze and nuzzle to her neck. But much to Lucy's relief, Wil had continued. "Lucy, our child is a gift from God and I don't really care either way, boy or girl." Remembering his response, Lucy smiled, knowing that he'd given her a glib answer, but was grateful nonetheless. Then she turned to the mirror again and an earlier concern returned. Smoothing her hands over her extended belly, she lowered her head. *Lord, this child comes from You. Thank you for the privilege of becoming a mother, but if I let my thoughts and fears take over, I'll be terrified. Mom has said that delivering a baby is the worst pain a woman can experience and the quickest forgotten, and I know You'll be with me in the midst of it...* Lucy raised her head, "...but, please, help me remember that," she added shyly.

Her prayer calmed her. Sharing her fears with God always did that, and when she spoke again it was with a lilt. "Let's go find your Daddy and see what he's up to."

Lucy leaned on the doorframe to the living room where she found Wil engrossed in setting his somewhat limited William Shakespeare collection on the shelves of the built-in bookcase. He'd painted the room three weeks earlier, but school demands and the painting of the other rooms had prevented Wil from putting his books back on the shelves. He'd stacked his collection in the middle of the room, waiting for school days to be over for the summer, but his actions had declared his impatience. He could wait no longer, and Lucy found him methodically opening the boxes one at a time and unearthing his treasures. She smiled, knowing how Wil's uncanny interest in literature and poetry had led to raised eyebrows in bewilderment, and even amusement from local townsfolk. But she had never questioned why he was so intrigued with Chaucer, Browning or William Shakespeare and found it rather captivating and romantic.

"Good morning. You're hard at it. Can't wait any longer, eh?"

Wil paused with a book in hand and turned to the sound of Lucy's voice. Lucy moved cautiously across the room and lowered herself to a cushion on the floor in front of an unopened carton. Wil's look changed to one of wonder and amazement at the miracle of life Lucy carried around so naturally.

"You're beautiful, you know that, Luce?"

"Sure I am! Twenty pounds heavier than normal and too many inches around to count," Lucy responded, turning up her nose as she opened the sealed carton and started to hand Wil the contents.

"You're still beautiful."

Shifting her legs to a more comfortable position, Lucy leaned against the couch and smiled. "Hope you still think so when I'm a grey-haired granny. What's that poem about growing old?" She laughed. "You know, the one old people quote to one another?"

"'Grow old along with me. The best is yet to be.' Robert Browning," he added, sliding a cushion behind his wife's back and kissing the top of her head.

"Our painting went well, don't you think?" Lucy acknowledged her husband's affections with a gentle stroke of his arm. "Or maybe I should say *your* painting went well. I'm still sorry I couldn't help you, but Doc was right. The smell was getting to me. I'm just glad we're done. The living room and two bedrooms, all *fini*." Lucy's gesturing and attempt at the French language leaned on the dramatic and Wil laughed at his wife's enthusiasm. "And Mom's been great. Supper every night this week, coming to help when she can and making sure I'm not around while you're painting. I can't believe how much she has come out of her shell these past weeks. It must be the baby. I can't think of any other reason, unless of course Lee has something to do with it."

"There's no doubt Lee has had an influence, and certainly the baby coming will have a major impact on her, but I've watched your mother as she's helped us empty rooms and move furniture out of the way. Sometimes her face is sad and then other times I catch her humming a tune. Telling you about her Jewish heritage has certainly played a big role in her coming around, but I'm not so sure she feels released from her past. Do you still think there's more?" Wil questioned as he filled the bookshelves.

"Absolutely! But for now, like you said a while ago, what she's shared will have to do. I can't help thinking, though, that if we're watching *her*, she's likely watching us. I know she saw a change in me when I got back on track with God, and she's admitted that she expected me to have a totally different reaction than I did when she told me I was Jewish."

"Bet she sees a change in you now." Wil squeezed his wife's shoulders and gently poked her belly, and then, thoughtfully, "Remember, Luce, God has never been a part of her life and she can't begin to understand how He could work things out. We both know she'd be a much happier person if she'd let God have a chance with her problems, whatever they are," Wil added, lowering himself beside his wife and stretching his legs. "Has she talked any more about the night she spent with Christina and Lee?"

Lucy twisted into a more comfortable position. "No. It's been months since that happened and I'm almost afraid to bring it up. I don't want to jinx the mood she's in and yet there's still so much secrecy. She told me about growing up, her parents, her grandmother, and changing their name." Lucy listed the items on her fingers and repeated them again, as she had done several times over the past six months. "But what about the torn two dollar bill? Apart from that one time last fall, she's said nothing else. I've wanted to ask her if she's read the Bible Lee gave her, but I can't help thinking I'd be intruding. The closest she has come to anything remotely spiritual is saying 'Confession is good for the soul,' but she's never elaborated on what she meant. Anyway, having this baby," Lucy laid her hand on her tummy, "is certainly putting a new slant on things. It's almost as though she's willing to let the past be buried in some deep cave and live only for now, looking ahead to the birth of her first grandchild, and maybe even a *different* friendship with Lee." Lucy added with a smirk, alleviating the frustration.

A few moments passed in silence before Lucy attempted to stretch her cramped legs. "Better help me up, Wil. Seems Little Lu is up to some serious somersaulting."

Wil helped Lucy stand and steady herself.

“You okay?” he asked, concern written all over his face as his wife teetered slightly.

“Hmm, bit of head rush, I guess, though this steady ache in my back doesn’t want to let up.” Lucy paused. “Come feel this.” Guiding her husband’s hand, Lucy placed it over her own. As they had on so many occasions, they marvelled at the aerobic performance going on unseen, in a warm, safe place. “I think I’ll go lay down for a while.” Lucy kissed her husband and left him standing in the middle of the living room watching her less-than-graceful exit.

“I’m going to be a Daddy,” Wil murmured and turned back to the half-filled bookshelves.

36

For God speaketh once, yea twice, yet man perceiveth it not. In a dream, in a vision of the night, when deep sleep falleth upon men, in slumberings upon the bed; then he openeth the ears of men.
JOB 33:14-16

The first two rings of the phone dissolved amid the blast when the sky opened up and released its contents. Awakened by the thunder burst, Evelyn had not heard the phone until the third ring. She glanced at her bedside clock. "Two thirty-five. Who could be calling us at this hour of the morning?" she whispered more to herself than her dog, despite Trickster's raised head. Her immediate thought was for her daughter, but Lucy had another two weeks before the baby was due, and then, surprisingly, Evelyn's mind raced to Christina. All this in the seconds it took to roll over and reach for the phone.

"It's a little girl, Evie. Lucy's just given us a little girl." Wil's voice shouted in excitement.

"A girl?" Evelyn's breath quickened.

"Yep, just minutes ago. Doc Bailey is still with Luce, but the nurse came out and told me we have a healthy seven pound, five ounce squirming, and shrieking, little girl. We're going to call her Annie, for no real reason except that we like it. Officially she'll be Anna Evlyna Louise Douglas, Annie for short." And Wil rambled on, oblivious to the inner turmoil being experienced on the other end of the phone.

"You still there, Evie?"

"Yes, I'm here." Evelyn paused for a moment before resuming, her voice a soft whisper. "Remember this day, Will. Always keep the memory of your first child's birth in a special place. Never forget it." Changing her tone, she continued. "How's Lucy feeling?"

"Just great. From what the nurse said, she was amazing. She'll be in for a week, but if I know Luce, she'll wanna come home long before Doc Bailey gives the okay."

"Well, you give her my love and tell her I'll come by the hospital tomorrow afternoon, and give my new granddaughter a kiss from her Nana."

"Nana?"

"Yes, I think I like that name. It has a nice sound to it."

"You're full of surprises, Evie. You can count on my delivering your kisses, but after mine. Okay?"

"Go to your wife, Wil, and welcome to the world of parenting." Evelyn added, smiling, as she heard her son-in-law react to the realization of being a new father.

Sleep returned quickly for Evelyn. Lucy had surprised her, going into labour early, but the baby was healthy, a little girl, and Lucy was fine. She could ask for nothing more. Being a grandmother proved to be a nice feeling, evidenced by the contentment and peace that had quickly settled over her, despite the steady rain blowing against her bedroom window. Now fast asleep, her smile had long faded as the world of the unconscious moved over her.

"Give him back! Please! Just give him back to me!" Her voice broke, weak with emotion.

Gentle but majestic hands reached down and lifted the baby from her arms. Slowly, calmly, the voice responded. "No, she's not yours. She belongs to another."

"That's not true. She's mine. No! He's mine. Why do you call him she? *I had a boy! I had a boy! You can't have him." Her voice filled with panic. "We've already named him."*

Over and over, voices sang in a monotonous yet angelic tone: "Annie. Annie. Annie."

"Stop that! His name's not Annie. It's Anthony. You can't have him. He's mine."

Desperation cloaked her.

An envelope and papers were placed in front of her. "Do you remember? You signed this. You can never have another." Again, slowly, calmly, but with each word the voices began to sound more and more like an old phonograph player slowing to a halt. "No more, no more, no more."

She grabbed the papers, missing the envelope. Ripping, tearing, shredding, her hands worked in a frenzy, but the papers were all blank. She watched as the child was carried away, fast asleep, the white envelope tucked in its blanket. The echo of her own scream filled the dark room where she lay despondent and alone.

Evelyn awoke terrified. The weight on her chest increased, and with each breath the pain intensified. Inhaling became impossible. The pounding of her heart roared in her ears as she grabbed the phone and dialed.

"Lee, please … come," she managed, her whisper barely audible.

Coffee in hand, Evelyn curled up on her living room couch watching Levi strike a match to light a fire in the grate. Her first instinct was to protest, yet despite the heat wave during the past days, Evelyn realized that the much-needed rain during the night had dropped the temperature enough to put a chill in the pre-dawn air. But she also knew that the chill she felt was more from her fright than from the temperature of her living room. The warmth of the fire proved to be a blessing, and she was grateful Levi seemed to understand her need.

"I'm so embarrassed, Lee. Please don't say anything to Lucy. I would never want her to know that the announcement of her child's birth put her mother into such a mental state that she thought she was having a heart attack." Even saying the words brought tears to Evelyn's eyes.

"You had a terrible experience. You shouldn't feel embarrassed. Bad dreams are like the common cold. We all know that germs are out there, somewhere, and we all hope they never find *us*. But they do, and we have to grin and bear it until the cold is over." Evelyn cringed at his choice of words and silenced him for a moment. "Sorry, bad analogy. So you didn't grin, but you get what I mean." Levi smiled and then continued on a more serious note. "Evie, no one really understands dreams, not really. There are a lot of theories about what triggers them. Sometimes our subconscious digs deep into our past, and other times it gravitates to a current event in life; but whatever the case, yours was certainly centred on the birth of your new granddaughter. How the details became twisted and distorted is just conjecture, but take comfort in the fact that dreams are dreams, and eventually we wake up from them. Sometimes they stay with us, other times we can't remember one thing about them the moment our eyes open, other than we just had a bad dream." Levi stoked the fire to encourage the new flames.

"But it was so confusing. First I had a boy, then he was a girl called Annie and then all that paper on my bed. I've ruined one of my journals. I have no idea what I thought I was tearing up. It was so confusing." Evelyn repeated herself.

Levi sat beside her, reached around her shoulder, and eased her into his side. Both sat gazing into the fire for some time.

"Sometimes dreams, good or bad, are given to us to help us sort through something buried deep inside, something that needs to be put to rest. I believe God uses dreams sometimes to help us unearth a pain that is crippling us from moving ahead with our lives. I also think that healing can come when we've had a dream that makes us think and then act on whatever it is that is affecting us, whatever it is that our unconscious mind is awakening."

Evelyn didn't respond.

"Seems kind of silly lighting a fire in the middle of June," Levi laughed, changing the subject. "But there's something to be said for a glowing fire in a fireplace. I'll see that it's out before I leave, but right now, I want you to shut your eyes and rest. No more talking."

"You're quite the guy."

"Hmm. You say something?"

"No, just *thanks.*"

"Any time. Now close your eyes and I'll remember to put the key back under the mat."

37

As arrows are in the hand of a mighty man;
so are children of the youth. Happy is the man
that hath his quiver full of them.
PSALM 127:4-5

Lucy arrived unannounced just as Evelyn was putting Trickster outside. She'd barely been able to shut the back door, preventing Trickster from nudging her way back in at the sound of the front doorbell and was delighted to see her daughter standing in the front hallway—albeit burdened down with baby and diaper bag.

"Well, look at you two," Evelyn smiled as she came to Lucy's rescue and lifted her two-week old granddaughter from Lucy's arms.

"She's sound asleep, Mom, but not for long, I hope. I've got a couple of hours to kill and I need to feed her before I head over to the school for show-and-tell." Lucy laughed as she exaggerated the words. "Can you believe my husband, the last day of school and he wants to show off his daughter. But she won't be happy if I don't nurse her first, and, for that matter, neither will I." Lucy rubbed the sides of her breasts. "They sure get sore when she doesn't nurse when she should."

Evelyn smiled, admiring her daughter's ability to speak so openly. "Will you have time for some iced tea? It's nice and cold."

"I'd love some, but I'd better have milk. Doc Bailey says drink milk, drink milk, drink milk. I have yet to figure out why I have to drink so much milk just 'cause I'm nursing a baby. The way I see it, cows don't drink milk, they eat grass."

Evelyn's laughter brought a stir from Annie, but not quite enough for the baby to fully awaken. She poured herself a glass of iced tea and one of milk for her daughter. She added a plate of Lucy's favourite cookies to complete the treat, all the while watching Lucy tickle her daughter's cheeks to help her wake up. Lucy had only been a mother for two weeks, but Evelyn could see she was a natural. There were no apparent misgivings about nursing Annie in front of her, and yet Evelyn kept her distance and gave Lucy the privacy needed for such an intimate moment.

"I read the other night that a man is most happy when his quiver is full. Doc Bailey had said that to me many years ago." Evelyn paused for a moment, surprised at how much less painful the memory had become.

"A quiver! Mother, that's in the Bible."

Evelyn glanced sideways at her daughter. Lucy's reaction was predictable, but Evelyn was not expecting her daughter to be so formal. Nevertheless, she remained nonchalant.

"I know. Are you planning on giving Wil a full quiver?" Evelyn knew her daughter well enough that Lucy would not consider it intrusive, and she masked a mischievous look as she watched her daughter digest the question, knowing its source. Besides, the humour in the timing of her question could not be mistaken.

"A full quiver. Hmm. We'll just have to wait and see, but first let's get Annie through high school." At that remark, they looked at the infant and laughed at the prospect of a two-week-old baby going to college.

Lucy lifted Annie to her shoulder and both mother and daughter smiled as the baby offered a gratifying burp. At the unusual sound, Trickster came and leaned against Lucy's leg, looking up with a gloomy disposition. Lucy laid Annie in the bassinet that had once been her own and lifted Trickster to her lap. "I think someone's nose is out of joint. If dogs could pout, I think you'd win the prize, Tricks." Obviously happy to be part of the affection that Annie received, Trickster circled a couple of times before flopping in Lucy's lap with a satisfying grunt.

Turning to her mother, she said, "Do you read the Bible a lot, Mom?"

"Some. I find it hard to understand and I'm not convinced it's relevant for today, but I'm keeping a journal of questions. Someday I'll start asking them."

"Got any for me now?"

Evelyn paused, conscious of one that had been nagging her since Annie's birth. "Can your God speak to you in your dreams?" Evelyn deliberately couched her words, and in so doing confirmed that the God of the Bible, the One she'd been reading about for six months, was still not a God she could call her own, or even relate to.

"Wow, that's a loaded question and a big topic. Let's see ... I know there are simple dreams that the Bible records, for example, when the angel of the Lord appeared to Joseph in Chapter One of St. Matthew—that's the first book in the New Testament—telling him not to be afraid to take Mary, the mother of Jesus, for his wife even though she was already pregnant—that's a *must* read! Then there are the more complicated dreams that required interpretation. For example, in Genesis 37 we read about Joseph, who dreamed he was harvesting wheat with his brothers and his sheaf stood taller than his brothers' sheaves. When he told his brothers about this and interpreted it to mean that someday they would bow down to him, it got him into a lot of trouble. It's a neat story and a lot of it has to do with dreams. Another great read!"

Evelyn smiled at her daughter's enthusiasm.

Lucy continued. "And sometimes God used dreams to reveal His will to certain individuals like the Magi—we call them the Wise Men. That's found in St. Matthew as well. Anyway, that's just off the top of my head. There's so much more on the subject and it's much more complicated than I've made it sound. Why do you ask?"

"Oh, I was just curious." She could not bring herself to share her panic attack the night Annie had been born, and turned the subject to a safer topic. "While I think of it, have you and Wil decided on what you'll be taking to the picnic on Saturday? With school freshly out, I'm sure there will be some very excited children anxiously waiting for the big day. I've invited Abby and Jake to join us at..."

"Mother! Why would you do that knowing Jake is at odds with Rob?"

"But Abby isn't," Evelyn quickly countered. "Lucy, I can't help feeling a little sorry for her and a great deal sorrier for Jake. He needs a friend. They'll be at the picnic anyway, I'm sure, so I thought I'd get a little ahead of them and invite them to join our meal time."

"But Rob and B.J. will be joining us."

"That's right, and now Abby and Jake will be, too." Evelyn's tone brought closure to the conversation as she tried once again to turn the subject to a safer topic. "What have you decided to bring for lunch? It would be nice not to duplicate if we can help it. I know how much Wil likes my potato salad. Would you like me to bring enough for everyone? I'm sure Lee and Christina will be joining us." Evelyn's thoughts wandered as she started to do a headcount. "My goodness, this is going to be quite a feast by the time everyone brings a favourite dish. I think it would be nice if we invited Ruth Norton to join us now that Jake and Abby are living out there with her."

"She'd like that, Mom, and I'm sorry about my reaction to Jake. I'm just surprised you're so drawn to them, especially Jake. He's got such a temper."

"Lucy, anger can be destructive. If I can be of any help in reconciling Jake and Rob, that would help me, too. I know the path Jake is on."

Evelyn waved goodbye from the front yard. After an hour of planning, the menu for the picnic had been settled and Evelyn had been left with the task of calling Christina for her input and inviting Ruth Norton to join the *Sherwood/Douglas and Company* gathering. Evelyn smiled, remembering Lucy's title at the top of the page when she listed the various items necessary for the meal.

"She's quite the organizer, Tricks."

At the sound of her name, Trickster squirmed in Evelyn's arms to be free to roam the bushes and garden in the front of the house. But Evelyn held her dog tightly as she watched Lucy reach the corner and head toward the school. One last wave and Evelyn turned back to the house.

From habit, she bent down and pulled a weed hidden among the new growth under the grove of white birch. Her thoughts drifted to the earlier conversation with Lucy about dreams, and the memory of her nightmare returned. With a deep sigh, Evelyn dropped the weed in an existing pile beside the walkway near the garage, closed her eyes, and shook her head in an attempt to clear her mind. But the dream would not let her go. And then, for the first time, she knew...in her heart, she knew what her dream meant. The whole idea of wondering if God could or would speak to her in a dream had troubled her, but it really didn't matter now. She now knew what it meant, but an inner resolve left her unwilling to do what needed to be done.

Still crouching in front of her garden, her grip tightened around Trickster until the dog yelped and jumped free from Evelyn's grasp. With a vigilant eye, Evelyn watched as Trickster enjoyed a few moments of freedom, unearthing a buried acorn and leaving a mound of earth in her wake. "Come on, Tricks, we need to leave what's buried where it is." And as though her own words gave her further resolve, she turned and walked slowly to the house.

PART SIX

38

All we like sheep have gone astray;
we have turned every one to his own way.
Isaiah 53:6

Maude Lasington owned Maudeville, even from the grave. As some would say, "Her hand reaches down from above and influences all that goes on in our town." And if some would say that, they would quickly add that it was all for the good. Maude Lasington had been loved, respected and honoured, and her memory was still revered among the most influential members of society long after her death.

Reared in the east under the controlling eye of an influential politician father, Maude escaped his domination and came west in 1877 at the age of twenty. Heading deep into the North Country, she braved the elements and landed in a small settlement in Central Alberta at the onset of winter. With enough money to lodge her through the winter months, she determined to remain free from her father's oppressive control and married the first drifter available. With a new last name,

Maude cut all strings and, with her freedom secure, she never heard from or about her father again, not even to inherit his wealth upon his death.

Clive Lasington may have been a drifter and he may have been a means to an end for Maude, but he proved to be a diamond in the rough, a soul waiting to be discovered, a man longing to marry and settle down. Maude married Clive and they remained happily married for thirteen years before his untimely death at the hands of an unscrupulous card shark. Only one son had been born. There were to be no other children. Maude never remarried.

She inherited the trading business that she and her husband had started, along with land they'd purchased through wise use of their money. Within two years of Clive's death, the obscure town was given its first name and Maudeville was born. A trading centre for hunters to bring their pelts, a general store that supplied the new settlers with their immediate needs to set up house, and a saloon that supplied the least desirables with a beverage that was usually behind more deaths than would have been necessary had the saloon not existed. As more hunters sought out the riches of pelts, families arrived: wives, children, mothers-in-law, and grandparents. The town grew. A school was established, sharing its facilities with the local church, and a bank was built to house the assets of those fortunate enough to obtain wealth from the land. Maude Lasington was the first customer of the bank, and the wealthiest.

When Maude was in her mid-forties, a sister town, Thystle Creek, was established fifteen miles to the west of Maudeville. Over the following decades there were many marriages between the two towns, and each year a First of July picnic was held to celebrate the bond of friendship that generation after generation enjoyed. Thanks to the memory of Maude Lasington and the generosity of Sherwood's

Hardware Emporium, who provided the prizes for the various competitions, the Maudeville/Thystle Creek annual picnic was a highlight of the summer months.

The weather report proved promising throughout the week, and the morning of the parade and picnic the sun shone warm and high in a blue sky. Old Mr. Lasington, the grandson of Maude and Clive, led the parade. With the help of Jim Broughton's tractor, Clive Lasington Jr. sat high and proud, alongside the newly married Josh Graham, waving at the large crowd that had evolved with the temporary merging of the two towns. Clowns bounced on large balls or skipped on thick rope, tripping as they went to the delight of the small children looking on. Older children scooted back and forth on their bikes and tricycles, decorated with streamers, teddy bears and ribbons for the occasion. Tears shone in the eyes of the elderly as they remembered years gone by, and laughter filled the air as parents shouted to their passing child and waved frantically from the sidelines. Folk who seldom saw one another from one year to the next chatted endlessly and then suddenly stopped to enjoy the Thystle Creek High School band as it marched by playing *When the Saints Come Marching In.* "That took a lot of practising," a voice shouted over the pounding of the bass drums. Everyone within hearing agreed and a spirit of pride filtered through the crowd.

Wil Douglas led his basketball team in a practice drill in the middle of the road, each player proudly displaying his new team uniform, compliments of the Emporium, whose well-known slogan was clearly seen across the back of each shirt.

Every year the parade and picnic brought something new, but every year one thing remained the same, everyone had one purpose: to eat, laugh, and enjoy the day.

Relaxing under the shade of an overgrown Manitoba maple tree with her granddaughter, Evelyn reflected back on the day she and Lucy had made plans for the picnic. A menu had evolved and excitement increased as they'd laughed and planned the day despite the misunderstanding regarding Jake Waters. *We're doing okay.* Evelyn smiled to herself and nodded. *It's been two years, and we're doing okay.* Her smile broadened and her heart filled with gratitude that the bond between herself and her daughter was able to withstand such challenges as their disagreement over Jake.

"Mrs. Sherwood, can I go skip stones at the creek?" B.J. came bounding up to Evelyn as she adjusted the netting around Annie's carriage.

"I think you'd better ask your father, B.J. He's over with Mr. Douglas judging the pie contest."

"I already did. He asked me to ask you 'cause he can't watch me. Will you?"

"I'm afraid I can't, B.J. I have to look after Annie for a few minutes and she's... "

"I'll go with him, Evelyn."

"Oh! You startled me, Jake. I didn't see you behind me."

"If you want, I can watch B.J. I'm kind of at loose ends. Abby's not here and I'm not interested in watching the little kids' three-legged race. But B.J. and I could shoot off a few stones, if it's all right with you."

Evelyn bent down and spoke softly to B.J. "Do you want to go with Jake, B.J.?" She had given thought to the possibility that the desire of a little boy to skip stones could be overshadowed by his previous experience with the one now befriending him. But instead B.J. nodded enthusiastically, and the reaction touched Evelyn's heart. *How soon a child forgives,* she thought, but before rising, Evelyn spoke softly one more time.

"It's very important that you stay with Jake. If he decides to come back, you need to come, too. The water's not very deep, but there are a few embankments that can be scary, and we both know all about them, don't we?

"Yes, ma'am."

"Off you go then, and Jake, please keep a close eye on him. He tends to wander more than he should. And don't be too long. Once the competitions and awards are over, we'll be packing up and heading home. It's been a long day."

"Not to worry Mrs. S., B.J. and I are buddies, aren't we B.J.?"

Evelyn watched with mixed emotions as the two wandered off toward the creek, making a mental note to call Abby and find out why she never attended the picnic.

"Evie, have you seen B.J.? His dad thought he might like to join in on the last of the races for kids his age." Wil had come ambling across the field to the grove of trees where Evelyn sat chatting with Ruth Norton. His message delivered, he'd bent down to peek under the netting to see his sleeping daughter.

"Not for some time. He and Jake left to skip stones at the creek."

"What?" Wil bolted upright.

"B.J. wanted to skip stones and I told him he had to ask his father, which he had already done. Rob said he'd have to ask me because he was busy with the pie contest and then Jake offered..."

"Evie, Jake's been over by the pie contest watching us for over half an hour."

"Well, where's B.J.? Jake said he'd watch him, and B.J. promised... Wil!"

But Wil had already turned and was racing back across the field in the direction he'd come from, leaving Evelyn standing by her friend, concern written on both women's faces.

"Ladies and gentlemen, boys and girls," Clive Lasington's voice quivered over the PA system. "Please, can I have your attention?" Parents turned from conversations, laughter ceased, children stopped in their play, and judges of contests put a halt to the activities before them. "It would appear that a child is lost. B.J. Adams has wandered off and has been missing for some time." Gasps filtered through the crowd. Women unconsciously searched the crowd for their own children. Men listened intently, waiting for further information and instructions. "We need the men to spread out and start searching by the creek in both directions. Ladies, would you keep your youngsters by your side until B.J. is found? We don't want to alarm anyone, but night is coming and we need to move quickly."

Under any other circumstance, Clive Lasington's choice of words, "move quickly," would have drawn a roar of laughter. Short and stocky, his ponderous figure waddled rather than walked, and many smiles followed him once he'd passed by. However, this occasion did not warrant a humorous response. Mothers whispered as they spoke to their young children, drawing them close, but at the same time sending their teenage sons to join the team of men looking by the creek.

The crowd dispersed quietly. In all the years Thystle Creek had hosted the annual picnic, the closure of the day had never been so sombre. Women packed up their lunch baskets, folded blankets, and collapsed picnic chairs. Children sensed the seriousness of the moment and whispered amongst themselves. "Maybe he's fallen in the water" was heard far too often, and mothers shuddered at the possibility. More than once the soon-to-be-setting sun was mentioned and further concern filtered through the group.

Clive Lasington encouraged those not involved in the search to make their way home, and a small train of mothers and children quietly wormed across the field. Moments lapsed before only three were left, waiting.

Heavy-hearted, Evelyn believed she was responsible for whatever happened to B.J. Lucy and Christina did all that they could to comfort her, but nothing would remove the guilt that was closing in with each passing moment. And unbeknownst to her daughter and friend, an old voice surfaced, drawing Evelyn deeper and deeper into a dark place, one she had not inhabited for many months.

"Mom, I need to get Annie out of the evening air and mosquitoes. We can all wait at your house, if you'd be more comfortable." Lucy's voice was full of compassion as she spoke with her mother before inviting Christina to join them, and Evelyn smiled at her sweetness.

"You go ahead, Lucy. I just need to wait here a little longer." Evelyn struggled to remain calm. "I want to be here when they find him," she whispered with tear-filled eyes.

"Now, now, Evie," Christina said, reaching her arm around her friend. "B.J.'s going to be just fine, you'll see. God's bigger than you or I can imagine, and He's looking over B.J. right now. Lucy, why don't you just ask God to keep B.J. safe?"

Lucy bent down and took her mother's hands in hers. "Lord, you know our hearts and you know we are a little afraid because we don't know where B.J. is. But we do know that wherever he is, You are with him. Please keep him safe until he is found, and would You please help Mom find some peace in all of this? Lord, she feels so responsible that B.J.…"

"They found him! They found him!" Making his way across the field to join Evelyn and company, Clive Lasington's voice broke the quiet moment—where he lacked in speed, he made up for in volume.

"He's all right. Doc Bailey and Doctor Morsman are with him." Pausing to catch his breath, the grandson of Maude Lasington took a moment to wipe his eyes and blow his nose. "Seems he wandered downriver, slid off one of the embankments, and rolled into the underbrush and thistles." Panting, he continued. "Got quite a hit on the head, must have been out when they found him. He's full of scratches from the thistles that stuck to him and his left arm may be broken, but just slightly," he added when he saw the women's reaction to the possibility. "But other than that he's all right."

Evelyn gasped for joy, then broke into tears when she considered the possibilities of his injuries. Lucy hugged Christina and then both women embraced Evelyn.

"Now isn't that a quick answer to prayer," Christina chimed the words gently, but purposefully, and Evelyn stopped abruptly and stared.

"Is *that* what it was? Is that what your God allowed? Is that what you call an answer to prayer?"

"I certainly do," Christina responded with an unusual firmness. "When I think of the alternative that we could be facing, yes, I certainly do call that an answer to prayer. Clive, where are they taking him?"

"Doc Bailey's office. He's already gone. Doc Morsman said they would take a good look at his arm there and if it was broken ..." Clive raised his hands in a calming manner. "... *if* it's broken, they'd take him to the hospital." The senior gentleman took the chair offered him while he wiped his brow and blew his nose one more time. "Seems we have another problem, though. Jake Waters has taken quite a thrashing from the young lad's father. Appears he's being held responsible for the boy's dilemma, leastwise that's what Mr. Adams is saying. When I last saw Mr. Waters, it appeared he needed some doctoring, too, but had refused it. This has been quite a picnic, yes sir, quite a picnic!"

Worry and concern for a lost little boy had replaced the small talk of the annual picnic. Few people becalmed their fears that evening, and it wasn't until word came through the grapevine that B.J. Adams had been found that the towns of Thystle Creek and Maudeville settled down for the night. Tucked safely in their beds, some children prayed for B.J.'s arm to heal overnight so he could play ball the next day. Others prayed that Mr. Adams would not give B.J. a whipping for disobeying. Still others, old enough to understand the seriousness of B.J.'s actions, assured their parents that they'd never wander off like that, "not in a million years." In the end, when children had given into the bewitching hour of sleep, many parents stood over their sleeping son or daughter and whispered a prayer of thanks, not just that B.J. had suffered no major harm from his adventure—for that was how some parents chose to describe it to their younger offspring—but that *their* child had not been the subject of a long and intensive search.

39

Commit thy way unto the LORD;
trust also in him; and he shall bring it to pass.
PSALM 37:5

Here, Wil, have some more potato salad. I've got enough here to feed most of Thystle Creek!" Evelyn Sherwood's lighthearted tone created a contrast to the tense moments she and the others had experienced a couple of hours earlier. The crisis had passed, as had the nauseous feeling that is experienced at the very thought of food—much less the consumption of it— when under such stress.

"Honestly, Evie, you'd think your mission in life was to fill my stomach!" Wil laughed as Evelyn offered him his second dinner of the day.

She smiled and placed the extra helping of salad on Wil's plate. In truth, she could never have imagined the scene before her a couple of hours ago. But B.J. was safe and sound, and it seemed a late supper was "just what the doctor ordered," as Levi had quipped when Evelyn invited the small group back to her home for some much needed food.

"Well, the little guy's fast asleep," Rob announced as he joined the group in Evelyn's living room after settling B.J. down in Lucy's old bedroom. "He's got his arm propped up over one of your many bears, Lucy. Hope that's okay?" Wil winked at Lucy when she cringed at the mention of her overabundance of stuffed animals, all of which had been forced to remain behind when she married Wil. "He was determined not to cry, but I helped him wipe away a few that got away just as we were saying prayers. When I'm ready to go, he'll be out for the night and an easy load to lift to the car." Rob turned with a smile that brought Evelyn to a halt. "Thanks, Evie, for letting him rest here for awhile."

Evelyn stood speechless, staring at her guest.

"Mom?" Lucy questioned her mother.

"What? Oh, sorry, Rob. You just…I was reminded…" Evelyn closed her eyes and shook her head before opening them again and smiled. "You're more than welcome. I'm quite sure the little guy is exhausted after the kind of day he's had."

Rob plunked himself down in a side chair. "That's for sure. And what a day it's been. Hope I never have another one like it." Everyone nodded, each realizing that the day could have had a very different ending. Evelyn handed Rob a plate of food and his instant pleasure broke the spell. Christina broke the silence.

"Rob, did B.J. tell you what happened? Why didn't he return to Evelyn when Jake left him?"

"Seems Jake got bored." Disgust filtered through Rob's voice. "He'd teased B.J. about going back to the picnic to watch me and Wil consume pies and then throw up because we might eat something that tasted awful. But B.J. wasn't interested. He said he'd go back to Mrs. Sherwood on his own. Jake left him standing by the water. That's where Jake made his mistake. I wouldn't have left a child, and Jake should've known better. Even if B.J.'s old enough to know what he did was wrong—and he certainly suffered enough for a bad choice—Jake still should've known better." Silence filled the room. No one mentioned the fight that had ensued when Rob confronted Jake, and although everyone understood Rob's reaction, emotions were already running high. No one seemed to want to broach the subject. "I'm just thankful that he didn't suffer more than he did."

Again a silence sifted through the small group. Eyes glazed over as thoughts seemed to focus on the many possibilities of what could have happened to B.J.

The front doorbell broke the silence and Trickster landed on all fours off Evelyn's lap when Evelyn stood to answer the door.

"Stay put, Evie, I've got it," Wil offered. "Can't be too important. Seems most of the town has gone to bed except for us and our unknown visitor," Wil said over his shoulder as he headed for the front door, smiling as Trickster once again claimed her spot on Evelyn's lap.

Evelyn remained in her chair but with the lateness of the hour, she couldn't shake a growing apprehension.

"Abby! Come in."

"No, thanks, Wil, I just wanted to see how B.J. was doing." Abby wiped a tear and turned toward the street.

Wil waited for her to continue, grateful for the front hall light behind him. *Need to fix this light,* he thought as he glanced at the darkened light fixture on the outside wall.

Abby turned back. "Is B.J.'s arm broken?"

"Doc Morsman can answer that better than I can, Abby. Just a sec. Hey, Doc, got a minute?"

When Levi Morsman appeared beside Wil, Wil tried to appear

lighthearted. "Doc, can you give Abby some reassurance that B.J.'s gonna be okay? She's worried his arm's broken."

"B.J.'s arm is *not* broken, Abby." Levi laid a reassuring hand on Abby's shoulder and spoke with a firmness that his profession demanded. "Just a bad sprain," he added with a smile. "At his age, his bruises and scrapes will be gone in a few days, and we can remove the stitches from his forehead in a week or so. For a little guy that took a big tumble, we have a lot to be thankful for. He'll be fine, don't you worry."

Relief filled Abby's face and once again tears filled her eyes.

"How's your hubby? I understand *he* might need some of my professional help." Levi spoke gently.

"He'll be fine, I guess. He's awful mad, though... at the world, it seems... anyway, I just needed to know how B.J. made out before I left."

"Left?" Levi turned a curious look to Wil who shrugged his shoulders.

"Yeah. I'm going back to Quebec. Maybe things will cool off when I'm gone and Jake won't be so mad. Just thought I'd give him some time to think things over. He should really come home, too, back to Quebec, I mean." Abby stumbled over her words as she repeated herself. "Anyway, my bus is due in soon. Please say goodbye to the others for me, especially Evie, will you Doc? She's been real kind to me. And tell Josh I'm sorry to leave him high and dry like this, but I guess I gotta do what's best, right? I've really appreciated all your friendships these past months and... well... I gotta go." And with that, Abby turned and walked into the darkened street. She never looked back.

"Wow..." Wil turned to Levi. "What should we tell the others?"

"Exactly what she asked: her thanks and her goodbye."

"Think Jake will follow her?"

Levi walked with Wil to join the others. "My guess is not likely any time soon, but God is the God of the impossible. Lives can change and Jake certainly needs some inner renovations before he can be the husband he should be. But he's got to want it and I think that's where he has a problem."

Having only heard muted voices, Evelyn studied the faces of both men as they returned to the living room. Her concern was somewhat abated when Levi mouthed the word *Later* from across the room and gave her a reassuring smile. Relieved, she turned to the question Christina had just put to Rob.

"Did B.J. tell you *why* he didn't come back to Evelyn, Rob?"

"Yep, it was a butterfly."

Everyone's voice responded in unison. "A butterfly?"

"The other day we were reading about monarch butterflies in a book we got from the library. Remember, Lucy, you met us there when you were visiting your mom." Lucy nodded, and Evelyn remembered how excited B.J. had been to see Lucy and Annie.

Rob continued. "B.J. saw pictures of how the caterpillar forms a chrysalis on a milk pod. We even talked about looking for some in the woods back by Doc Bailey's house sometime next month. He was quite enraptured by the whole story and thought he could find some milk pods at the bottom of an embankment to surprise me. I guess he didn't realize it was a little early in the season. Anyway, he tripped over the branch of a fallen tree halfway down the embankment. He remembers rolling a lot, and from what Jim Broughton told me when he found him, it appeared B.J. had rolled through the thistle bushes and landed near a rotten log with lots of undergrowth to cover him.

That's when he must have hit his head. He doesn't remember doing it, but he asked me if I'd take him back to where it happened. He wants to make sure he never goes there again." Rob smiled a weak smile, as did each of the others listening to the story. The innocence of B.J.'s request fell heavily on them and for a long time they sat in silence, once again absorbed in their own thoughts.

"Yep, some day I will, I told him." Rob's whisper broke the stillness. "I can't help thinking how different this day would have been had Holly been here. There have been many times over the past three years that I've wanted to talk with her about raising B.J., especially when Jake points an accusing finger."

"You can't put a lot of thought into what Jake says," Lucy interjected gently. "He's so mixed up that he has to find fault with what others do, especially if it's a reflection on how he's chosen to live."

Rob looked at Lucy and was about to say something, but Levi broke in.

"I think Lucy's right, Rob. I'm sure Jake must feel terrible for what happened to B.J., but he's pointed such an accusing finger at you that those feelings can't surface. Somehow he needs to let go of the past and move on. Abby is such a sweet girl, but Jake can't see that. If your wife were sitting here right now, I'm sure she'd agree with me. Unfortunately, the only comfort Jake's getting right now is in believing *you* feel responsible for what happened to B.J. It seems he'll never admit his role in what happened today because he'd have to be accountable for his own negligence."

The sweetness of age and the gentleness of her spirit prompted Christina to ask Rob another question. "Would you like to tell us about your wife?"

A smile broke through his tears, and as he wiped the moisture from his face, he started to talk about his wife.

"Holly was my angel. Heck, she was everyone's angel. A day never went by when someone wouldn't tell me how lucky I was to have her for my wife. People just saw something in Holly that was special. Her kind spirit. Her soft voice. When I watched her sing songs to B.J. as she stood over his crib, it seemed that everything around me just stopped. It felt like I was in space, floating, with just the sound of her voice keeping me buoyant."

Rob paused and pinched the inner corners of his eyes in an effort to dry the tears that had yet to fall. "Holly loved to plant vegetables. Flowers weren't enough for her. 'I have to benefit from all my hard work,' she'd say more than once through the summer months. She would plant, weed, prune, and water and never complain, never once. She'd spend the fall months harvesting what she grew and then proudly display her wares. Canning became her speciality. B.J. and I still have some pickles and tomatoes she canned the year before she got sick. We've decided never to open them. We'll just keep them as a reminder."

"Rob, did you and Holly go to church?" Wil asked out of curiosity.

"No, not in the beginning. Our families were simple folk. As I've mentioned before, my parents were older when I was born and there didn't seem to be time for church. Farming was my father's life from sunup to sundown, and Sunday was his day of rest. Holly's family went to church, but not on a regular basis, just special occasions, Easter, Christmas, times like that. But after B.J. was born, we began to wonder if we should be having some kind of spiritual influence on him and any other children we'd have. We didn't turn out too badly from not going to church, but we wanted more, especially for our children. So, we began going and we both enjoyed it. Lots of times we'd comment to each other about the things we'd missed growing up and were glad we'd made the decision to join the little church. Then Holly got sick and our lives changed forever."

For a moment, Rob seemed lost in his memories. Life had been difficult for him, but it was evident to those listening that he'd landed on both feet. Evelyn especially felt her heart pull toward this young man who had lost so much.

"During the early months of Holly's illness, my mom had a stroke and never regained her health. She died three months after my dad's fatal heart attack when B.J. was two. I suppose our church friends became our family. I can't begin to tell you the kindness we were shown. They held a special prayer meeting for Holly when they first heard about her illness. They brought us meals when she was taking treatment, arranged for babysitters for B.J. when I needed to be with her at the hospital. We really saw their love through that time, and I learned what trusting God was all about. Holly made me promise before she died that I would always expose B.J. to a solid church family."

Annie stirred in her bassinet and Lucy uncurled her legs to look after her, but Wil placed his hand on her shoulder. "I'll get her," he whispered. Lucy resettled herself beside Christina.

Evelyn listened closely as Rob continued to share his life with Holly. There was no missing it. Holly Adams would have been the kind of a person that most women would want to know better. She heard stories about Holly's interests, decorating her home, reading to her son, even when he was asleep, and her constant teasing when Rob would twitch his feet like a grasshopper when he was overtired. Evelyn joined in the laughter when Rob demonstrated this habit.

She learned that Holly dreamed a lot, and sometimes her dreams were overwhelming; other times, Rob admitted, her dreams were so far over the edge of logic that all he would say was *hmmm* or *ahhhh,* just to prove he was paying attention. This often ended in a mini fight with a pillow landing on his head. “She was quite feisty and had good aim.” Again, a chorus of gentle laughter filled the Sherwood living room.

“Rob, what did you mean when you said you learned what trust was all about?” Evelyn spoke softly and her question would have been missed had it not been asked during a lull in the conversation.

“It’s hard to explain. I suppose it’s something you have to experience, like today, for example. I was terrified when B.J. went missing. But at the same time, I had a sense of peace that comes from trusting God to do what only God can do: everything *right!* I’ve learned over these past few years that God doesn’t make mistakes, no matter how difficult something may be when it comes into your life. I could have blamed God for Holly’s death, even cursed Him, but both Holly and I had come to accept that He is sovereign and there’s nothing so sweet in life than to trust Him for everything that touches you.”

40

And ought not this woman, being a daughter of Abraham,
whom Satan hath bound, lo, these eighteen years,
be loosed from this bond on the sabbath day?
LUKE 13:16

The humming was faint, but so angelic that Evelyn paused in her conversation with Rob and turned to the senior member of the group. Christina's eyes were closed; a smile radiated from her face as she leaned her head on the back of the couch and began to sing softly. *"Tis so sweet to trust in Jesus, just to take him at his word..."* The quietness of the room enveloped everyone, and, as so often in the past, Evelyn was drawn to the gentle spirit of her elderly friend, and to the words. *Is this the same trust Rob is talking about?* The song concluded and before Evelyn could ponder further, Levi appeared in the kitchen doorway with a tray of cookies and clean cups.

"Lee, you didn't have to do that!" Evelyn rose to assist him. "I didn't even see you go into the kitchen."

"You looked so comfortable, and even at the expense of missing an enchanting solo," he smiled in his mother's direction, "I didn't want to disturb you. And you're right, I didn't have to do it. I wanted to." Levi turned, with tray in hand and a voice to match the occasion, he announced, "Coffee, tea, anyone?" He winked at his mother. *Beautiful!* he mouthed.

Evelyn saw his look of pride and admiration and felt a sense of admiration of her own, only directed to Christina's son, not Christina. *Can't go there,* she thought, climbing behind her invisible wall. Feeling on safer ground, she watched Christina resettle herself beside Lucy, lean forward, and ask Rob her fourth question of the evening

"Does B.J. look like Holly? I see a small resemblance of him in you, but not a strong one. Perhaps he's more like your parents, or Holly's?"

"If you'd met my father-in-law, you would've been glad there was no resemblance." Everyone laughed at Rob's honesty despite his efforts to be serious. "And I'm adopted..."

"You're adopted?" Lucy's reaction broke the intimacy of the moment.

"Yes, I am. I don't think about it much, though. I know for some it's a negative thing, almost a stigma on their lives that they're ashamed of. But I'm not. In fact, I'm grateful to my birth mother. Obviously she had good reasons for doing what she did when I was born and I've had a good life with my adoptive parents. So, there's not a chance B.J. resembles my folks unless there's some kind of osmosis of the genes as you grow up, eh, Doc?" Rob laughed at Levi's reaction. "Actually, B.J. looks a great deal like Holly, both blessed with freckles; but Holly's freckles were her thorn in the flesh—she thought so, anyway. I thought they were beautiful. She had reddish hair, maybe auburn, and despite exposing the freckles further, she always wore it back off her face in a ponytail or scarf. Funny though, if we were going to church, she'd always wear it down on her shoulders. I don't have many pictures of her when she was little, but I do have one I carry with me all the time. It was taken just before we were married. Holly and I went to our annual fall fair and I had her picture taken holding the stuffed poodle I'd won for her. I think I did it more so I could brag that I actually won something, but now I'm very glad I have it. I carry it with me all the time."

Rob placed his cup and saucer on the coffee table and reached in his back pocket for his wallet. Before opening it, he paused and looked at his friends. "You know, when you experience something like I've experienced today, you're reminded how precious friends are. I can't thank you enough for all that you've done, not just today, but over the past few months. Helping out with B.J., welcoming us into your families… I've never really thanked you."

"Okay, already! Enough or you'll have every woman in this room bawling," Wil exclaimed, lightening the mood. "Let's see that picture of B.J.'s mother."

Sliding the picture from the flap, Rob dropped a piece of paper that fell at Lucy's feet. As she handed it to him, she stopped.

"Rob, I've… "

"Oh, thanks, Lucy. Wouldn't want to lose that. I've carried it since I was eighteen. It's part of my life before I knew it."

"Before you knew it?" Lucy whispered.

"Yeah." Rob held the piece of paper and caressed it gently. "When I turned eighteen, just before I married Holly, my parents asked me to invite Holly over for dinner. I thought it was just their way of giving us an engagement dinner, but what they gave me was much more than that. It was the best gift I could ever be given, apart from B.J," Rob added with a smile. "My parents knew that Holly and I would be leaving for the city so I could go to Teacher's College, and they wanted me to have their gift before the wedding, and before we left town.

"What was it?" Wil teased. "Your college tuition?"

"No, better than that. They gave me an envelope."

Mixed reactions circled the room. Wil continued on the same vein. "An envelope? Was it full of money?"

"Something far more valuable. It contained a letter, and this." He handed something to Levi. Christina rose quietly from her position and stood behind her son.

"Why, that's a piece of torn money," she whispered, mystery saturating each word.

"That's right. It belonged to my father."

Evelyn gasped and dropped her cup to the floor. Her hands flew to her mouth as she struggled to breathe. Lucy jumped to assist her mother, but Levi had already sprung into action. Evelyn's breath came in short gasps as her face drained of colour. Everyone watched, helpless to know what to do, while at the same time grateful Levi was by her side.

"Lucy, get your mother some water!"

Lucy turned toward the kitchen.

"Stay with your mother. I'll get it." Wil had already spun into action, his earlier humour long since abated.

"Take a breath, Evie. Breathe deeply. Close your eyes. That's it. Breathe. Again," Levi spoke from a bent position holding Evelyn's hands as he checked her pulse. "That's good. You're doing fine. Look at me." Evelyn opened her eyes and tears emptied onto her face. "No, don't look around the room. Just look at me." Levi smoothed a strand of hair from Evelyn's face and smiled. "Whatever happened is passing. Just breathe slowly. That's it. You'll be fine. Thanks, Wil." Levi took the glass from Wil and held it for Evelyn. "Here, sip this."

Moments passed. No one moved. All eyes were fixed on Evelyn, not realizing she had just experienced something that would change her life forever, not realizing she was fighting a losing battle of denying God's existence, not realizing she had just experienced one of God's miracles and she was in the centre of it.

41

But my God shall supply all your need
according to his riches in glory by Christ Jesus.
PHILIPPIANS 4:19

Annie's crying broke the tension. Lucy lifted her daughter to her arms and reluctantly left to nurse her in the privacy of her mother's bedroom. Wil joined her, and in so doing prompted Christina and Rob to leave Levi and Evelyn alone.

Several minutes passed before Evelyn appeared in the doorway of her bedroom, her composure still unsettled.

"Mom, are you all right?" The alarm in Lucy's voice touched Evelyn deeply and she walked over to her daughter and bent down. Trickster immediately joined her and nuzzled against her hand.

"Too much excitement for you, eh girl?" Evelyn stroked the head of her faithful pet before turning to her daughter, conscious of her son-in-law nearby and the contented sounds of a nursing baby.

"Lucy, I'm not sure how I'm feeling. A wall in my life has just crumbled before me and I'm standing in the middle of it, seemingly unscathed. That in itself is a miracle. I do know there is something I need to do that will take every ounce of my being to do it, and I'd appreciate your prayers."

"My prayers!" Lucy's voice broke at the realization of her mother's request.

"Yes, dear, and there's something else I need. I need you with me when I go back into the living room."

"Sure, Mom, Annie's finished." Lucy raised her sleeping daughter to her shoulder for the desired burp. "We were just going to give you some time with Lee before we came downstairs."

Evelyn rose and walked to her dresser. The lid of her jewellery box was open when her daughter's voice broke through her thoughts.

"I know, Mom."

Evelyn turned to find tears rushing down Lucy's face. "You know?"

"I didn't mean to, but I found it when I was twelve, the day I wore your grandmother's pearls when I was baptized. There was an accident and I knocked your box on the floor and it fell out. Daddy found me holding it. He told me the story, but, did Daddy know about ... ?"

"No." Evelyn returned and crouched down once again at the feet of her daughter. "I've buried it deep in my life, believing it would remain there forever, a secret to be shared with no one."

Wil ran his fingers through his hair. "That explains so much, Evie. Lucy has said more times than I can count, 'There's more, Wil. I can feel it.' And she was right."

Evelyn turned to her daughter. "Lucy, I need to go downstairs. Can you and Wil come with me?"

Wil took Annie from Lucy's arms and Lucy embraced her mother.

"Do you have any idea how proud I am of you? Come on, let's go. I can't wait to see the faces of those we've left wondering what in the world has happened to you."

Both women wiped their eyes and headed for the door.

"You feeling better, dear?" It was Christina that spoke first as the three entered the room. Levi immediately went to Evelyn's side and Rob stood, unsure what to say or do.

"Thank you, Christina. I'm much better than I was a few moments ago. I need to apologize for my behaviour, but what I have to say will explain it."

Lucy settled Annie in her bassinet and stood behind her husband as he sat in a chair. Wil started to rise, but Lucy whispered, "I'd like to stand. I'm fine."

Christina settled herself in her favourite chair by the fireplace, Levi joined Rob on the couch, and Trickster jumped up on Wil's lap, triggering smiles around the room. Everyone watched Evelyn in silence and, for those in the know, prayers reached the heavens.

Seconds stretched into minutes. Trickster jumped down, settling herself at Wil's feet. Finally, Evelyn walked over to where Rob was sitting and crouched down.

"Rob, I have something to show you, but before I do, I need to tell you a story about a girl I once knew."

All eyes were on Evelyn, especially Lucy's.

"Missy, I can't wait much longer. If you haven't finished your letter, you need to do it right away." The nursing attendant spoke gently and the young girl knew that the time had come.

"Is he ready? I mean, is he… can I see him one more time?"

"I'm sorry, dear, that wouldn't be wise. As difficult as it sounds, it's best this way. His new mother and father have arrived and are ready to

make the round trip back home today. If you've finished your letter, you can seal it and leave it with me. I've spoken with the director and she has agreed to hold it in trust until the baby's of age. It will be mailed to his new parents when he turns eighteen and they'll give it to him.

Missy's nose ran unattended. She wiped it with the sleeve of her hospital gown and reached into the drawer of her side table. Several letters had been kept safely sealed in a brown envelope and tied with a string. Untying the knot, Missy searched through the letters until she found what she was looking for and then broke down.

Breaking from the story, Evelyn explained. "The letters were all addressed to her boyfriend, Bobby, with an address in England. Bobby's mother sent the letters to Missy, along with some of his personal belongings that his mother thought Missy should have. She'd received them from the Army following her son's death. She never understood what she was sending; she just felt that her son's girlfriend should have them."

Evelyn continued her story, standing in front of the fireplace beside Christina.

Compassion ruled the moment and the nursing attendant helped Missy open the chosen envelope. Sifting through the pages, the torn bill fell on her bed sheets.

"This was Bobby's half," Missy said, expecting the nurse to understand. "We tore a bill the day he left for England and we promised each other that we would join it the day he returned. It was our secret. We didn't tell anyone 'cause we thought they'd laugh at us, but this piece of

ripped bill spoke volumes." Missy choked as the tears fell freely. Holding the torn bill, she shared the rest of the story with the one woman who had spoken as her mother might have, had she known of her daughter's plight. "This was our way of staying connected. When we tore it, we each kept a piece and it kept us together and now I need to give Bobby's half to his son. So we'll always be connected. Do you think that'll be all right?"

The nurse blew her own nose before speaking. "I think it would be the best gift your baby will ever receive," and she gently took the bill and slipped it in the envelope for Missy before it was sealed.

"Wait!" Missy raised her hand and held the envelope as though it had a life and dropping it would end it. Tears fell on it as Missy raised it to her lips and laid her last kiss to her son on the back flap. Shuttered breaths escaped. "Goodbye my Baby Child." She handed it to the nurse, turned her back to the door, and wept the pain of a broken heart.

Evelyn bent down once again in front of Rob. "*Missy* was the name given to the eighteen-year-old girl by the nursing attendant. It was not uncommon to use a generic name to help girls in the unwed mother's home maintain some privacy. But it was not her real name." Unbridled tears flowed down her cheeks as she unfolded her closed hand and revealed part of a two dollar bill. Rob took it from her hand and held the two pieces together, matching their torn edges. He stared at what lay in his hand. Evelyn watched as he looked from her face to the money and back again, and then she watched as realization dawned and tears fell on the money.

"You're ... my ... !"

"... birth mother? Yes. I gave birth to you and hid it from the world, including my parents, my husband and my daughter, and I wrote the letter and included your father's half of the torn bill."

Rob fumbled for his wallet and removed some worn handwritten papers. "I never showed this when I took out Holly's picture." He sniffed back tears and Christina quietly handed him a tissue. More composed externally than internally, Rob continued.

"May I?" Seeking Evelyn's permission to read the letter written so long ago came unexpectedly. Evelyn stood and felt lightheaded. Levi jumped up and took her elbow to steady her as she closed her eyes and nodded her head to Rob. Levi slipped his arm around Evelyn's waist and held her tightly.

Rob cleared his throat and began.

Halifax, Nova Scotia
October, 1942

My dear Baby Child,

I call you this for I have relinquished the right to call you my son—

What I'm about to do is going to be the most difficult decision I'll ever make in my life, but also the easiest because it's the right thing to do.

I love you with all my heart and your father would have loved you the same. He died not knowing you were going to be part of his world. He died fighting for the freedom you will enjoy as you grow up. He died knowing that I loved him more than I can put into words in this letter.

We loved each other very much and you were the result of that love. In the eyes of some, we may have committed a sin, and perhaps we did, but the threat of years of separation and the fears that come with war ended in a moment of passion, and you were conceived. We intended to marry on his return home from the war, but your father was killed in a battle on the shores of France. I never had a chance to tell him I was carrying his

> child, and you will never have the chance of knowing one of the most wonderful people you would have ever met, so I'd like to introduce you to him.

Rob paused and looked at Evelyn. Her face revealed the trance she was in, almost as though she was reciting the letter as it was being read. Lowering his head, he continued reading.

> Bobby Jenkins was his name. He was a wonderful man, tall, handsome, fun-loving and compassionate, and I can see his eyes in you. The hint of a dimple on your left cheek is in the same place as was on his face, a face that smiled just thinking that someday he would be a daddy. His hair was curly, sandy in colour that turned very light in the summer sun. He loved life, sang crazy tunes he would make up as he strummed his guitar. He played baseball from when he was a little boy and loved watching young children as they ran around a baseball diamond. You would have been proud of him, proud to call him father.
>
> Baby Child, I have chosen to give you to a couple who will raise you as their own, a couple who are unable to have their own children. I know in my heart they will love you, and if they love you half as much as I do, you will be happy. Not a day will go by in my life that I will not think of you.
>
> With love from your mother, the other mother in your life who gave you birth and died a little when she gave you to another.

"You signed it 'E'...for Evelyn."

"Actually, it's really Evlyna, but that's another story for another day." Evelyn felt Levi's encouraging squeeze and it helped steady her enough that she slipped from his side and bent down again at the feet of her son.

"Rob, I have carried your birth deep in my heart, behind a very high wall. I wasn't ashamed of you. You are an extension of my first love. Earlier tonight, when you smiled, I saw Bobby and didn't realize it. You have his smile, his faint dimple. I can't imagine never having given birth to you. But life was complicated back then. The war was still on. My parents were hundreds of miles away and we were at odds with one another. I left home when Bobby went overseas. My parents wouldn't give us permission to marry and I was very angry with them. I've never been in contact with them since then." Evelyn bowed her head at those words and waited until she could continue.

"Bobby had insisted we exchange our love and vows before God, the very God I've blamed for all that's gone wrong in my life. As soon as he left for England, I moved to Halifax to work in the factories, to do anything to help with the war. I never dreamed Bobby would die." Taking a deep breath, Evelyn continued, mindful that this news was being heard by her daughter for the first time. "By the time I realized I was carrying his child, our communication had been cut off. And then I received word he had been killed."

Evelyn's voice broke. Rob laid his hand on her shoulder and his smile through his own tears encouraged her to continue.

"The dread of separation overpowered our reasoning and, rightly or wrongly, you were conceived." Evelyn echoed the words she had written many years ago. Taking the torn money from Rob's hands with a sacredness that came from the depth of her heart, Evelyn continued. "This represented our separation and we vowed that our love would last and we would join these two pieces together."

"Well, it looks like that's exactly what's happened. They are a perfect fit," Rob said, helping Evelyn stand to her feet. "Evie, thank you for my birth. Thank you for the letter that tells me how much my birth parents loved each other and how much my father would have loved me. I've never held any resentment against an unknown woman for giving me up, but I have to admit that I've often wondered what she was like, especially after I became a parent myself. Holly would often read this letter to me while we lay in bed at night and we would wonder what she...*you* were like. Holly often said that one day I'd meet you. I never believed her." Rob bowed his head. "But God saw to it that I did. You know, some people might call this a coincidence, but I remember a former pastor back home saying that a coincidence is when God wants to remain anonymous. I stand here utterly amazed at the path He took to orchestrate tonight. Not one I'd have taken, that's for sure. Holly's death. Moving west, and to Thystle Creek, of all places, right where you live. And then B.J. being lost—I guess I can't be mad at him now."

Everyone laughed and the tension broke, somewhat.

"I heard recently that even though life may be unfair, God is not. That no matter what happens around us, God is in complete control and He will work things out according to His own pleasure. Even though we may benefit from His actions, the glory all goes to Him."

"I'm afraid I'm not on that spiritual page...yet. But I'm working on it," Evelyn added, to the delight of those listening.

Such words held promise, and for one in particular, a future where he would help in the healing of a soul that had suffered, perhaps more than necessary, but nevertheless suffered.

EPILOGUE

Having many things to write unto you,
I would not write with paper and ink:
but I trust to come unto you and speak
face to face, that our joy may be full.
2 JOHN 1:12

Rob and Lucy exchanged awkward hugs, but only for a moment.

"Well, Sis..."

"Well, indeed," Lucy responded with a second hug and a kiss planted firmly on Rob's dimpled cheek. "Nice to meet you!" Her laugh was infectious and Rob couldn't help smiling.

Christina stood, wordless delight written all over her face. "This has been a very exciting day, but I for one am exhausted. Wil, I'd welcome a lift home if it's not an imposition. It appears my son is otherwise occupied." Christina smiled and nodded in the direction of her son as he headed toward the kitchen door.

"No problem, Christina. We need to get Annie in her own bed anyway. Morning comes too soon when the midnight hour finds you still up. Can I pull you away from your brother there, wife? There's always tomorrow," Wil teased with some reluctance as he watched his wife share one story after another with an exuberance not befitting the late hour.

"I'll just be a minute, honest, Wil. Rob and I want to say good-night to Mom. I think she's in the kitchen with Lee." Both turned to find their mother on the phone.

"Hello Papa, this is Evlyna... Yes, Papa, your daughter, Chava." Evelyn's free hand trembled as she clasped Levi's and turned at the sound behind her. Arms linked, Rob and Lucy were wiping tears and smiling at their mother. "I'm sorry it's so late, but... you don't mind? Yes, I know. You've waited a long time."

AUTHOR'S NOTES

Questions I've been asked while writing *Come Find Me*…

Q. *Why did you write a novel?*

A. It just happened. I had been trying to write my memoirs for several years—still am, for that matter—and at one of our earliest writer's group meetings, I responded to a picture/homework assignment and ended up with an outline for *Come Find Me.*

Q. *Can you elaborate?*

A. As we were choosing our pictures to write about, Lisa placed one in front of me and said, "I thought you might like this one since you're writing your memoirs." It was a picture of a brunette women and a little blonde girl running through a field. That's how I met Evelyn Sherwood and her daughter Lucy. Several months later, I responded to another picture/homework assignment and met Lucy as a married woman expecting her first child. I never want to see these pictures in their proper element. I'd be devastated! They have been in front of me at my desk for almost five years. I eventually had to laminate them because they were beginning to show signs of wear! I would love to have included them in my book, but I'm afraid I'd be breaking some copyright rule.

Q. *Did any of the various events really happen?*

A. This is a hard question. I'm learning many things in writing a novel. One point that has been stated repeatedly is that a first-time novelist will draw on his/her own life for inspiration. I have this neat book called *Turning Life into Fiction* by Robin Hemley and have learned a lot on how to incorporate your everyday world into a novel. For example, how to embellish the truth (I don't recommend this in real life)! When you do this in writing fiction, it releases you from the confines of what really happened and allows you to go off in another direction. So, in answer to your question, yes, some of the events are authentic. Lucy's speech, for example—certainly the opening—was a speech I gave in Grade Eight and won the public speaking contest in the Regional Public School Competition. It came from an article written for the Department of Lands and Forests, where my older brother was working when I was a young teenager. Another example is Wil's father keeping his children waiting on Christmas morning while he shaved. Just ask my husband or my kids about that one! And just a few more: our street number when I grew up, 1151; my dislike for winter is an understatement; the icebox and wringer washer my mother used and how glad she was to have them replaced; and my engagement ring disguised in a Cracker Jack box. My interest in World War II has a direct relation to my father going overseas when I was a baby. Oh, and one more thing: the quote that Evelyn hears in church came from Pastor Mark who shared it in his Christmas message. I was so excited when I heard it that I wrote it down, had him confirm it, and then asked him if I could quote it in my novel. He just smiled!

Q. *Are any of your characters 'real' people?*

A. No. Each individual character is a 'mixture' of people I've known: family members, new and old friends, people who have crossed my path over my lifetime. Some have stayed with me, others were just passing through. The character of Cliff Moses, to some degree, would be my only exception.

Q. *Can you expand on him?*

A. Well…I suppose I can say that when I picture Uncle Mo, I envision an older gentleman I met several years ago, a man that some might think a little gruff. I came to think of him as my friend. It's been several years since I've seen him, but when I think of him, I picture a gentle, kind man with a servant's heart whose Christian walk affirms his love for the Lord and heightens my respect for him. When I wrote, "when Cliff Moses said goodnight to his nephew, neither knew it would be their last goodnight," I cried. I really did! Uncle Mo was such a solid man, so caring, that I knew he would be missed, and I really did miss him in the rest of my story. I see a lot of my friend in Cliff.

Q. *How did you come to use a Jewish element in* Come Find Me*?*

A. Two years into my novel, I spoke to a publisher at a writer's conference. I was bold and determined, yet at the same time terrified! When I presented a synopsis of *Come Find Me,* he gave me some positive direction. I needed something fresh! About a month or two later, I said to my husband, "I'm going to make Evelyn Jewish." And that was it. Nothing profound, nothing particularly motivating. I suppose, if I had to think of an explanation, I would lean toward my interest in WWII and the Jewish annihilation, plus the fact that I grew up with several childhood friends who were Jewish. That's how I came to love *matzoh*!

This turn of events has been a blessing in the form of Sharon, a Christian Jew who met the Messiah early on in our friendship. She is a joy to know and has her own spiritual journey worth writing about! She willingly read my novel before any other eyes saw it, and her words of encouragement, "How did you get into the head of a Jewish woman?" thrilled me, encouraged me, and motivated me. My only regret: I moved a year or so after meeting her, and we are forced to maintain a long-distance friendship, which we do!

Q. *Tell me about Trickster. Why did you include her?*

A. I love dogs! I couldn't imagine not having one in my story. And, isn't she cute? I've had ten dogs over my life (nine of which were mine), and it didn't seem natural not to have one in Evelyn's life. I never had one quite like Trickster, but I have a friend who does and although Rosie is black, her character and personality (yes, dogs have personalities!) are built into Tricks.

Q. *Who's your favourite character?*

A. Wow...that's not fair! That's like asking a mother who's her favourite child. She shouldn't have favourites! I like them all for various reasons, even Mae! They serve a purpose and, I hope, add some fibre and excitement to the storyline. Obviously, the one I focused on the most was Evelyn. When I first met her, I found her self-absorbed, almost annoying. I felt sorry for Lucy and Lewis. But as her character and life story evolved, I began to feel sorry for her. I began to understand her more: her anger, her pain, her guilt. By the end of the story, I missed her in my life. I've been known to say, "Evelyn is the kind of person I'd call a friend and would enjoy having a cup of tea with." But, no favourites, except, of course, Uncle Mo!

Q. *What's your favourite section?*

A. The last paragraph.

Q. *How did you feel when you were finished?*

A. What is finished? I have spent over a year and a half finishing my story: editing, rewriting, editing some more, and rewriting some more and more and more. I doubt there is ever a finishing point. However, when I first finished my story, I made five different phone calls to share this wonderful news. No one was home! I even had to leave a message on my husband's cell phone! So I ran an elaborate bubble bath, made a hot drink, took a large chocolate bar, spread it out on the edge of the tub and climbed in! "Here's to me," I said, and laid the portable phone nearby just in case someone returned my call!

Q. *Have you received any special advice while writing* Come Find Me?

A. Every person who writes poems, drama, music, fiction or non-fiction should be open to well-grounded advice. One of my highlights in writing *Come Find Me* was a half-hour spent with Christian novelist Jeanette Oke. When I shared my outline with her, these were her words, "Ruth, don't get caught up with how many books you will publish. Remember where your story came from. It's your responsibility to write it the best that you can. It's His responsibility to find the readers. And if only one person reads your book and a life changes because of it, then that's why you wrote your book." I've taken her advice to heart.

Q. *Will you write a sequel?*

A. My husband and several friends keep asking that!

Q. *Why the title? Why the verses? Why the ending?*

A. As Levi would say, "Whoa, rein it in a little! That's three questions on top of each other!" Actually, they are the most important questions I've been asked.

First, the title: It came on the morning of my first draft. Since then, I've added and deleted ideas and characters many times, but the title never left. I've always imagined God calling out to this troubled woman, *"Come find Me,"* stretching out His hands, ready to offer her a new life full of His love, His forgiveness, His peace. It would be a life with new purpose, not without pain, not without sorrow, but a life lived with God in control. The title had to stay. Jeremiah 29:13 was a natural fit.

The verses: Putting Bible verses at the beginning of each chapter was, at first, just a chosen style. Then as my chapters developed, I began to search for verses that would be a lead into the theme of the chapter. The most exciting verse I used was the one for the epilogue. It was not the original one. I discovered this verse during a sermon or my own reading, I can't remember which. It seemed to jump off the page and I knew it had to be used.

The ending: Being careful not to spoil the story for those who just have to read the ending before the beginning... Evelyn hasn't arrived yet, but is on her way 'home.' She is finally breaking down the wall that has stood so high for so long.

Thanks for asking!